CITY OF WHISPERS

IMPERIAL ASSASSIN BOOK 1

KATT POWERS

First edition

ISBN: 978-0-6450855-1-8 (hardcover)
ISBN: 978-0-6450855-2-5 (paperback)
ISBN: 978-0-6450855-0-1 (ebook)

Book cover design by designedbyboots.com
Copy editing by Nikki B
Proof reading by Gadget

www.kattpowers.com

BOOKS BY KATT POWERS

Imperial Assassin Series

City of Whispers

Valley of Lies

The Night Lily (Coming mid-2021)

The Diamond King (Coming late-2021)

Be first to hear about new book releases *and* get exclusive content
like prequels, short stories and offers by signing up for the
Assassin's Team at http://bit.ly/Assassins-team.

A NOTE FOR US READERS

This book is written in United Kingdom (UK) English.

This means words like *color* and *favorite* are spelled *colour* and *favourite* as is standard in UK English. It also means you'll see phrases like: *she walked towards the door* rather than the US *she walked toward the door,* and *whilst* sometimes used in place of *while.*

However, several other less common UK English terms also appear, and I've listed these below.

In UK English the word *storey,* as in *'the tavern was a two-storey building'* is used, describing the number of floors (storeys) a building possesses. In US English, this would be a *two-story* building, meaning the building had two floors.

Mould, as in *'the bathroom walls were covered in black mould'.* In US English, this would be *mold.*

The swear word *arse* is, of course, used in place of the US 'ass'. *Ass* is used to refer the donkey-type animal.

For Gary, without whom this book would never have been written.

CHARACTER LIST

Main Characters (pronunciation)

Dhani Karim (*DHAR-nee kar-EEM*)

Parvan Gorshayik (*par-VUN gor-SHAY-ick*)

Tizraki (tiz-RAH-kee) Characters

Abil Beriktiin (*AY-bill beh-rick-TEE-IN*)

Esmille Beriktiin (*EZ-mill beh-rick-TEE-IN*)

Fikret Beriktiin (*fick-RET beh-rick-TEE-IN*)

Jursek Cerevin (*jur-SEK che-ree-VIN*)

Temek Huyurgal (*tem-ECK HOY-ur-gal*)

Ziraat Olucik (*zir-ART oll-OO-chick*)

Milej Tarovik (*mill-EDGE taro-VICK*)

Erdogal Timoyucik (*er-DOE-gal tim-oe-YOU-chick*)

Kyvil Yenidogat (*KYE-vil yen-ee-DOE-gat*)

Jhiriyan (jih-RHEE-yan) Characters

Behzad El'Meshid (*BEY-zad el-mesh-EED*)

Ismail Hanrif (*iss-MAY-EEL han-REEF*)

Aydan Khasain (*AY-dann kha-SAY-EEN*)

Bethsehal Shalamir (*beth-seh-HAAL shall-a-MEER*)

Rulers, Jhiriyan Noble Houses and Gods

Safid Ereldemore (*sah-FEED eh-reld-eh-MOOR*) - the Jhiriyan Emperor

Sharafaa Ereldemore (*sha-rah-FAAR eh-reld-eh-MOOR*) - Safid's daughter and heir

House Nohirrim (*noe-RHEEM*) - the Jhiriyan Empire's former ruling house

House Rumahlah (*rue-MAA-lah*) - a Jhiriyan house with business interests in the Colonies

Prince Attomir Suydan (*at-OE-meer SOY-daan*) - the current ruler of Tizrak Yirda

Duyjarit Lurgak (*doy-JUH-rit lur-GACK*) - the Majapayit (*mar-jah-PYE-EET*)/ruler of Izurum

Father Ulgan (*ull-GAN*) - the male aspect of the Tizraki primary (temple) god

Mother Yamir (*ya-MEER*) - the female aspect of the Tizraki primary (temple) god

*For pronunciation of places, titles and general terms, please see the glossary at the end of the book.

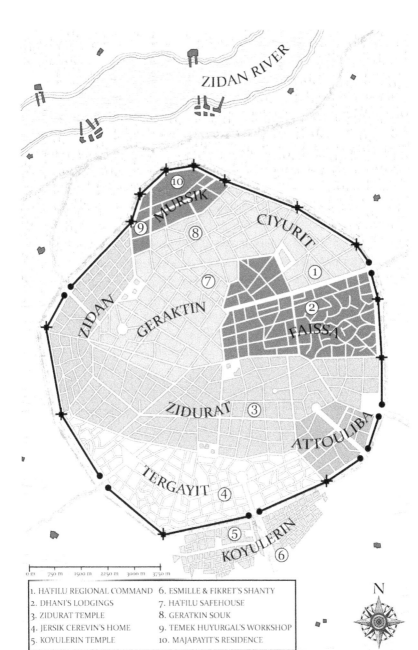

ZIDAN RIVER

MURSIK

CIYURIT

ZIDAN

GERAKTIN

FAISSA

ZIDURAT

ATTOULIBA

TERGAYIT

KOYULERIN

0 m 750 m 1500 m 2250 m 3000 m 3750 m

1. HA'FILU REGIONAL COMMAND	6. ESMILLE & FIKRET'S SHANTY
2. DHANI'S LODGINGS	7. HA'FILU SAFEHOUSE
3. ZIDURAT TEMPLE	8. GERATKIN SOUK
4. JERSIK CEREVIN'S HOME	9. TEMEK HUYURGAL'S WORKSHOP
5. KOYULERIN TEMPLE	10. MAJAPAYIT'S RESIDENCE

N

CHAPTER ONE

SPRING 1493 (JHIRIYAN CALENDAR) IZURUM,
Talmakhan Region, Imperial Colony of Tizrak Yirda

No one expected a group of figures to burst out from the temple's bone-white walls, revolvers in hand— shiny new pieces, gun-metal grey, oiled, and glistening.

After all, no one expected to die at a wedding.

Certainly not the priest, suddenly standing cheek-to-jowl with two black-clad, pistol-wielding men, nor his attendant as he was thrown head-first down the steps. More men streamed out from the temple's cloying darkness, others stormed in through the compound gates. The priest's mouth opened in a horrified, round-lipped gasp.

For a gut-squeezing moment, Dhani Karim stared through the heat shimmer, watching the scene unfold. The band stopped playing. The fiddler's cheeks paled. A long way away, like a voice calling out across a field, her mind added the words *nationalist cult* to *wedding* and came up with *massacre*.

Then, the shooting began.

Wedding guests scattered from under the marquee, cried out, and fell. Chairs flew sideways, a platter piled with naan and a jug of wine wobbled and shattered on the ground. Beyond the dribbling fountain, Fikret grabbed Esmille and scanned the crowd for little Rivek. His shoulders sagged in anguish. The child was nowhere to be found.

A woman shrieked the nationalist cult's name: *"Yevengik cu Bapa!"* and then, *"RUN!"*

After that, the hiss and sizzle of people hurling the killing Flame at their attackers turned the afternoon fiery red.

A bullet smashed into the wooden arbor a hand's breadth from Dhani's ear. Splinters and crimson bougainvillea stung her cheek; blood blistered on her skin. A bolt of scarlet flame scorched the air just metres away, close enough it tugged at her solar plexus. Her knuckles popped as she reefed a blade from its holster.

Now would have been a good time to develop the ability to hurl Deenjah or some other kind of magic. *Creator above!* She'd settle for tossing sparkly pink fairies if it gave her an advantage. She stole a glance at her olive-copper skin.

Nope. Not going to happen. Still a Jhiriyan Homelander. Still mute to the Flames. Blades and batons would have to do.

She crouched low and ran, retracing her steps beneath

the bougainvillea-covered walkway. A bullet whizzed past. A man screamed and cried out to the Gods. Burned hair and charred skin choked her nose, making her gag. Sweat stung her bleeding cheek.

At the end of the walkway, she made a hard right, angling for the temple's western steps. A desperate flanking move, sure, but one that might—*might*—just save lives.

Especially if she could get her hands on a gun.

On the temple balcony, the priest had somehow fallen over. His ample form lay prostrate on the tiles, his legs peddling frantic circles in the air. Slowly—somewhere around the speed of waterlogged continental drift—he rolled onto his belly and began to elbow his bulk towards the temple's main chamber.

As people scattered, an old man and a small boy, both wedding guests, stumbled and fell, blocking her path to the temple steps. A ginger cat tumbled out of the child's arms and onto the dirt. It froze, arching its back and hissing.

A hooded man rushed in to cut off the pair's escape, wielding a pistol. Dhani skidded to a halt.

Time *could* have slowed if the Creator, Father Ulgan, Mother Yamir—heck, even a long-forgotten, one-eyed tortoise god with foot fungus—had even the slightest sense of compassion.

Time didn't slow. It zeroed in for a direct collision, delivered to the gut with a bull camel's kick.

The hooded man wheeled, aiming the pistol at the old man's head.

The small boy bounced to his feet, screaming for his

Bopa—his great-grandfather—and *Selti*—a common name for Tizraki cats—to run. Tears glistened on the child's pale, dirt-streaked face. His bright blue tunic had a rent down the centre, exposing a grazed belly.

Dhani unclipped her steel baton, testing its weight in her hand. Adrenaline flooded her mouth with a sharp, metal tang.

Behind the mask, the gunman's eyes bulged like fearful saucers. He gripped the gun with both hands, its muzzle cutting a shaky arc from the old man to the boy to the spitting ginger cat. Dhani took aim. *Maybe the Gods cared after all.* Either that or the gunman feared their judgement in the afterlife.

"Please, don't!" the old man begged, trying to rise on trembling arms. His great-grandson cowered, now wailing for his mother.

Shots popped off on the other side of the temple courtyard. Women, men, children screamed. A blaze of red Flame rent the air. *Another.* The wedding marquee fell, ballooning inwards like some great, dying sea beast.

Dhani drew back her arm, muscles tense, mind narrowed on the gunman and his shakier-than-a-twig-in-an-earthquake aim. The gunman twitched the weapon from the old man to the boy—then pointed it instead at the hissing, spitting cat.

Her entire being cinched. *Oh no, no, no, you don't.*

No one—*no one*—killed a cat in front of Dhani Karim.

She flung the baton with every fibre of strength she possessed. It spun through the air as the pistol cracked, the cat—

The cat!

4

Hindquarters bunched, the cat sprung *upwards*, a prodigious leap, claws extended, fangs bared, and attached itself to the gunman's thigh at the exact moment the spinning metal baton crunched into the side of his head.

The man dropped as if his bones had leapt clean out of his body leaving behind a fleshy sack. The pistol fell from his grasp, clanged on the paved walkway, and spun, coming to rest next to a potted miniature lemon.

The child's jaw swung, though whether it was at the sudden appearance of a blonde-haired, copper-skinned Jhiriyan in a sea of raven Tizraki heads or the baton strike to the gunman's skull, Dhani couldn't say. She moved at once, ready to offer a hand up to the old man.

A *click-click* stopped her before she'd taken a second step. Another masked man emerged from behind a trellis on her left, pistol clutched in a white-knuckled grip. Its cold, dead eye glared directly at her head.

"Time to die, Metalskin bitch."

CHAPTER TWO

Two days earlier…

Dhani Karim strode towards an arbor covered in eye-watering crimson bougainvillea. The morning sun stung her neck, hot and raw with the promise of a skin-blistering day. A fly buzzed her ear. She punched the insect to oblivion with a white-knuckled fist.

The bastard had frisked her. *Frisked her!*

Even after the five-minute march across the compound, fury still burned on her cheeks.

Reporting for duty at Izurum's Regional Command should have been easy. Standard Ha'filu—*Secret Service*—protocol, outlined in precise and excruciating detail within the Service manual, no space for ambiguity. She'd present her orders at the gatehouse then hand over her knives, her dagger, her metal baton, and the bracelet on her wrist that doubled as a garrotte. In return, the security detail would hand her a receipt.

But to be frisked by a bull-necked local with over-friendly fingers?

Not on today's agenda. Not on *any* day's agenda.

Likewise *not* on the agenda—ever—had been having her breasts groped, her butt grabbed and her crotch fondled. The guard responsible had at least one cracked rib after her elbow had suddenly *slipped*, but it offered little consolation. Sooner or later, she'd have to return to the gatehouse and retrieve her weapons from Touchy-Feely the guard. Maybe this time, she'd crack his head. *Ai Creator! Happy days.*

And today of all days, she didn't need the attention.

Her gut tightened at what lay ahead. In response, her heart began to pound. She cycled through a well-worn mantra, drawing solace from a fast-dwindling supply.

No emotion. No weakness. No retreat.

Her destination loomed at the end of the arbor-sheltered walkway: a squat, single story blockhouse shaded by a wide verandah. The building boasted the same tired, complete-the-form-in-triplicate colonial architecture she'd encountered the length and breadth of Tizrak Yirda: rows of louvered glass windows covered by insect screens, a lone entrance door likewise shuttered behind a screen. The stone and timber verandah posts, the terracotta tiles, and the potted geraniums—she'd seen it all before. Even the blowfly battering the door's wire screen like a tiny, single-minded siege engine was nothing novel or new.

Thump. Thump. Thump.

She drew breath, inhaling dust, heat, pinyon pine, and cinnamon. Her fingers brushed a communique in her pocket—brusque and short—commanding her presence at nine bells. She squinted up at the sun. By her calculation, she was ten minutes early. She forced her shoulders to relax, attempting to ease the tension in her neck.

Four hundred and twelve days. An entire year in purgatory at the Empire's steaming arse-end, pushing paper about a desk. Her sole opportunity to clear her name, and even then, there were few guarantees.

The General claimed this was the only option the Service's brass would accept. She'd never quite believed him. A flick of a pen, a slight perceived by some faceless Kishaat caste bureaucrat she'd never met, and any chance of rejoining the Ta'Hafiq, the Imperial Assassins, would be gone forever.

And Creator only knew, in her life—lowly Gishatriya caste, the child of a drunk and a money-laundering dockside bar owner—certainty had never been a friend.

But what choice did she have?

For the time being, she was an unranked Secret Service operative—a dirt-level, lowlife pond scum *nothing*.

She pulled the screen door open and stepped into the building's cool. A foyer with the usual array of Imperial regalia greeted her.

Behind a lone battleship of a mahogany desk, a thin-faced local adjutant stared back at her. Several years her junior, the adjutant wore a charcoal grey uniform and sported a scruffy goatee. Affixed to the wall behind him was a two-metre tall Jhiriyan coat of arms, the Empire's sinuous gold dragon superimposed over its royal blue cedar, gloss enamel on polished brass. Elsewhere, a large wall clock, also enamel over polished brass, emitted an imperious *tock-tock-tock*.

Alongside the Imperial arms—predictably—hung a pair of sepia portraits: one of the Emperor Safid, the other of Tizrak Yirda's current ruler, portly Prince Attomir. The Prince beamed out at the world through his unruly two-tone beard, happy with his lot in life. The Emperor didn't smile. Safid Ereldemore never did. His thin lips and weary gaze simply pressed down on Dhani, damning her to her predicament.

No use delaying. She snapped the papers from her pocket and offered them to the waiting adjutant.

"Operative Karim reporting for duty. I have an appointment with the Regional Controller at nine bells."

The sudden scowl on the adjutant's face read like a newspaper headline: a twist of the lip and a cool, thousand-yard stare. She knew the look immediately, knew the familiar sting of guilt as well. Despite two hundred years of famine-ending colonisation, the occasional piped sewer, *and* a standard currency, there were still Tizraki nationals who resented the Empire and every Jhiriyan Homelander who'd ever drawn breath.

"Your appointment has been moved to ten bells, Operative Karim." The adjutant tapped his writing nib on an open register, a gesture equal parts *go away* and *I-don't-give-a-fuck.* "There's your name, second from the top, inked in at ten. The handwriting's mine."

It took less than a moment to scan the man's precise calligraphy—perfectly straight, perfectly neat, *perfectly smug*—and decide they'd never be friends. It took another moment and a slow, calming breath to stop herself reaching out and squeezing his neck.

The wall clock ticked out three seconds. She sucked on a cheek. Let her fingers drift over the empty knife holster on her thigh. Had second, third—even fifth and sixth thoughts about what to do next.

Perhaps this was an omen. *It wasn't too late to leave.*

Not too late to flip both the Secret Service *and* Safid Ereldemore's tired sepia stare a resounding middle finger. With her skills, work wouldn't be hard to find. Here on the Continent, there was always someone willing to pay an assassin or a discrete, highly trained thief.

Instead, her boots rooted themselves to the lifeless grey tiles.

Call it duty, call it loyalty, call it *stupidity*. Even she wasn't cold enough to tear out the hearts of the only people who cared. She owed the General and his wife the blood in her veins, the breath in her lungs, her name, her honour, her fealty. To herself, she'd made a blood promise, *clear your name of the heinous crime you didn't commit.*

The adjutant sat back in his chair, waiting. His beady gaze flickered to the door and back, once, twice, and again.

"Will there be anything else, Operative Karim?"

Dhani eyed the short, windowless hall that ended in the Regional Controller's closed door, hair on her still-sweaty neck prickling. *But what had she expected, really?* Bethsehal Shalamir had to know by now that her newest unranked operative was a disgraced former assassin. *Pond scum, indeed.*

"As a matter of fact, there is something else, Adjutant..." She searched the desk for a nameplate, found it half-hidden by a newspaper and a small brass statue of a Tizraki horse-and-snake hearth god she couldn't name. *Ziraat-something. How ironic.* Named after a Tizraki folk hero famous for his continent-sized ego and outrageous red hat. "Perhaps Adjutant Ziraat, you could explain why I wasn't informed of the change earlier?"

"I only know what the Regional Controller told me." Ziraat's too-sharp chin and its fine black fluff jerked to the left. Clearly, he wanted her gone. "Seat's in the corridor if you care to wait. Your partner's not here yet though."

Her partner. It took two full breaths and a clenched jaw just to keep the fury contained. She'd never needed a partner before. She didn't need one now. *Another slap to the cheek.*

"I'll wait," she said.

"Suit yourself."

Ziraat's lips flattened, unhappy with her decision. His rodent-gaze flickered to the screen door and lingered, before finally settling on the empty knife holster strapped to her thigh. He squirmed in his seat as if caught thieving, *guilty* tattooed in his narrow, shifting gaze.

Dhani glanced back at the screen door and beyond but there was no-one there. The blockhouse courtyard stood empty save for the trellised walkway and its garish crimson bougainvillea. She scowled at the bougainvillea. Everywhere Jhiriyans went it was always the bloody same: bougainvillea, Imperial portraits, records, ledgers, and accounts. *Oh, had she mentioned bougainvillea?* A shrug and she let it pass.

Nothing she said or did would change a thing. She was a tooth on a tiny cog, an insignificant, nameless component in the great, hulking gears comprising the brass, iron, and steel of the Imperium. *A low caste nobody. No living family. No home. The name she now used not even the one she'd been born with.*

With a final glare at Ziraat-named-for-a-bloviating-hat, she turned on her heel and took the first seat in the corridor. Resting her head against the wall, she closed her eyes.

First battle completed. Let the year in purgatory begin.

—

The Regional Controller's office matched her personnel file, a space so ordered and predictable, Dhani stifled a yawn.

Three floor-to-ceiling bookshelves filled with manuals and ledgers but devoid of personal effects. Two chairs were upholstered in utility brown. On the far wall, maps of the Continent and Tizrak Yirda hanging plumb-line straight. A desk that suggested an obsession with neatness, bearing nothing more than a set of orders carrying General El'Meshid's signature, two gold writing nibs, and a bottle of ink.

Behind it, Regional Controller Bethsehal Shalamir sat waiting, lips neatly pursed on a cut-glass sharp, perfectly proportioned face. Coming to attention, Dhani fixed her stare on a point just above the Regional Controller's golden blonde head. To her right, her new partner did the same. Overhead, a ceiling fan clicked.

"I'll make this brief," Shalamir began, voice crisp as the white silk scarf draped around the high collar of her periwinkle blue shirt. She didn't offer them a seat; Dhani hadn't expected it. "General El'Meshid gave me no choice but to accept both of you into my command, so I'm going to tell you the same thing I told him. I don't want either of you here. I have no time for traitors or..." The woman's cobalt glare drilled holes in Dhani's skin. "Murderous criminals."

A long pause followed, the fan's errant click counting out the passage of seconds. If the *oversight* with the appointment had been a prelude, the dry, stale taste in Dhani's mouth foretold the main act.

Before leaving the capital, she'd read Shalamir's file and tried not to fall asleep. Shulim—*earl* in Jhiriyan—Bethsehal Shalamir, thirty-six years old, unmarried, youngest child of a noble House of middling rank. Despite her relative youth, Shalamir had carved out a reputation in the Ha'filu as a *fixer*—an officer sent to restore order in places where Imperial discipline lacked. Her record read like a romance of rules, protocols, and tradition complimented by two dozen perfectly executed covert operations. The file held no surprises about what to expect during her year in Izurum working under Bethsehal Shalamir: *boredom, more boredom, paperwork, paperwork, paperwork, and sore feet.*

"Very well, let's get this finished and the pair of you out of my sight." Shalamir turned her attention to the looming figure at Dhani's right. "Captain Gorshayik, I've had a brief look over your personnel file."

"Yes, ma'am," came the rumbling reply in deep, Tizraki-accented Jhiriyan.

Street thug had been Dhani's initial impression when

13

she'd first set eyes upon Parvan Gorshayik. The fleshy scars on his throat and cheek didn't help, nor did his oak-tree arms or bear-sized height. That he'd once been a historian in a university archive was as hard to imagine as him working undercover on some highly classified secret mission. He looked like he belonged in a dockside bar, throwing unruly patrons out by the scruffs of their necks.

Gorshayik shifted his weight and the Regional Controller continued, "Five operatives under your command died because you chose a course of action you'd been advised against, Captain Gorshayik." Shalamir's eyebrow lifted. "You will not repeat that kind of treacherous insubordination here."

"No, ma'am."

Shalamir tipped her chin towards the Emperor's portrait hanging behind her desk. One delicate eyebrow arched. "I may not agree with the current regime on many things, but I do understand why they've given you a second chance, Captain. The Service needs Colonials like yourself, natives who *fit in*." Her fingers brushed her scarf again, smoothing out a crease. "Personally, I've always found you Tizraki lazy and far too fond of food and wine to be reliable, but who am I to question the Imperium?"

Gorshayik didn't react to the insult. Shalamir didn't seem inclined to care.

"Operative Karim." The woman's gaze settled on Dhani. A knife-like smile thinned her lips but it held no more warmth than a thousand-year-old corpse. "I'm not privy to the misdemeanour which had you thrown out of the Ta'Hafiq but given what little of your somewhat

14

unorthodox personnel record I've been permitted to read, I can only assume it was a vile and despicable act."

Dhani set her gaze on the Emperor's sagging jawline and bored stare. Her gut churned. *A farce. A complete lie.* In her head, discipline shrilled the Ta'Hafiq's mantra: *no emotion. No weakness. No retreat.* The reason she'd been suspended from the Ta'Hafiq—the Imperial Assassins— was classified information, privy only to those in the oxygen-starved heights of the Secret Service far beyond Shalamir's rank. Not that *that* would deter a noble from asking and, of course, expecting an answer she'd never get.

"You don't want to be here, Karim, and we both know it," Shalamir continued when the silence grew too grim. "Eight years in the Ta'Hafiq and fifty-three confirmed kills. You think you're too good for Internal Affairs, don't you? But if you ask me, a failed assassin is nothing more than a liability to the Imperium, a festering canker that needs to be lanced."

Dhani met the challenge with an impassive stare. Shalamir had the first part correct; she didn't want to be here at all and she *was* too good for Internal Affairs, but the words *failed assassin* set her blood aflame. She flared her nostrils, staring at Shalamir's white silk scarf and its embroidered House motif—some kind of pudgy, leaping antelope. Ten years ago, rebuking a member of the Shaliaat —Ihiriyah's noble caste—would have been unthinkable. Indeed, in the Homeland even now, she wouldn't have dared. But here at the Empire's far-flung edges, after years of busted bones, burned brain cells, blood and sweat, she refused to be cowered.

"May I ask a question, ma'am?" Dhani fixed her gaze on the wall again, her voice a droll, clipped monotone, a polite register of Jhiriyan, low caste to high.

Shalamir waved a dismissive hand. "Go ahead."

"Did you support the old regime, ma'am?"

The woman's olive-copper skin blanched. Beside her, Parvan Gorshayik inhaled a sharp breath. Dhani tightened her jaw. *Let Shalamir suck sour lemons on that.* A noble in Shalamir's position should have known better than to mention her political allegiances at all—especially to a junior operative from a lower Homeland caste.

"You know very well what House Shalamir thought of the Emperor Mishal's removal, *unranked* Operative Karim." The blade-like smile returned to the Regional Commander's lips, chasing the moment of surprise from her face. "But it's ancient history, fifteen years past. House Nohirrim is gone and House Ereldemore ascendant. The Empire has moved on. And besides, we've all sworn an oath to serve the Imperium, haven't we?"

Dhani studied the Emperor's portrait again. The thrill of a meaningless victory coursed through her veins like a Deenjin's Flame. *Score one for Karim.* Another notch to carve on her favourite embroidery hoop.

"Indeed we have, ma'am," she said, toneless and flat. *"May the sun never set on the Imperium."*

Beyond the window, Ziraat the adjutant passed by, locked in animated conversation with a brawny man dressed in a pauper's blue tunic. The Regional Controller frowned at the pair, checked the time, then cleared her throat.

"Captain Gorshayik, Operative Karim, enough of this

pleasant banter." She opened a drawer and removed a brown folder. "A man named *Scythe* has information pertaining to a case one of my senior operatives is working on. I want you to find Scythe and bring him in." She pushed the folder towards Parvan Gorshayik. "This is what we have on Scythe, Captain."

The big Tizraki took the folder, opened it, scanned the documents inside, and snapped it shut.

"Ma'am?" he said.

"Yes, Captain?"

"The case Scythe has information on? What is it?"

"Not your concern, Gorshayik. Find Scythe and bring him in. That's your mission."

Gorshayik offered the file to Dhani. She accepted the folder and studied its frugal content. *Well, that was interesting.* A single page. *Nothing, nothing, and more nothing.* She closed the file and found Bethsehal Shalamir watching her.

"That's it, ma'am?" she said. "Four names and the same half-paragraph of nothing we've just been told?"

The Regional Controller rolled her eyes and laughed. "Oh, my dear. You have a lot to learn, don't you? This isn't the Ta'Hafiq. You won't be treated like some kind of deity and handed encyclopaedic case notes researched by a suite of operatives whose names you'll never deign to ask. You're the operative here. You walk the streets, you flap your jaw at the inns, the souks, the caravanserais, and ashishqa dens. You saddle your behind to a chair and do your own research." Her gaze wandered towards Parvan Gorshayik's coal-dark hair. "I'm sure your *new* partner will be happy to refresh your memory regarding basic Secret

Service procedures." Shalamir's expression cooled. She flattened her palms to the desk, fingers spread. "Now, both of you are dismissed."

Dhani inclined her head and saluted, touching the fingertips of her right hand to her heart. Her scalp prickled, her mouth dried and soured. *Too simple, too easy.* For all of Shalamir's posturing, all she wanted them to do was find someone and bring them in? There had to be a catch.

It came as they reached the door.

"Oh, and by the way," Shalamir said in a voice like a trap snapping shut.

Dhani paused. Gorshayik froze, his deep brown eyes twin points of flame. When they turned about, the Regional Controller's lips had thinned to a razor-smile behind her elegantly steepled fingers.

"I'm returning to the Homeland for my brother's wedding," she said. "I want this Scythe found before I leave."

"And when would that be?" Dhani asked.

"Three days." Shalamir beamed, showing her neat, white teeth. "And Karim?"

"Ma'am?" The honorific stung her throat.

The woman switched to Court Jhiriyan, a hard, hacking register only nobles were permitted to speak. "Fail to find Scythe and I'll slap a court-martial on you for insubordination so fast, you won't be able to blink."

CHAPTER THREE

The office they'd been allocated resembled a broom closet, only twice as cramped. Located in a grim, flat-roofed blockhouse near the compound's centre, Dhani cracked open the door and stuck her head inside the room. One look and she inhaled dust, dirt, gloom, and claustrophobia in that order. She shoved at the door. It banged against something unseen and refused to budge, forcing her to turn sideways to squeeze through.

More of the same awaited within.

Two heavy desks jammed together—one obstructing the door—both scoured with cuts and ink smears. A pair of threadbare, lumpy chairs. A set of faded maps of the Continent and Tizrak Yirda, years out of date, hanging next to a grimy window with a torn insect screen. A brass lamp ancient enough to qualify as a museum relic and a bottle of desiccated ink, no lid. On one corner of a desk lay a dead cockroach, legs crossed skyward in eternal repose— probably succumbed to depression—and everywhere a layer of fine, red desert dust. Dhani wrinkled her nose.

Three days, Shalamir had said. Given the size of the office, she'd be lucky to last three minutes.

Behind her, Parvan Gorshayik grunted at the door, shoved it twice, and forced his way in. Dhani stepped back to make way and collided with a chair.

"Welcome to paradise," she said with a sweep of a hand. The chair settled back on all four legs.

"How did you get here?"

"I beg your pardon, Captain?"

He glared. "How did you get here? To Izurum? Your personnel file doesn't mention you being deaf."

She arched an eyebrow at the rebuke. Not quite the response she'd expected. Was he pissed off about the office? The heat? The unfortunate brown roach on the desk?

A glance at him said *no to all of the above*. Gorshayik's eyes burned holes in her skin, his expression that of a man so perpetually angry at life, fury had engraved its autograph on his being. Otherwise, he looked little different to any other Tizraki man: a strong jaw, olive skin, glossy black hair, and a full, neat beard. A straight, slightly broad nose, lips neither full nor thin. The devotional horse-head necklace at his throat said he followed Father Ulgan, his deep blue tunic with its white and gold embroidery on the cuffs and seams smacked of expensive tastes. She cocked an eyebrow. Either he'd dressed to impress Bethsehal Shalamir or he had a penchant for fine clothes. A tunic like that had probably cost at least a week's wages.

Time began again as he tossed the file onto a desk. It slid towards her, clearing a path in the dust—a revealing gesture, forceful but measured, an act of will. Parvan Gorshayik was that kind of man.

She caught the file before it collected the roach. The insect didn't deserve the disrespect.

"I believe I asked you a question, Karim."

So that was how it was going to be. She raised her chin. Parvan Gorshayik wouldn't be the first—or last—bully she'd worked with. "I came to Izurum the same way you did, Captain. Steam train from Istanakhand to Dursay, coach from Dursay to Talmakhan, then another from Talmakhan to here. The coach down from Talmakhan was delayed a day because the River Gilgit flowed out of season. Desert's full of surprises."

"Your orders were to travel with me."

Dhani sucked on a cheek. Either it was an oversight on his behalf or an outright lie. The only orders she'd received had been the formal letter instructing her to '...*report to Ha'filu Regional Command in Izurum*' and a date.

"Orders?"

"Standard operating procedure. Partners who work together, travel together. You're supposed to know these things."

She flexed her jaw. Released the tension from her cheeks and smoothed any trace of emotion from her face. *Difficult*, was how the General had described Parvan Gorshayik, *difficult, damaged, but underneath, a good man and a valuable operative.* None of the latter was on display as Gorshayik watched her, probably trying to anticipate her next response and outmanoeuvre it. Heat flared in her gut. *Good man, difficult man*, it didn't matter either way. If they were to survive a year working together, it was going to begin with respect.

"My apologies, Captain," she said, forcing a too-sweet smile. "But if you check my personnel file, you won't find *mind reading* listed amongst my skills."

"Lose the attitude, Karim."

"Attitude? Are you always this rude or did seventeen angry hornets fly up your arse and sting you?"

His cheek twitched but he didn't respond to the insult. Instead, he continued the rapid-fire interrogation. "You're not staying at the safe house in Geraktin. Why?"

"In my experience safe houses are rarely safe."

"You don't trust the Service?"

She flared her nostrils. Who she trusted and who she didn't were none of his business. Needless to say, his name wasn't on the list. "I don't trust anyone, including the Imperium."

"Yet, you work for the Empire. I assume you've sworn an oath to serve it?"

"I work for the *General*. That's all you need to know." Dhani folded her arms and studied her nails. They needed a trim. "I've run missions in Izurum before if you must know. I have my own lodgings in Faissa."

"You're going to relocate."

"No, I'm not." She jerked her chin about and returned his glare. This was going nowhere and they didn't have time to waste. "If you're done with the power games, Captain, can we get on with the mission? The clock is ticking."

The comment hung in the air between them. Dhani counted five seconds and then ten. Gorshayik watched her with a force so smothering, every hair on her body registered the threat, and of its own accord, bristled in defence.

Then, he moved, his fists slamming down on the nearest desk.

"Karim, listen to me."

The uncanny prickling on her flesh vanished. She released a breath she hadn't been aware of holding.

"I know you don't want a partner," he continued, "and I don't particularly want *you* as a partner either, but for the time being neither of us have a choice."

"Impressive, Captain. Are you always this perceptive?"

Gorshayik swore under his breath, the desk groaning beneath his weight. His attention fixed on some point on the wall beyond her, his mouth thinned to a hard line. He drew a long, slow breath.

"Very well," he said. "Let's clear the air. I'm sure you're aware of the recommendation I'm supposed to write regarding your behaviour? The one you'll need to rejoin the Ta'Hafiq?" He paused for effect. Dhani refolded her arms. Of course, she knew. The Review Board's request for an *independent recommendation* was the only reason she'd agreed to the posting at all—one frail thread of hope in a tapestry of deceit. "After we've worked together for nine moons, I'm to provide commentary on your rehabilitation along with evidence you've demonstrated remorse and compassion after your…" His tone darkened. "*Indiscretion.*"

Her cheeks cooled. Through the window, a pair of Homelander women ambled down a covered walkway, their pace suggesting they were locked in an all-consuming conversation. Their neat, blonde braids and subdued black clothing had *Ha'filu* written all over them.

So he knew. Parvan Gorshayik knew about the slave woman and children she'd been framed for murdering in the rotting backstreets of Casa-del-Toro, the world's most dangerous city. That he knew the entirety of what happened that night—of the betrayal from within the Ta'Hafiq's ranks, of a mission gone to hell and the gaping hole in her heart—was doubtful. The Ta'Hafiq was an organisation shrouded in secrecy. A covert operative in the Secret Service's general ranks would never be privy to such information.

Gorshayik continued, "I'm willing to concede there was a reason for your actions in Casa-del-Toro, otherwise General El'Meshid wouldn't have given you a second chance. I'm also aware that the General and his wife hold some deep affection for you." He paused long enough for the silence to become uncomfortable. "I'd hate to inform them their trust has been misplaced."

The women in the courtyard disappeared behind the walkway's crimson bougainvillea. Dhani cycled through three calming breaths. Parvan Gorshayik was right on both counts. The only person she'd killed in Casa-del-Toro that night had been the man she'd been ordered to kill. And Behzad El'Meshid—sober, stern and caring—had pulled her broken body from a pile of refuse a decade earlier, given her a new name, a new life, and most importantly, a purpose. In comparison, her real father—a cheerful but ineffectual man—donated sperm then hurried off to celebrate at the nearest whiskey vat.

"Very well, Captain," she said at last. "You've made your point."

"Then we can move on."

"We can." She turned away from the window. "But let's get a few things straight. First, I'm not moving to Geraktin. I use the lodgings in Faissa for several reasons, anonymity being one of them."

He gave a curt nod. "Acceptable. And the rest?"

"I agreed to this partnership as a means to an end, nothing else. I don't do small talk, I'm not here to be your friend, and I keep my private affairs to myself. I don't know you, and don't assume you know me from what's written in my file or the rumours you've heard. But I promise you this. Whatever our differences, we *will* find a way to work together. I intend to clear my name and rejoin the Ta'Hafiq."

"Understood."

Someone passed in the hall outside, footsteps slowing as if to eavesdrop before quickly hurrying on. She waited until they'd faded before speaking again.

"You should also know the General briefed me a little about your *condition*…" She hesitated. The words tasted like cold ash in her throat. Her mother's voice ghosted from memory, chastising her for being too blunt and direct. In the end, Dhani simply lowered her head.

"I'm also sorry about your wife and son," she said.

Gorshayik's fingers curled. The glint of a gold wedding bracelet on his right wrist caught her eye and she looked away. *Eight moons was still too soon*, she guessed. How did anyone ever recover from something like that? Most likely they didn't. Little wonder he had a *condition*.

"Thank you," he said, low and hoarse.

Dhani cleared her throat. "So, this operation?" She opened the folder and pushed it towards him. "Four names and three addresses. Not a lot of information."

He made a noise somewhere between a grunt and a sniff. "I suspect there is no Scythe and this is a fool's errand to keep us busy until Shalamir figures out a better way to get rid of us."

"Well, at least we can agree about that." She studied the file again. "Where do you want to start?"

"At the Service archive. We'll see if any of these men have files." He tapped a finger on the last name on the list. "*Papat Yenidogat.* A priest shouldn't be hard to find."

Dhani frowned. "*Yenidogat?* I've heard the name before."

"You said you've worked in Izurum previously?"

"I have." She'd worked in Izurum a number of times over the past few years. Regularly enough to have several caches containing weapons, clothing and a handful of cash hidden in the city and its shantytown, Koyulerin, just beyond the southern wall. Like most Ta'Hafiq missions, however, those she'd conducted here were brief: *locate target, eliminate or obtain target, get out quick.* She couldn't claim a local's deep familiarity with the city or its inhabitants.

"Do you have contacts you could call on for information?" He looked up in earnest, the first time he'd expressed anything other than frustration with the entire arrangement. "*Scythe* is an unusual nickname for a Tizraki," he continued. "The kind of name that begs attention. If this person exists, someone will know them."

26

"There's one or two people I could ask."

"Good." He pulled a brass pocket watch from a pocket and checked the time. He held it for a moment, gaze lingering on the piece before tucking it away again. "Let's head over to the Service archive. After lunch, we'll start talking to the people on the list."

"So…that's the plan? Talk to them?"

"That's the plan. Unless you have some other suggestion?"

For the sake of peace—and the recommendation he eventually had to sign—Dhani shrugged acceptance. *Don't piss off the Tizraki bear with a bag of hornets up its arse on the first day.* There'd be a year's worth of days, four hundred and twelve to be exact, in which to do the same.

"Talking is fine." She tapped the list of names. "I'll take Erdogal Timoyucik and Jursek Cerevin. Their addresses are in Tergayit on the southern side of the city. You can take Temek Huyurgal and Papat Yenidogat. I'm sure a Tizraki priest would rather talk to a Tizraki than a gods-denying Homelander, anyway."

The fires-of-hell look flickered in his eyes once more and disappeared. He stared at the file, at the cockroach, at smears of dust on the table. "We're partners, Karim. We do this together."

"This partnership will work better if I work alone, Captain."

"This isn't the Ta'Hafiq."

Dhani ground her teeth. A hall clock elsewhere in the building chimed a muffled eleven bells. *Three days.* Surely even a man as stubborn as Parvan Gorshayik could understand efficiency? She found her most begrudging smile and painted it on her lips.

"In three days, I'm facing court martial, Captain Gorshayik. It might not matter to you, but I'll wager a hundred dironi that Bethsehal Shalamir already has an execution order drawn up and a firing squad etching my name on their bullets. I don't have time to waste."

"You should have thought about that before you gave *Shulim* Bethsehal lip."

"Shulim Bethsehal should have kept her mouth shut about her political allegiances. I'd rather not know her underwear gets hot and sweaty over an emperor deposed for nation-sized embezzlement."

Gorshayik muttered something unintelligible under his breath. When he looked up, his gaze locked with hers and held. "Have you ever run an intelligence mission before, Karim?"

"A number of them."

"From the beginning? Gathered the facts, created an evidence matrix, mapped out a relationship diagram?"

Checkmate. She sucked in both cheeks. *But how hard could it be, trawling Izurum's streets for people with bad pseudonyms and shuffling paper about a desk?* Her first year in the Ta'Hafiq comprised the same basic training as every other Secret Service operative when it came to gathering intelligence. Give her a week, a re-read of a few Service manuals and she'd be equal to anyone else working in Internal Affairs. After all, as an assassin she'd sweated blood, pulled muscles, bent bones, and busted her brain harder than any ordinary operative ever would—all in the name of carrying out the Imperium's darkest biddings.

"I've fifty-three confirmed kills as an assassin, Captain Gorshayik. Finding someone with a bad alias shouldn't be too much of a problem."

Gorshayik stared her down, unmoved. "This is Internal Affairs, Karim. You can forget about pulling a blade here anytime soon unless it's in self-defence." He brushed a finger along the scar on his cheek, drawing it away just as quickly. "For now, we run this mission by the Service rulebook, which means we do it together and we do it under my command."

So they were back to stalemate again. A caustic voice in her head told her to get used to it. "There are four names on that list, Captain. You take two, I take two. I don't see anything wrong with that."

Gorshayik straightened to his full height. That she had to look up when she was as tall as—or even taller than—most Tizraki men was vaguely irritating.

"This isn't a democracy, Karim. I'm the captain and *you* follow orders. If that's too hard to understand, then think about the recommendation I have to write in nine moons." With that, he took a single stride and banged open the door. Not looking back, he flicked a hand at the file. "Bring the list. We're going to the archive and then we're going out *together*, whether you like it or not."

Dhani snatched the list from the desk and shoved it into a pocket. She didn't need her mother's ghost to tell her this was going to be the longest of very long years

CHAPTER FOUR

Erdogal Timoyucik didn't have a file. The second man on the list, Jursek Cerevin, did.

The Registrar, a young Tizraki man dressed in a crisp, black uniform, locked the archive door behind him and dumped three tattered files on the desk. Creases, dirt, and greasy thumb prints attested to their frequent use.

"Jursik Cerevin is known," the Registrar said, not making eye contact, "for money-laundering, fencing stolen goods, operating an illegal whisky still, public obstruction and attempting to organise a protection racket." His voice rose in inflection as he read the next name off the list. Dhani arched an eyebrow. The Registrar sounded...*surprised*. "Temek Huyurgal, master cordwain. No file."

The last file he set down was so thin it couldn't have held more than a single page. As the Registrar spoke the name, his fingers drifted to a bone horseshoe pendant— another of Father Ulgan's devotional symbols—touching it briefly out of respect. "Papat Kyvil Yenidogat, priest of

Father Ulgan's temple in Zidurat. Biography only. No known misdemeanours or political affiliations."

The man pushed the register across the desk then tilted his head up to meet Parvan Gorshayik's gaze. "Sign here, Captain. Should you make additions to any of the files, please inform the duty Registrar upon their return. Understood?"

Gorshayik nodded and signed the register in neat Tizraki calligraphy. He scooped up the files, turned on his heel, and marched in silence under the stinging sun back across the compound, returning to the flat-roofed blockhouse and their cat-sized, dust filled office.

Dhani spent the next hour combing Cerevin's files, trawling through case notes and interview extracts whilst Gorshayik made jottings and lists on a pad of lined paper he'd found in a drawer. After reading a few pages of Cerevin's file, her gut feeling was that he likely knew nothing about Scythe. The man was merely a serial entrepreneur of the wrong kind, an easy target for Ha'filu operatives when beginning a new case.

Just after midday, Gorshayik pulled out his pocket watch and grunted. He set the pen down, rose from the chair, and announced, "I'm going to midday prayer. I'll meet you at the Ciyurit temple's north gate at half-one. After that, we'll go looking for Erdogal Timoyucik and Jursek Cerevin."

Then he left.

His footsteps faded along the corridor's dusty tiles. The blockhouse door groaned open and then slammed shut.

Dhani eased back in the chair, ignoring the springs drilling holes in her butt. She stared out the window. The

Tizraki's mincing strides and broad back appeared briefly beneath the bougainvillea-covered walkway and vanished from sight.

Across the compound, midday heat shimmered off a collection of dreary, flat-roofed blockhouses, all as uniformly neat and orderly as Bethsehal Shalamir's desk. Beyond the compound's wall, the city threw up thousands of rectangular buildings, few taller than three stories, all of them the same tiresome ochre brown. Punctuating the city's low relief were several dozen white towers topped with onion domes, marking temples belonging to Mother Yamir or Father Ulgan, some domes summer blue, others tiled in deepest black.

She tapped her fingers on the wood, cracked her knuckles, rolled her shoulders. The cockroach still lay upside-down on a corner of the desk, six legs crossed in eternal repose, dry and brittle as kindling. *Dead, like her career.* She blew out a breath.

Half a day gone. Four hundred and eleven-point-five to go. But who was counting?

She locked the office door, collected her five throwing blades, her baton and talon-shaped dagger from a guard who wasn't Touchy-Feely at compound's security office, and left. Lunch was spiced lamb kofte from a nearby street stall washed down with strong, bitter-sweet kaffai. Then, she made her way to the ebony domes and whitewashed walls of Father Ulgan's temple in Ciyurit, tugged a dark blue scarf from a pocket, and tied it over her head.

Tizraki might have loved their food and wine, but above all, they loved their gods. Prayers were three times each day, sunrise, zenith, and sunset. Most Tizraki attended at least one of those services. The devout attended all three. The least she could do as a foreign woman from a conquering nation was to show her respect by covering her head.

Ten minutes later, Parvan Gorshayik strode out amidst a stream of faithful wearing a dark blue temple turban, a good head's height above the rest of the crowd. He paused to return the turban to a small child who'd appeared beside him. The child took it with a nod before scampering off to a teenage boy at a street stall hiring turbans and scarves to those who needed them.

Gorshayik came to a stop before Dhani, a shaft of sunlight illuminating the raven gloss of his hair. He took in the scarf on her head, the hand of blades holstered on her thigh, the dagger and metal baton in her belt. His mouth thinned, but he made no comment.

"We're going to see Erdogal Timoyucik, Captain?" she said.

"We are." He didn't quite smile, but the corners of his lips twitched.

Dhani nodded. It wasn't much, but a glimmer of hope sparked within.

Even she could work with that.

—

The mid-afternoon sun stung her skin like whisky set aflame. It took an hour to cross the city and find Timoyucik's address amidst the maze of unnamed, unnumbered streets in Izurum's less-than-salubrious

Tergayit district, and Dhani was glad for the scarf covering her head.

Eventually, they found the crumbling, high-walled adobe compound where Erdogal Timoyucik lived, a place whose occupants largely comprised elders with faces like ancient leather and mouths filled with questionable dentition. After several minutes of eliciting nothing from a cluster of sun-wrinkled, white haired and apparently *deaf* women seated around a courtyard well, Dhani pulled a gold dironi from a pocket and held it aloft. In Tizraki culture flashing wealth about was rude, but in her experience, money—especially the Empire's coin—loosened tongues nearly as well as a knife to the throat.

"Erdogal Timoyucik owes me fifty peshak," she called into doorways and windows surrounding the well. "A gold dironi to anyone who can tell me where he is."

Gorshayik swore and grabbed at her, but she sidestepped and avoided him. "Karim! Gods forbid, you know—"

"*Dead*," a sudden voice called from above. "Timoyucik is dead."

A woman appeared at a second storey window, broad-faced and middle-aged, her head part-covered with a fine blue scarf as if she'd just come from a temple.

"Timoyucik had a heart attack yesterday morning," the woman said. "Dropped dead right in this very courtyard. His family buried him at midday. I've just come from Mother Yamir's temple, tidying up after the service."

Suddenly, the cluster of crones found their tongues. One old woman raised a walking stick and pointed at the low, circular stone well. "Old Timoyucik died right near the well just last week. One-hundred and thirty-three, he was."

"Ai! Noori," the toothless woman next to her said, spraying a mist of spittle as she spoke up. "He were one-hundred and thirty-*five*!"

"He was old as a tortoise," another crone wheezed. This one wore a very fine, bright red temple tunic. Her head was covered in a matching scarf. "Two hundred years at least!"

"He was *five hundred*," Noori declared again, tapping her stick. "Probably more."

"Gods above! He was one-hundred and twenty-five, and big as a whale!" The woman in the window shook her head. "He ate too much pork fat and his heart gave out. Those crones went to the funeral this morning and they've forgotten already." She scowled down at the one wearing the red tunic and scarf. "No one lives two hundred years, Milya. The Gods give us one-hundred and thirty years and that's *that*." The woman's gaze returned to Dhani. "Hai, you! Metalskin! I've told you what you wanted, now throw me up that coin."

Dhani tossed the coin up at the window. The woman snatched it from the air like a hawk diving on a glittering, gold mouse. She glanced down at her hands and their olive-copper skin with its faint metallic gleam. Some Homelanders took offence at being called *Metalskin*, but after seven years living on the Continent, she'd long since grown accustomed to it.

"You would be wise to refrain from such improprieties in future," Parvan Gorshayik said in a dangerous tone as they left the courtyard and headed towards the address they had for Jursek Cerevin. "I'm sure you understand Tizraki customs about such things."

She scuffed her boots in the grime, chewing over the least offensive answer as they turned out of an alley and into a wider street. Every street in this part of Izurum looked much the same: scarcely wide enough for two carts to pass, flanked by rows of adjoining, high-walled compounds in various states of decay.

"It worked, didn't it?" she said, finally. "We can cross one name off the list."

"It was ill-mannered."

She arched an eyebrow. "I guess you'd be the expert on that."

"*Karim*." His glare was hot enough to scorch brick.

She curled her fingers and released them. The urge to slap Parvan Gorshayik, to call him out as rude and insulting before his own gods, came and went. "They saw exactly what they expected to see, Captain. An ignorant Homelander waving her money about in the company of her hired thug, come to collect on a debt." She sidestepped a chicken too lazy to give up the cockroach it was pecking in the middle of the street. "And now we know exactly where Erdogal Timoyucik is."

Gorshayik slowed his pace. "Hired…*thug*?"

She cast a glance his way. His jaw flexed, his nostrils flared. It was difficult not to stare at the fleshy, pink scar marring his neck. *Sensitive about his looks,* she guessed.

"Bodyguard, then," she said. "Someone an uppity Homelander would hire to accompany her to less savoury parts of the city."

He didn't reply until they reached the next corner,

where he stopped and pointed a finger at her chest. "Cerevin lives in Kergot Lane, just down here. Keep your mouth shut and let me do the talking."

Jursek Cerevin was so happy to see them, he threw a bucket of night soil out his window and onto the street. Dhani grabbed Parvan Gorshayik's sleeve as soon as footsteps began drumming inside the house, hauling him off the front porch and around the corner of the building. A moment later, a metal bucket sailed out the window, its contents exploding onto the dusty street with a resounding *plish!* The stench was instant and rich.

"We need to talk, Cerevin," Gorshayik called back.

"You come here again," Jursek Cerevin screeched in a whining, high pitched voice, "and the next thing through the window is a shotgun. Fuck off, whoever you are. *Sarmek?*"

"I can go around back and get inside." Dhani nodded at the rear fence of Cerevin's house, a two-metre-high adobe wall covered in flaking white paint. It didn't look as if the man had hired thugs of his own, just the fence, a solid back door and a pair of smoking refuse piles left to burn on the hard-packed dirt. Something in the man's whining tone told her the shotgun was a bluff, too. Odds on, he'd have an ancient muzzleloader hanging above his mantlepiece that hadn't been cleaned or fired in years. "Blade to the throat or the balls, I'm sure he'll change his mind."

A puff of wind chased the stink of shit and stale urine along the street. Gorshayik wrinkled his nose, eyes tracing circles in the dirt at his feet. He muttered something under his breath. It sounded like *complete waste of time.*

"We'll come back later." He glanced at the hand of blades on her thigh. If he didn't approve of her openly carrying weapons, he'd so far held his peace. *And those were just the weapons he could see.* In the side of her boot was another blade, the skewers holding her bun in place held metal points. The tiny lock pick and rake hidden in her brassiere didn't count as weapons, but she went nowhere without them.

"Come on," he snapped like a bear trap slamming shut. "We're talking to Temek Huyurgal before he shuts up shop."

—

By the time they'd made their way from Tergayit over to Mursik in the city's north where Temek Huyurgal's workshop lay, the sun was drawing long, golden shadows across the city's streets.

Unlike the confusing web of lanes and unpaved alleys in Tergayit, Mursik sat upon a low rise in Izurum's north. The streets were laid with cobbled blocks made of a rust-red local quartzite and boasted newly piped sewers and drains. Dhani squinted up at the well-maintained family compounds and businesses on the hill. Someone had probably paid the Majapayit Lurgak, Izurum's current ruler, a tidy sum for streets as neat as this. Given that Mursik was home to the city's finest artisans—such as high-end tailors, hosiers, and milliners—it came as no surprise. The wealthy looked after their own, no matter what your nation's name.

Temek Huyurgal ran a large cordwainery not far from

Mursik's main souk. The word *factory* came to mind when she adjusted her scarf, ducked, and followed Parvan Gorshayik's broad back in through the building's low stone door. A quick count of raven Tizraki heads inside the structure told her at least forty people worked for Huyurgal, turning out fine leather sandals, boots, and delicate temple moccasins from rows of orderly, hand-cranked sewing machines, workbenches, and leather rollers. A few of the workers traced careful red Flames over leather, using Deenjah to inscribe intricate designs into leather.

A reluctant Huyurgal agreed to speak with them. He was a man in his early sixties wearing a turquoise earring in one ear and a stained jute apron over a plain, dark blue tunic. His beard was obsidian, his charcoal eyes deep set, his mouth etched with a few early lines. His right hand lacked two joints of its little finger. Even more unusual, Temek Huyurgal was sweating, far more than even the warm spring sun on the arid savannahs suggested he should be.

"You from the Office of Revenue?" the cordwain demanded, looking Parvan Gorshayik up and down. His gaze settled on the scar on the big Tizraki's left cheek.

"Should we be?" Gorshayik replied, completely stone-faced. Dhani cocked an eyebrow, impressed.

Huyurgal's eyes flittered away. A tooth sawed at his bottom lip, he shifted balance between his feet. "My apologies. Quarterly tax just slipped my mind. I'll send my son up with the money tomorrow." He returned to the leather roller he was repairing. "I'm busy. You going to stand there all day and stare?"

"We're not from Revenue," Gorshayik said.

The cordwain's head jerked up. His cheeks drained of blood. Dhani tensed, ready to react. Temek Huyurgal looked like a hare caught in the open, about to bolt for cover.

"Who sent you?"

"Is there somewhere private we could talk?" She offered a smile, hoping to reassure him. "Perhaps an office?"

Huyurgal licked his lips. He studied the hand of blades on her thigh before his attention drifted upwards and settled on her face. "Anything you've got to say, you say it here."

"Very well." Gorshayik folded his arms. The stance made his chest and shoulders seem broader than they already were. The description *thug-like* warred with *bear-like* in Dhani's mind. Again, she settled on *angry bear with a hornet up its arse.* "We're looking for a man named Scythe. Perhaps you've heard of him?"

"Never heard of him."

"You're certain about that?" Gorshayik said.

"I'm certain." Huyurgal tapped the hammer on the machine and didn't look up. "You people Imperium?"

"*Ha'filu.*"

Any blood left in the man's cheeks packed up its belongings and fled. His forehead glistened with a new flush of sweat. He banged the hammer twice on the roller before speaking, each blow harder than the last. Dhani studied the hammer, keeping her expression completely blank. *Scythe* was a name Temek Huyurgal had clearly heard before. Any fool could see that. Perhaps they'd both been wrong and the mission wasn't a wild goose chase, after all.

"Look, I don't know anyone called *Scythe* and I'm sorry about my quarterly tax. Like I said, I'll send my son with the payment tomorrow." Huyurgal tapped the hammer against the metal again. "Now, I'm busy. It's nearly closing time and I need to get this fixed. We've a rush of orders to get ready in time for the Equinox festival next week."

"If you remember anything." Gorshayik offered the man a slip of paper. "This is where to find me."

Temek Huyurgal stared at the slip for a moment then took it. "I won't, but thanks."

They turned and retraced their steps through the noisy workshop. When Dhani turned back, Huyurgal was staring at the paper.

The cordwain's hands were shaking.

CHAPTER FIVE

T he sun had dropped below the city's western wall
as they left the cluster of lanes around Temek
Huyurgal's workshop and headed back down the gentle
slope of Mursik's main street. The evening air had cooled
from blast furnace hot to simmering soup, and red-liveried
lamplighters scurried about with ladders, priming the
Deenjah-emitting rods within lamps affixed to iron
lampposts or attached to buildings.

Dhani lowered her head when one lamplighter caught
her staring, murmuring an apology under her breath. Like
the cobbled streets and sewers, the deenjili lamps spoke of
wealth and privilege residents elsewhere in the city
wouldn't see for a generation—if at all.

They soon joined a forest of people on the street,
Tizraki mostly, save for the golden heads of a few tall,
willowy, golden-haired Homelanders also dotting the
crowd. These were the well-to-do returning home from
offices, workshops, and businesses, whilst others hurried
towards the Mursik Souk whose food stalls filled the air

with spices and the mouth-watering aromas of roasting lamb, goat, and pork.

Dhani checked over her shoulder, scanning faces in the crowd. Her pulse kicked up a notch and she held her breath. *Old habits.* She scanned for a tail, for those who looked away a little too swiftly, those who turned suddenly down a lane or hurried into a shop. She found no one suspicious and refocused her attention on the street ahead.

"Your thoughts, Karim?" Parvan Gorshayik asked after a long silence. They passed a cross street that lead to the souk—a long, rectangular space thronging with light, food stalls and people. The scent of spiced meat grew strong. Dhani's stomach rumbled. "Was Huyurgal scared or lying?"

"Both." She lowered her voice. "We should go back and wait. Corner him when he leaves the workshop."

"A merchant like that should have had a file." An eyebrow lifted. His lips parted as if he were going to add something but he thought better of it and held his peace. "I find it odd he did not."

Dhani nodded. Keeping records was something the Ha'filu excelled at. After visiting Temek Huyurgal and his workshop, she agreed. The cordwain should have at least a biographical sketch, even a single page, like the priest's. "Agreed. It's strange. Perhaps the file was checked out to someone else and the Registrar simply didn't bother to look?"

Gorshayik shrugged, withdrew his watch from a pocket and frowned at its face. A flicker of something came and went in his eyes, too swift to read. *Urgency?*

Impatience? If she hadn't known better, she'd have sworn he had somewhere else to be. She shrugged and let it go. Most likely, checking his watch was just another habit in a library catalogue that included *rudeness, bullying, arrogance,* and *pig-headedness.*

"We'll pay him another visit tomorrow," he said. "See if he's more forthcoming then."

"So where are we going now?"

"Back to Tergayit to talk to Jursek Cerevin."

She raised an eyebrow, unable to keep the surprise from her face. "Back to Cerevin? Why not the priest?"

"The priest can wait."

Dhani stared into the crowds, bunching her fingers into a loose fist. *It made no sense.* Why backtrack all the way across the city to Jursek Cerevin and his night soil when all they had to do was wait for jumpy Temek Huyurgal to shut up shop? It was a complete waste of time—time they didn't have.

She said, "We should go back and lean on Huyurgal whilst we're here in Mursik. Like you said, he knows something."

"We're going to see Cerevin, Karim. We still haven't crossed him off the list."

The list? She rolled her eyes—it was impossible not to—and slowed her pace. *Gorshayik's methodology here was to work his way down an arbitrary list?* In order, without deviation. It took some effort—and another eye roll—not to turn about and smack him in the head.

"My guess," she said, "is that Jursek Cerevin knows nothing. His name is on the list simply because he's an easy target. He's probably tired of Ha'filu turning up and

44

questioning him about every other misdemeanour in Izurum." She sidestepped a missing flagstone in the pavement. *Ai Creator*, she knew she was right. They could string Jurvik Cerevin up by the left testicle and slice his little fingers to the quick and he'd tell them nothing…*because he had nothing to tell.*

She kicked at a stone and watched it scamper along the street. Temek Huyurgal, on the other hand, needed a knife to the trachea in a dark alley when he least expected it. And if blade to the throat didn't work, a dagger to the genitals would. "What if I go back and wait for Temek Huyurgal and find out what he knows? Whilst I'm doing that, you find a cab down to the southern gate and talk to Papat Yenidogat?"

Gorshayik didn't so much as break stride. "Which part of *partners* do you not understand, Karim?"

"The part where we have three days to finish this mission."

"Last time I checked, I was running this operation, *unranked* Operative Karim."

She clenched both fists. *Four bloody Winds!* What was wrong with him? A *condition* was one thing, but running about Izurum like a chicken missing its head because of a *list?* That crossed into the realms of obsession. *Or insanity.* She eyed the puckered scar on his left cheek. Perhaps this *condition* had screwed Parvan Gorshayik sideways in the head a little more than the General wanted to admit.

After a few more steps, Dhani drew a steadying breath. She counted off another four strides and chose her next words carefully. "Captain Gorshayik, would you care to enlighten me as to what your plan is here? Because from where I'm standing, what we're doing makes no sense."

Gorshayik's jaw flexed. He murmured *Father Ulgan give me strength* and began to walk on again at a brisk pace. His strides were so long, Dhani had to jog to catch him.

"Karim," he said when she reached his side. He made a deliberate point of not looking at her, but past her, at some unfortunate building on the other side of the street. "In nine moons, I have a report to write about your behaviour. Remember that next time you're about to open your mouth."

"A report. I see." A flush of anger warmed her cheeks. *The bastard.* He was going to take every opportunity he could to hold that over her head. She curled her fingers. Well, he wasn't the only one being asked to write a report on their partner's ability to undertake their duties. "Just like the monthly reports I have to send the General about your *condition* and its effect on your ability to carry out your duties?" Gorshayik stiffened. The knife-edge smile thinning her lips was pure spite. "But unlike some, I'm not so petty as to play games with someone else's career."

He turned just enough that his gaze met hers. The expression was so scorching, so damning, she missed a step. For an instant, there came a hint of something dark, something deep and pervasive, the same kind of smouldering madness she'd once glimpsed in the eyes of a deluded priest convinced of his own godhood moments before she'd put a dagger in his heart.

"Don't push me, Karim," he said in a voice no more than a rattling hiss. "Assassin or not, you'll live to regret it."

—

They caught an open cab back to Tergayit's outskirts, a twin seater sulky drawn by a pair of bored mules whose driver sang love songs to his animals in a quavering tenor.

Dhani sat on the back seat of the sulky, listening to the driver's serenading of his animals, pretending to ignore Parvan Gorshayik. The big Tizraki sat rod straight, his knees jammed hard against the driver's seat whilst he alternatively glowered at some point in the gathering gloom or at the inscriptions on his pocket watch as he turned it over and over in his hands.

She tightened her grip on the sulky's side and stared at the darkening street. Inside, she fumed.

Don't push him or she'd regret it? What did that even mean? An empty threat or was he in fact asylum-certified, opium-addict-deluded, no-oars-in-the-water *mad*? And she had an entire *year* of this ahead.

She traced her fingers over the cold, hard steel of her throwing blades and recited the Ta'Hafiq's mantra in her head. *No emotion. No weakness. No retreat.* If she could survive the murderous betrayal of Casa-del-Toro, a childhood raised in a bar and life as a fugitive on the streets of Jhiriyah's most notorious city, she'd survive *this*.

"This is as far as I go," the driver said after a time, reining his mules at a cross street where shops with tattered canvas awnings gave way to grubby family compounds. He pushed his cap back and flashed a nervous smile. Dhani returned it. The man's top incisors were missing, putting his age somewhere around fifty. His second set of adult teeth were just making an

47

appearance in his gums, ensuring he spoke with a pronounced lisp.

"Any further into Tergayit and I'll have to pay the racketeers or risk a knife between the ribs." The man's gap-toothed smile flashed again. "That'll be two peshak, sir."

Gorshayik nodded, giving up a faint groan as he unfolded his legs and swung out of the sulky. He surprised Dhani completely, offering a hand to help her down. She stared at it for a moment then shrugged. *No use holding grudges.* She took the offered hand and jumped to the dusty ground.

After paying the driver, they worked their way through Tergayit's tangle of alleys and lanes, stopping several times to ask directions or to bypass groups of young men who seemed to be lingering—*malingering* more likely—at various intersections.

Along with the unfriendly locals, packs of mange-ridden dogs prowled in piles of refuse, whilst stringy white chickens squawked over maggots, mice, or roosting places. Lamps, where they existed at all, were powered by oil rather than deenjili rods imported from a foreign land at great expense. More often than not, the area's residents simply raised balls of bluish white Deenjah from their fingertips and set them to float in the air a metre or so in front of their heads.

They were halfway back to Jursek Cerevin's home when Dhani noticed the tail: a pair of slab-faced, beefy men wearing temple turbans and grubby, dark blue tunics. Every time she checked over her shoulder, the pair looked away and started talking. Their attention, however, remained affixed to her and Parvan Gorshayik.

"We've got company," she said after they'd taken a second turn and the pair still hadn't disappeared. "Two men wearing temple turbans."

Gorshayik glanced back, frowned, then swung left as soon as a lane presented itself. "We'll lose them."

The sound of boot leather slapped down the lane. Dhani looked over her shoulder again. Turban One and Turban Two hadn't caught up yet, but their scurrying footfalls announced they weren't far away. "Wouldn't you rather know why they're following us? There's only two of them. You take one, I'll take the other."

He looked up at the pink-smeared cobalt sky. The light was fading swiftly now the sun had set. "We don't have time."

She almost missed a step. *Don't have time?* It was the second time he'd said as much. Did that mean he'd finally decided the mission's timeframe was slim and they had to hurry, or had she been right before and he had somewhere else he needed to be?

Before she could ask, a distraught wail filled the evening gloom.

A wooden door in a compound wall was flung open and a young man ran out, colliding with Gorshayik. The big Tizraki's frame absorbed the impact and he staggered only a step before regaining his balance. A group of women poured through the arched doorway after the young man who'd bumped into Gorshyik, all crying, each pleading with him to come back inside. The man didn't move.

For three heartbeats, Parvan Gorshayik stared down at the tear-streaked man. The man stared back as if Gorshayik were a wall or a lamp post or some other non-human, immovable object. In his arms, he held a small bundle: an infant swaddled in a blood-stained cotton sheet.

Dhani drew breath and lowered her head. *A tiny infant. Newborn. Blue-lipped. Unmoving.* Clearly dead.

Time began again as the man whirled away and lurched off down the lane, wailing. The trio of women called after him, begging him to come back.

Gorshayik didn't so much as flinch. Instead, he stood statue still, cheeks pale, staring into space as the grieving father's sandals slapped out an unsteady rhythm on the unpaved street. A dog howled behind a nearby compound wall. A child squealed. The women remained rooted to the spot, clutching each other as they sobbed and wept.

Then, the big Tizraki made an immediate about-face.

Without a word, Gorshayik, turned on his heel and began to walk *back* the way they'd came—surprising Turban One and Turban Two who'd just entered the lane. Dhani drew a knife. Her gut tightened. The pair of turbans came to an abrupt halt and exchanged a wary glance.

"Where are you going?" She grabbed a fistful of Gorshayik's tunic, slowing him down. "Cerevin's house is back that way and our *friends* are blocking our way."

"Alley. Here," Gorshayik said, stiff, like his jaw had rusted shut and it was an effort to speak. "*Go.*"

He squeezed into a narrow space between two compound walls, nose wrinkling at the overpowering stench of rotting fruit, piss, and shit. Dhani followed, the

General's words echoing in her head as she slid along the flaking adobe walls, spoken the same afternoon she'd been given the choice that had been no choice at all. *Parvan Gorshayik is an empty carapace imploding upon itself.* It had seemed a strange turn of phrase at the time, yet right now, after the encounter with the stricken father and his stillborn child, she knew exactly what Behzad El'Meshid meant.

The alley ended abruptly, opening into a shadowy courtyard, a square of no man's land surrounded by a number of high-walled compounds. At the courtyard's centre—predictably—was a public well encircled by a calf-high brick fence. A wooden trapdoor covered the well, keeping out the bugs, rats, and dust. An alley on the other side of the square, slightly wider than the one they'd just emerged from, offered the only other way out.

Behind her, a grunt and a whisper told her the pair of tails had entered the alley and were on their way down. Warm evening air stirred her skin. Her pulse kicked up a notch in her veins.

"*Hurry,*" she hissed to Gorshayik, who'd stopped dead in front of her. "They're not far behind us."

Instead of moving however, he sucked in a sharp breath. A faint *swish* in her ears and a tug beneath her ribs warned of him raising the Flames. Tightening her grip on the blade, she tracked his gaze.

The blood froze in her veins.

At the opposite side of the courtyard, less than ten strides away, three men stepped out of the shadows, left hands blazing with the blood red of the killing Flame.

CHAPTER SIX

Dhani spun about. The pair of turbaned tails were now halfway along the narrow lane, just visible in the deep shadows between the buildings. One grunted as his boot connected with something unsavoury and he kicked it out of the way. The other one guffawed, making a lewd comment about rotting fruit and rectums.

She fixed her gaze on the approaching pair. Rolled and loosened her shoulders, exhaled the tension from her chest. Whether the tails were connected to the thug triplets advancing across the courtyard or it was some random, flip-you-the-middle-finger coincidence, she couldn't say. Right now, what mattered was that overfed and under-groomed Turban One and Turban Two stood between her and a fast exit.

Not for long.

Her stomach contracted. Her mind emptied, narrowing to a single point on the throat of a shadowy, moving target. The blade's familiar weight felt cold and sure in her hand, perfectly balanced. *No emotion. No weakness. No retreat.*

Turban One was less than five metres way. Belly cinched, shoulder drawn, she took aim and launched the blade.

The man had no time to register the spinning knife.

No time to react.

There was a soft *thunk*, a gurgling scream and a sudden, frantic scuffle of clothing and boots. She'd aimed for the soft space beside the man's trachea where the carotid artery lay. Throwing knives only maimed or slowed a target down; rarely did they end a life. The best outcome was that she'd struck true and he'd bleed out over a number of minutes.

Which seemed to be the case.

The man lurched forward, hacking out a series of wet, sucking shrieks. He clutched at his neck, trying to staunch the blood gushing from his throat, whilst his other hand made frantic tugs at the blade, attempting to pull it free. His companion grappled with him, desperately trying to hold him upright as his knees began to buckle and his turban fell from his head. She pulled another knife, its familiar grey, cloth-wrapped hilt smooth against her skin. The man's companion roared at him to keep his hand on the wound. One corner of Dhani's mouth kinked back. *Nice to see they were friends.*

An instant later, a fierce surge of the Flames tore through her middle, sending off warning bells in her head. Behind her, Parvan Gorshayik drew up *askandhli,* the blue Flame of maintaining, and shaped it into a shimmering, protective shield. Dhani winced. This close, raising the Flames felt like someone had grabbed a fistful of stomach and tried to haul it out through her skin.

"Get in close," Gorshayik hissed. "Karim, quick!"

The courtyard's gloom vanished before a sudden, blazing blue glow. Every instinct screamed *run*—a fight with the Flames was no place for a Deenjah-mute Jhiriyan —but a decade of Ta'Hafiq training took over.

Her pulse banged in her ears, adrenalin shot a metallic tang into her mouth. She connected with Gorshayik's back and pulled her elbows in, sending the Creator—that great amorphous, unknowable *force* all Homelanders believed in —a silent prayer, *Ai, Creator's vast and all-powerful, mighty sparkling balls, don't let this be my final mistake.*

Truth was, she had no idea how strong or skilled Parvan Gorshayik was when it came to hurling Deenjah— not a single clue. As Tizraki, he'd be able to command Deenjah up to the fifth class of elements, called *Sha*. She *could* make the assumption that Gorshayik, given his previous posting as a covert operative, had better-than-average skill with the Flames; that he could wield the *Li*— the forms used to shape and direct Deenjah's Flames— with some considerable finesse. Right now, however, she had front row tickets for the thug triplets versus Captain-I-have-a-condition-Gorshayik. And a three-on-one in a fight with the Flames was a losing proposition in any arena.

As if sensing his chance, Turban Two chose that moment to give up waltzing his partner and let the stricken man slip to the ground. He scurried out of the alley and into the courtyard, expression wild.

Dhani didn't hesitate. She hurled the second blade just as a red glow appeared around Turban Two's hand, aiming for the soft space just beneath the man's ribs—the place where Deenjah entered and left the body of those who could wield it.

The blade spun through the air and struck, slicing deep into the man's solar plexus. Turban Two cried out as the knife speared him, grabbing at his middle. At once, the red glow of the killing Flame disappeared from his hand.

But it didn't stop his advance.

He reefed the knife from his flesh and charged, brandishing the blade, teeth bared.

Dhani pulled a third knife, swearing under her breath. *Four bloody Winds, nothing could ever be easy, could it?* Her heart pounded in her ribs. Her chest cinched, and she focused again, cycling through several long, slow breaths.

Behind her, a brilliant red flare of Deenjah lit the courtyard—one of the thug triplets launching an assault on Parvan Gorshayik's shield. The flash stole Dhani's vision momentarily, blinding her and thickening the air with a breath-searing, butt-clenching, hot wind. At the same time, Gorshayik stumbled backwards, absorbing the assault, knocking her nearer to the alley and the oncoming man.

Turban Two, however, wasn't so lucky.

Gorshayik's shield deflected part of the fiery strike, sending it sizzling in all directions about the courtyard. One of those directions happened to be the alley's entrance and Turban Two as he roared out of it, knife in his hand, intent on Dhani.

The man's beard and clothing burst into flame and he screamed a sudden thin, inhuman wail. The blade dropped from his hand with a soft *ping* on the hard-packed dirt. He threw himself forward, diving for open ground in the courtyard, rolling over and over, beating at his head and tunic, trying to dowse the flames.

The threat from behind gone, Dhani whirled about, a third blade ready in her hand. She scanned the courtyard, assessing the threat.

The three men who'd emerged from the shadows had fanned out in a flanking manoeuvre—no surprise there. Burly locals, they all appeared to be several decades older than her; hard-faced men with tattered blue tunics and scuffed boots. One held a wooden baton, another a long, curved knife. The one currently hurling Deenjah was empty handed. She bounced on her toes, resetting her weight. *A robbery, for certain.* These men had *clumsy, desperate thieves* tattooed on their foreheads. It was sheer bad luck Parvan Gorshayik just happened to choose the wrong alley to turn into.

She narrowed her gaze, picking a target. The centre man licked his lips, hesitating—most likely grappling with the Tizraki aversion to killing on religious grounds. His left hand twitched, warning he'd come to some decision and was ready to draw the Flames. On his right, the man with the knife stood lathered in sweat, his jerky, careless movements betraying his fear. The third man fidgeted with his baton, his nose wrinkling at the stink of burning hair and flesh. Dhani rolled her shoulders, shifted her weight again, and chose the nervous, sweaty man.

There was little time to think about anything else. The man in the centre hurled another red flare at Gorshayik's shield, sending light and heat sizzling about them. Dhani instinctively ducked her head.

Burning air hissed past, again sprayed wide by Gorshayik's shield. Turban Two's clothing reignited and his screams began anew. He called to Mother Yamir, five separate hearth gods and then to Father Ulgan before his voice trailed off to a trembling whine. Nearby, several dogs answered his cries with a fury of barking snarls. A woman's voice called the hounds back, cursing them with the kind of language that started generational feuds.

The moment the Flame subsided, Dhani ducked around Gorshayik's glowing shield, found the sweaty man, and hurled her blade. She aimed for the solar plexus again, and the shallow ganglia of nodes which channelled Deenjah into the bodies of Deenjin.

The man registered the blade at the last moment and tried to pivot. The knife spun and struck him near the liver. He recoiled, staggering back, gaping at the blade protruding from his gut.

His face paled. He pulled the blade from his side, goggled at the sight of his own blood, and wavered on his feet. Without a backward glance, he turned and sprinted into alley from which he and his friends had presumably entered the courtyard. His staggering footfalls slapped out an unsteady rhythm, ceasing as he stopped to vomit loudly and then dry wretch.

Three down. Dhani pulled a fourth knife as the man nearest to them drew back his arm to hurl a third flare of Deenjah. Eyes wild and jaw tight, he had the look of someone set to throw the Flames with every last shred of mortal strength he possessed. For him, she guessed, this had just become personal. She'd just wounded his friend.

"*Gods above,*" Parvan Gorshayik hissed. His voice was dry and hoarse. "This is going to—"

His words vanished beneath a desperate pull of the Flames as he called up whatever reserves he had left. The shield flared into place just as his assailant's pummelling spray of red fire stuck, knocking them both several steps back.

Dhani stumbled, cinched in her belly, and found her balance quickly. The man who'd thrown the Flame staggered and almost fell. He took two shambling steps to right himself before sagging with hands on his knees, shoulders heaving. Before her, the blue shield faded, with Parvan Gorshayik breathing as hard as his adversary. Near the well, Turban Two gave up a deep, guttural moan and writhed about on the ground. Behind a nearby wall, the hounds of hell continued to snarl and gnash.

A flicker of movement caught Dhani's attention—the man with the baton lunging.

"*Look out!*" she shouted.

Baton man had used the seconds where his partner had hurled the Flames as a decoy, advancing on Gorshayik, swinging the weapon up towards his head. A man of middling height and ample girth, he had more than enough weight behind him to inflict lasting damage with a wooden club.

At the last moment, Parvan Gorshayik threw up his arm to deflect the blow. The courtyard echoed with the *smack* of wood on bone and flesh. The thudding impact was solid enough that Dhani felt the jarring blow reverberate in her chest.

Gorshayik took the hit, neither flinching nor giving up so much as a single step. Dhani exhaled relief. *So he'd taken unarmed combat during basic training.* Better than nothing, given he'd probably exhausted his ability to draw the Flames fending off the last all-or-nothing attack.

Not waiting to see what happened next, she stepped out from behind Gorshayik and advanced on the man who'd hurled Deenjah. Upon sighting her, he raised his fists and hunched into a street brawler's defensive stoop. His eyes took in the blade in her hand and he shifted his weight, balancing on the balls of his feet.

She lunged twice with the knife, first left then right. The man dodged and did exactly what she'd been expecting—he struck out with a well-placed right jab. Behind her, a solid *thwack* sounded. Parvan Gorshayik grunted and a body hit the ground.

Dhani let the man's next jab slide past her left cheek and grabbed his arm whilst still extended. With the blow's momentum, she pulled the man around, reefed his arm down then twisted it upwards. There was an audible *snap* as his elbow dislocated.

The man howled in pain. Dhani released him, changed stance, and kicked him hard between the legs from behind.

He dropped like a meat sack down a well, hitting the dirt where he rolled and groaned and gasped for air. After a few moments, he came to rest on his side, dislocated right arm hanging at an odd angle, his left hand cupped about his genitals.

Satisfied, she turned about. Both Parvan Gorshayik and the man with the baton were on the ground. Gorshayik was bleeding from a cut to the temple but had managed to get hold of the baton. The other man was out cold.

She blew out a breath, walked over to the big Tizraki and offered him a hand up.

He took two swipes to grab it, blinking and shaking his head. She sawed on her lip. *Not good.* He'd probably earned himself a concussion. It took a further two tries before he caught her hand and she groaned. He weighed as much as a log stuffed with lead, and her muscles screamed before she finally hauled him to his feet. He stumbled immediately. She grabbed his arm and led him to the wall.

"Did you black out?" she asked.

He grimaced. "No."

She studied the cut on his temple. It wasn't serious, but it was the width of her hand and would require stitches. More worrying was the swollen, black bruise beneath the wound, already the size of a small egg. His unfocused gaze and wavering balance told her everything she needed to know. Parvan Gorshayik needed a healer and quickly, just to make sure he didn't have a serious head injury.

"That cut needs attention," she said, steadying him with her hands. "Have you got a medical kit at the safe house? Or do you want me to try and find a *drukilyi*?"

He winced and closed his eyes. His brows cinched together before he reached into a pocket and drew out a bright blue kerchief which he pressed to the cut. "Find me a cab."

She frowned. "A cab?"

"Yes, Karim, a bloody cab. Are you deaf?"

Her nostrils flared and a spark of anger warmed her

cheeks. "A shame that baton didn't knock some manners into you along with some sense." Gorshayik scowled. She rolled her eyes. "Fine. We'll find a cab. Can you walk?"

He grimaced and pushed himself off the wall.

"I'll manage," was all he said.

CHAPTER SEVEN

P arvan Gorshayik stumbled three times before they
reached the narrow alley. After his second stumble,
Dhani tucked herself under his right arm, shouldered his
granite-boulder weight and began to manhandle him
across the courtyard. As he tried to pull away, she ground
her teeth and shoved him sideways with her hip. He
grunted something under his breath less than
complimentary

"Karim, I'm perfectly capable—"

"You're not. Trust me on this."

His lips pressed together hard, pain whitening their
edges. He made a sweep of their surroundings, frowning.
"You killed…how many?"

She surveyed the courtyard. It bore a strong resemblance
to the aftermath of fight in a less-than-reputable bar. Turban
Two lay on his back, clothes still smouldering, whimpering
up at the deepening sky. A cursory glance suggested he'd
live, but with a few burn scars for his efforts. The man with

the dislocated elbow remained in a foetal position, moaning and gasping for air. Dhani cocked an eyebrow. Given his good hand still cupped his nether regions, her guess was that he wouldn't be fathering children anytime in the next few days. A few metres away, Baton man lay on the ground, out cold and unmoving. She didn't care enough to take a second look. Behind the wall, the pair of dogs continued to snarl like they'd been stung by ten thousand angry wasps. Her nose wrinkled, inhaling burnt cloth, singed adobe render, charred hair and faintly, blood and sweat.

"I killed one of the tails in the alley," she said after a pause, and feigned innocence, staring up at the cobalt sky. The first stars were already twinkling overhead. "Self-defence, of course."

"Of course." Gorshayik scowled, but whether it was at his wounds, the splitting headache he most certainly had or the mess of bodies strewn about them, Dhani couldn't say.

At the alley's entrance, she stooped to retrieve the blade Turban Two had dropped, wiping it clean on her pants before sheathing the weapon. A few strides on, Turban One lay dead, slumped in a pool of his own blood. One hand still clutched her knife, slick and wet and bloody. His other was outstretched, the sleeve peeled up to reveal a religious tattoo, a dancing black horse with a serpent coiled about it.

She paused before reclaiming her blade, studying the tattoo's design. Whilst Father Ulgan's prancing stallion was a common tattoo for Tizraki men, the additional serpent was not. Tizraki generally despised snakes with good reason: many snakes in the colony delivered lethal bites.

After a moment, she shrugged and dismissed the coiled serpent. *Each to their own.* Besides, there were dozens of local hearth gods here in Izurum, all lesser manifestations of Mother Yamir and Father Ulgan, the main Tizraki temple gods. The stallion and snake could signal devotion to any one of them.

With a grunt, she peeled the knife from the dead man's hand, wiped it on his tunic and tucked it into the holster on her thigh. Her fingers hesitated over the missing blade, lingering in empty space. The knife she'd put into the liver of the thug triplet was as good as gone. *A day's wages lost in a moment.* Grunting, she reset her balance, shouldered Captain Gorshayik's weight again, and started the journey along the lane.

Perhaps she'd send Bethsehal Shalamir an invoice for the blade.

—

It took a half hour to locate a cab after she'd managed to steer Gorshayik out of the lane.

They found one waiting outside an alehouse a few streets away, a horse drawn jig with a single bench seat whose torn and patched leather was as uncomfortable as its rigid springs. The surly driver, a woman with a square jaw and an ancient flintlock pistol nestled in her lap, took one look at Dhani and curled her lip before adding a third again to the price. Obviously, she didn't like Jhiriyans.

Dhani didn't bother arguing. It wasn't going to improve her day.

Gorshayik gave the driver orders to head for Geraktin Souk. The woman nodded once, turned the bay horse about and flicked her switch on its rump. The horse swished its tail and took off at a brisk trot. The sulky groaned and bounced over Tergayit's unmade streets, then clattered and jarred when it found the flagstones in Mursik. The suspension was so stiff, Dhani was certain her skull would rattle off her neck. Creator only knew how Parvan Gorshayik felt, riding with his head buried in his hands, the blood-stained kerchief still pressed to the wound. The lump on his forehead now resembled a duck's egg.

Just before Geraktin they passed through Faissa, where her own lodgings lay. Gorshayik unexpectedly called the driver to a halt. The woman glowered over her shoulder and said through clenched teeth, "No discount on the fare if you change your mind about where you're going."

"I haven't changed my mind. Geraktin Souk is where I'm going," Gorshayik snapped. He turned to Dhani. "You can get off here."

Dhani sat up straight, brows puckering. As far as she knew, they were going to Geraktin Souk to find a healer. "I beg your par—"

"Out, Karim. This is where you leave."

She studied his cold, flat expression. The big Tizraki wasn't joking. He wanted her gone. It made no sense, but then very little he'd said or done this afternoon had. *His condition?* She could only assume it was. "Wouldn't it be better for me to come with you? Head wounds can be—"

"I said *out*." He jerked his head aside as if he couldn't bear the sight of her any longer. "I don't need an audience."

"What about finding a healer?"

"I'm perfectly capable of doing that myself."

She glared at the street for a moment. *Breath of the Creator! What now?* With or without the head wound, Parvan Gorshayik's behaviour could only be classed as *erratic*. The horse swished its tail and stomped a hoof. Her attention drifted to the driver, whose face bore the same sour-milk stare she'd worn for the duration of the journey. Dhani switched to Jhiriyan, hoping the woman wouldn't understand. "And our *duties*, Captain? What about them?"

"I'll see you at the safe house tomorrow morning. Seven bells."

"What if you're not well enough—"

"I said seven bells, Karim. Now get out."

Her gut churned several times. She massaged her back, certain it wouldn't thank her for the uncomfortable ride. "And until then?"

Gorshayik bunched his hand into a fist so tight, his bones stretched the skin. He didn't turn his head. "Eat. Drink. Sleep. I don't care, Karim. *Just go away*."

—

A few minutes later, she made her way along a street lined with ashishqa dens, the sweet scent of poppy smoke and musk swirling in the air, the occasional blissed-out patron lolling in a doorway, smiling at things only they could see. The warm evening air caressed her skin, balmy, comfortable, reminiscent of quiet evenings she'd spent in Istanakhand between missions, an embroidery in her lap, a purring marmalade cat winding its soft body about her shins.

She kicked at a stone and watched it roll along the street, vanishing into the gloom. One day gone, and nothing to show for it save a head wound and a missing blade. Her hand coiled into a fist.

Screw Parvan Gorshayik five times in the head with a rusty nail. They'd walked all over the city wasting time. They'd been lied to, followed, attacked, and now Gorshayik was checking out.

Sure, he had an injury and needed to get it seen to, but his unpredictable, rude, disorganised and outright *irrational* behaviour pointed towards one conclusion and one conclusion only. *He wasn't fit for duty.* She found another stone and kicked it hard. What exactly was his *condition?* The one the General had been reluctant to tell her too much about? The stone's momentum failed and it rolled to a stop in the dust. If she asked General El'Meshid, there'd be no answer—and she decided then she didn't care. *Screw Gorshayik fifty times sideways with the same rusty nail.* If she had to, she'd find Scythe herself.

She reached the lodging house and slipped inside. Nondescript and block-like, the building boasted the same reddish brown adobe brick which characterised most of the city's compounds, homes, and souks. Two stories high, the building was conveniently situated above an ashishqa den—an opium house—and a watchmaker's shop. Some of the upstairs rooms were offices, but others were small apartments rented out on a weekly or monthly basis. She'd taken one of the apartments, paying a week's rent in advance.

After a week here, she'd move to another apartment elsewhere in Faissa, then another one after that. As much as she hated to admit it, if she stayed in Izurum she'd eventually have to find a permanent place to live, and Faissa was as good a place as any. The thought made her shoulders drop.

What she wanted…

Don't go there, she warned herself. But it was too late. She'd torn the scab clean off the half-healed wound and there was no turning back.

In another life, the one before the ill-fated mission in Casa-del-Toro, she'd hoped for a cottage of her own in the olive groves overlooking the azure waters of the Osmancik Sea. A walled garden with frangipani trees, geraniums, and a marmalade cat. A place to escape the disciplined days and ceaseless nights of the *next mission,* a place free of the stink of blood, splattered brains and opened guts, a place where you'd never need to look over your shoulder and wonder who was watching. *A real home, with Zandolan's arms wrapped about her. Perhaps in time, they'd adopt a child. He always said he wanted children.* She'd never been sure, and besides, Jhiriyan women rarely gave birth to a Deenjin's child. Either they miscarried or bore children who succumbed to fever and brainsickness before their fifth nameday.

A chill ran the length of her spine. Dhani's skin blistered with gooseflesh. The staircase opened out ahead of her, leading upwards into gloom. She slowed and for a moment, closed her eyes.

What did any of it matter now? Zandolan was dead. They'd been betrayed by someone within the Ta'Hafiq, accused of a crime she hadn't committed—and couldn't even defend herself against—and been exiled to the Empire's sweltering-arse end. The cozy cottage, the frangipani trees, the marmalade cat would never be. *And children?* Who was she kidding?

She finished climbing the stairs, thrusting Zandolan from her head and focusing on the door to her room at the end of the corridor. The space smelled of lye soap, a hint of sweet ashishqa and cinnamon-scented tabac.

At the door, she paused, checking the jamb for the single strand of hair she'd placed over the lock's tongue when she'd left this morning. A small thing, scarcely noticeable if you weren't looking for it. The hair couldn't be dislodged unless the handle was turned and the door opened.

Dhani frowned and double checked. The skin on her neck shivered. *The hair was gone.*

Her heart tapped at her ribs, her pulse raced in her veins. She drew a blade, sliding it noiselessly from the leather holster on her thigh. *Someone had been in the room. Perhaps they were still inside.*

She pressed herself into the wall, inhaled, and listened.

Five minutes passed. Then, another five.

There was no sound within. No tell-tale creak of floorboards, no scrape of clothing on walls, no squeak of boots or bed springs whilst a bored assailant shifted their weight, awaiting her return.

She relaxed a little, shoulders softening. Her attention fell to the blade in her hand.

Time to find out who—*if anyone*—was in the room.

Back pressed to one side of the frame, she grasped the door's handle. It was a cheap, curved brass lever, offering no resistance at all as she eased it down. She cocked an eyebrow and froze. *They'd left the door unlocked.* The mark of a careless assailant or a thief in a hurry. Far better to leave a door locked and use the sound of the key in the lock to warn of impending entry.

She counted off five seconds then finished turning the handle and gently pushed the door open.

The door groaned as it swung inwards. Dhani drew a slow breath, fingers tightening about the blade. Counted ten heart beats. There was neither sound nor movement inside the room.

Blade ready to hurl or slash, she rushed into the room.

And stopped dead.

The room looked like a tropical storm had ripped through it.

Evening light filtered in through the lone window, revealing her clothing strewn about, most of it torn to shreds. The mattress had been thrown off the bed, the bed frame lifted and turned on its side, the bedside table upended. A brassiere, ripped in half, had been tossed onto an overturned boot. There was no sign of the brass lamp she'd purchased just two days before. Whoever had made the mess had most certainly taken it with them. The room's mahogany cupboard, an ugly whale of a thing, had been shifted halfway across the room and left with its doors ajar, a task that would have required at least two people, likely men.

She took a single step and something rustled beneath

her feet. A scan of the floor revealed the newspaper she'd bought the previous day, pages dismembered and scattered across the room.

The creeping sensation on her scalp said this wasn't a random robbery—she'd been followed and targeted. That there was a connection to the turban-wearing men who'd followed her and Parvan Gorshayik wasn't unimaginable, but more worrying was *how* she'd been found.

Three fingers accounted for the people who knew she was staying here, all of them Secret Service. A new rush of gooseflesh crawled across her skin. It was all too coincidental, too uncanny.

Was it Bethsehal Shalamir, trying to scare her off?

Her gut argued *no*. Shalamir wouldn't smear her reputation with something as messy as torn clothing, an upturned bed and a stolen deenjili lamp. A court-martial written in triplicate, delivered by some Kishaat-caste marshal and a snooty, brown-nosing court clerk—that was how Jhiriyah's nobility exacted vengeance.

This—whatever it was—had the stench of something else completely.

Dhani sighed and closed the door, resigned to cleaning up the mess—then froze. Another chill ran the length of her spine.

On the back of the door was a note, pinned in place by one of her own blades.

Next time, the note said in an unpracticed Tizraki hand scrawled in dribbling black ink, we ~~kum kame~~ we COME for you.

CHAPTER EIGHT

D hani cursed the pillowcase slapping her back in four different languages. For good measure, she cursed it three more times in tongues she didn't actually speak but could swear fluently in. With her pack gone and clothing shredded, she'd had no choice but to steal the shit-brown, lowest-point-of-low-Tizraki-fashion pillowcase from her room to carry her belongings in.

She'd got as far as the lodging house's roof before regretting the choice.

She backstepped, measuring the gap between the buildings. The pillow cover bounced, smacking at her right shoulder. Ignoring it, she took a running jump off the roof. The child-sized space sailed past beneath her and she landed, cat-like, on the roof of the adjacent building. Overhead, a veil of stars shimmered, still and distant in the warm evening air.

She quick stepped to regain her balance then raced into a forest of clothing strung on lines across the rooftop. Dark blue tunics, pants, long skirts with tiny bells, bone-bleached underwear, brightly coloured petticoats all flashed past as she hurried to the roof's other side. Another short leap, and she landed on a third rooftop, again weaving her way through garments stiff, dry, and warm from the baking spring sun.

After the fourth leap, the external staircase she'd located on her initial reconnaissance of the area came into view. She hurried down the stairs, two at a time, the boots in the pillowcase stomping bruises into her back.

The stairs ended in a darkened courtyard. Here, she stilled her breathing and stopped to listen.

Nearby, a hand pump clanked as someone drew water from a well. Pots and pans clanged. Children laughed, a small dog yapped, a man sang in a high, quavering tenor. Woodsmoke, spiced lamb, garlic, cloves and cardamon mixed with the sour scent of her own sweat.

Nothing out of place. No sharp, thudding footfalls or muffled curses marking pursuit. Just the familiar ambience of an unhurried Tizraki evening. She rolled her shoulders and exhaled, taking a moment to relax.

In truth, she hadn't expected to be followed. Unless the mysterious room-wreckers been paid to look up, she'd bet her mother's stone-cold, dead heart they'd only be watching the lodging house's exits and nearby streets.

If they were watching at all.

Still, the thought offered little comfort. She'd left the apartment with a dozen questions spinning in her head. *Had it been a random burglary? A set up from within the Ha'filu? The mysterious Scythe trying to scare her away?* Or something far less sinister: another resident in the building who didn't like Jhiriyans and simply wanted her gone?

After all, whoever had ransacked her room hadn't been particularly thorough.

They'd taken only the most obvious things: a well-worn leather pack containing her fourth-best set of throwing blades, fifty peshak in Tizraki notes, a stash of false identification papers. *And the brass deenjili lamp.* She swore, slipped out of the courtyard, and stepped into the laneway beyond. The bloody lamp had cost her an outrageous *thirty-five* peshak. In Istanakhand, the Tizraki capital, she'd have been lucky to pay fifteen.

To their credit, the thieves had ignored her current embroidery piece, a garden scene featuring a quaint Jhiriyan bungalow set amongst frangipani trees, and her quilted embroidery bag. Both had been tossed in a dusty corner but were no worse for wear. They'd shredded most of her clothing but left her underpants intact. Her second set of boots had been completely ignored. Amusing, given they were worth twice as much as the stolen pack.

After returning the bed frame to all four legs, she'd levered up a loose floorboard and blown out a sigh of relief. The small leather case carrying her real identification papers, a handful of dironi notes and the set of custom-made blades Behzad and Zala El'Meshid had gifted her when she'd been accepted into the Ta'Hafiq, were all untouched.

The lane ended abruptly, opening on to a tidy street lit by flickering oil lamps. Dhani scanned both directions, then turned east. She needed to find somewhere else to stay, ideally somewhere no semi-literate, fourth-rate, garlic-sweaty thief would think to look. Several suitable lodgings came to mind, places she'd stayed during previous missions to Izurum. She decided on one in the shantytown, Koyulerin, just outside the city's southern gates. First, however, she needed to head over to Ciyurit and her nearest equipment cache to pick up more clothing, local currency, her Ta'Hafiq leathers and a replacement pack.

She made her way along the street, passing a row of two-storied guesthouses and a handful of well-kept family compounds. Faissa was where most non-Tizraki took lodgings or made their homes in Izurum—another reason she'd chosen the location. Here, a jade-eyed, ash-blonde Jhiriyan wouldn't look out of place.

In the street ahead, she picked out a family of slender, olive-skinned Erissi, a cluster of tall, noisy Homelanders like herself, and several mixed-race couples holding hands, all likely heading for a meal at Geraktin Souk. A sphere of bright, bluish-white light marked a pair of powerfully built, curly-haired Yargan women heading towards her. The pair nursed books in arms corded with muscle, paired with sabres and pistols on their hips. Every person in the street gave them a wide berth. Dhani did the same, studying the pavement and holding her breath as they passed.

A faint waft of sweet *ulaya* oil, cloying *chhadi* incense and a few syllables of their sing-song language, and the women swept by. Dhani released the air from her lungs. A moment later, she shot a wary glance over her shoulder

Ai, Creator! Yak-fucking, continent-conquering, Deenjah-wielding Yargans. Some claimed they were the most dangerous people in the world. Others simply called them demons. As far as she knew, both were true. With the

Flames, Yargans could burn bone to ash and bullets to slag. Could cure disease and heal wounds using methods defying the very best of the Empire's surgeons. And they could blow holes in city walls without the need for heavy artillery. Only a knife in the back from the Imperium had stopped them conquering all of Soolaith—the Continent's actual name—a century before.

Turning back to the street ahead, Dhani picked up her pace and hurried on, thoughts circling back to the ransacked room. *What would she say to Parvan Gorshayik about the burglary and note?* Oh, there'd be some Ha'filu protocol buried in a footnote within an obscure Service manual for sure, instructing her to inform her immediate superior about any such incidents *and* the moment she changed her residence. *And there'd be paperwork.* If there was one thing Jhiriyans worshipped above all else, it was forms, records and papers, all of them in triplicate.

She passed a lane where the scent of roasting meat and garlic teased the air. Her gut churned twice, once in hunger and once with resentment. *What to do?* The whole idea of having a partner to report to, to vet her actions and question her decisions was one she liked about as much as a bullet to the head. And, given her snide comment about safehouses rarely being safe, telling Gorshayik *anything* felt like a hard slap to her own face.

A few strides on, however, *it* struck her.

An idea that hadn't previously crossed her mind. *Had Parvan Gorshayik's room been ransacked as well?* What if he'd returned from seeing a healer, found his bed upturned and his gold-embroidered tunics torn to shreds? What if he'd been left a similar threatening note? Wouldn't that suggest they needed to take this Scythe person a little more seriously?

Though there were much more pleasant activities to occupy her time—like slamming her head against a wall repeatedly—finding out whether Gorshayik's room had been ransacked might answer at least a few of the questions circling vulture-like in her head.

Dhani puffed out a sigh and took a right turn, heading away from Geraktin, towards Ciyurit and her hidden cache. Once she'd picked up her clothes, her assassin's leathers, and a replacement pack, she'd pay Captain Gorshayik a visit.

—

An hour later, she stood in Parvan Gorshayik's darkened room, alone, lock pick in hand, listening to the slow, sure sound of her own breathing whilst staring at a perfectly made, perfectly empty bed. The pack she'd retrieved from the Ciyurit cache sat near the door, half full of clothing. The spiced after-taste of hastily downed lamb kofte lingered in her mouth.

Either Captain Gorshayik was the tidiest man alive, or he hadn't been back to the room here since leaving it that morning. There were no signs of a clumsy burglary, no notes from anyone threatening to kum kame or COME for the big Tizraki scrawled in dribbling black ink. The drapes were wide open, letting in the quarter moon's silvering light, revealing a ruthlessly neat space.

A carafe of water and a half-filled glass sat on a low bedside table. A nightshirt lay neatly folded atop the pillow. At the base of the bed was a battered suitcase, secured with a pair of tiny padlocks. Three books—Tizraki histories with excruciatingly long and dust-dry titles— were stacked on the floor beside the bed. A notebook lay on the bedside table, a silver nib resting atop it on a diagonal slant. Dhani sniffed. *Once a historian, always a historian,* she guessed.

She took several halting steps around the room, double checking to make sure Gorshayik hadn't been back. Her gaze fell upon a metal frame atop the books, no larger than her hand. *A framed photograph set face down.*

Her scalp prickled. Her fingers twitched. What kind of photograph would Parvan Gorshayik have on his bedside table? *His dead wife? His parents and siblings? Or something else even more revealing?* Certainly, it was prying but it wouldn't hurt to take a look.

She knelt down and lifted the frame. The moonlight was enough to reveal a sepia daguerreotype of Gorshayik wearing an embroidered wedding kurta and turban, standing next to a young woman who wore an even more fanciful kurta and headdress. The woman was seated, her handsome face wearing a serene half-smile, her hands gathered loosely in her lap. Gorshayik's hand rested on her shoulder, his posture stiff and formal, his expression a mix of pride and satisfaction. Though he'd aged little since the photo had been taken, he looked like a completely different man. Young and hopeful, with the better part of a century ahead him. A man looking forward to a life filled with children, grandchildren and great-grandchildren, cousins, nieces, nephews, laughter, food, and wine in his ancestral home amongst the olive groves of Bayti, in the hills above the Osmancik Sea.

For a fleeting moment, she wondered what kind of man he'd been then, *before* his wife and newborn son had died, *before* whatever had slaughtered his team out in western Erissat. Before he'd become an empty carapace, driven by some darkness only the Gods understood.

Then, she caught herself. Her breath snagged, her cheeks flamed with guilt.

Yes, this was prying and it was wrong. She set the frame down and exhaled.

A glance about the room stirred a creeping, spidery tingle within. Her eyes fell to the photograph again. Her throat tightened.

There was something far too personal, far too revealing about the image—a glimpse of Parvan Gorshayik's innermost, private hell. A flicker of her own darkness answered, shades of a murdered brother, of parents burned in their beds, of a grandmother she hadn't seen in over a decade, of a homeland to which she could never return. *The sure, sharp pain of Zandolan sacrificing his life for hers, a half-healed scab.* Dhani's fingers curled, she bit down on her lip. *Best she'd never seen the photograph at all.* Best she wait for Parvan Gorshayik's return elsewhere in the building.

Without a backward glance, she left the room, locking the door behind her.

She took refuge in a secluded corner down the hall from Gorshayik's room, an alcove near the first-floor landing with a comfortable lounge and a handful of books and newspapers on a shelf. If anyone asked what business she had there, she had her Ha'filu papers on her, though she suspected no one would. Settling into the lounge, she scooped up several copies of the *Imperial Pennant*, a somewhat disreputable but entertaining weekly purveyor of Colonial gossip, half-truths, and scandal, and immersed herself in its pages.

Nine bells came and went. As did ten and eleven. Parvan Gorshayik did not return.

By twelve bells, she'd waited long enough. The big Tizraki wasn't coming back and she had no idea where to look for him, and zero inclination to do so. Gorshayik could be anywhere: tucked up in a hospital bed, carousing with a whore, drunk in an alehouse, or stuffing his face at a late-night food-stall in Geraktin Souk.

He might even be dead.

None of it, however, solved her dilemma.

Time was slipping away. She was no closer to finding Scythe and giving Bethsehal Shalamir a large and resounding middle finger, nor had she figured out who'd ransacked her room.

As well, she needed to head out to Koyulerin and arrange new lodgings, though a glance at the wall clock declared it was far too late to disturb a family with small children. Best she leave that until morning and spend the time working on the mission instead.

She stared down at the story she'd been reading for the past ten minutes, an article about an ancient town uncovered by a landslip on the Erissi Plateau, east of Tizrak Yirda, located in the Empire's oldest colony, Erissat.

No one, apparently, could figure out just *who* had built the town until a young archaeologist pulled an all-nighter and solved the riddle. Adessan Venkaiwala was the woman's name. Whilst everyone else slept, Venkaiwala spent a frigid night at high altitude, excavating a doorway her superiors had dismissed as inconsequential. By sunrise, Venkaiwala had figured it out.

Dhani stood up. She'd never heard of the *Merishkopti* people who'd built the town, but that didn't matter. What mattered was that, like the young archaeologist, she had the night to herself. She could either waste it waiting for Parvan Gorshayik—wherever he might be—or use it to her advantage.

Her gaze met that of Adessan Venkaiwala, a raven haired Erissi with a brilliant smile and sparkling eyes even the smeary black and white photograph couldn't dim.

Play by your own rules, assassin, Venkaiwala's smile said. *Let's start with Jursek Cerevin.*

CHAPTER NINE

At two bells after midnight, Dhani stood at the foot of Jursek Cerevin's bed, fingers knotted in the silky hair of a small Tizraki boy. One hand held a bejeweled ivory blade, pressed against the child's exposed throat. The other held his arm, twisted upwards behind his back. The child's breaths huffed against her skin like a frightened dove's wings, hot and hard and swift.

Before her, Jursek Cerevin, a portly man in his mid-fifties, lay sleeping. The bed covers were pushed off his bare and ample torso, his fleshy legs tangled in the sheets. A stout woman lay next to him—his wife, presumably—spooned about his back, her long raven hair a dark stain on the pillow. Both of them exhaled the long, satisfied breaths of those in the deepest of slumbers.

Behind a black Ta'Hafiq hood, Dhani smiled a predator's thin smile. One she'd smiled a hundred times before. A crooked half-smile, one corner of her mouth tugged back. *Perfect.*

After leaving the Ha'filu safehouse, she'd donned her assassin's leathers and hood and jogged back across the city to Jursek Cerevin's. Parvan Gorshayik wouldn't approve, but right now, he could go roast his nuts in the fires of the Ninth Tizraki Hell. She had a point to prove: interrogate Cerevin, find out *nothing*, and tick him off the Captain's time-wasting list. Tomorrow or the next day, once she'd solved the case alone, there'd be time to wipe Gorshayik's face in it.

Her night improved when she discovered Cerevin didn't have a dog or a pair of thugs guarding his back door. It improved again as she scaled his back fence, picked the three locks securing his kitchen door in under five minutes and then slipped along the central hall inside. Like a wraith, she slid into the first bedroom she encountered and found *exactly* what she needed.

There, sleeping side-by-side in single beds were Cerevin's children, two small boys.

Perfect, indeed.

She dragged the smallest child from his bed whilst he'd still been half asleep. After grasping a clump of his hair, she'd put the smooth bone blade to his throat and pushed him into his parent's room, stopping at the end of the bed. The boy woke up and promptly wet himself.

"*Wake them,*" she said, hissing into the child's right ear.

The boy coughed and in a thin, quavering voice said, "Mama! Papa! Wake up! *A demon is going to kill me!*"

Both parents were awake in an instant.

The woman raised a ball of bluish white Deenjah, scowling and blinking off sleep. Cerevin wrestled with the sheets and swore in the despairing tone of harried parents well-accustomed to small children waking them in the deep of night.

It took the woman a further half second before her eyes bugged wide open and she screamed.

"What the…? No!" the woman shrieked. "Let him go, you monster! Jursek, do something!"

Cerevin kicked at the covers but didn't quite manage to free his legs. Or perhaps he didn't care. Eyes bulging, he raised his left hand—the hand which wielded Deenjah—as if he were going to hurl the killing Flame. Upon registering the blade at his son's throat he immediately thought better of it. The red glow vanished and his hand curled into a tight fist.

"Father Ulgan's balls," Cerevin spat. His voice sounded like a wining gear that needed oiling. Dhani pitied his wife, listening to that racket. "I'll burn your fucking—"

"Stop," Dhani said in a rasping whisper. She pressed the blade deeper into the boy's throat. Right now, his flesh would be turning white. *"Listen to me."*

Cerevin and his wife froze. The boy's body shivered. The acrid smell of urine filled the room along with the sweet scent of perfume. The woman had a collection of delicate glass bottles on her dresser, far more opulent than the occupant of a forgettable terrace house in a rundown section of a backwater city should have possessed. Clearly, Cerevin's suite of illegal business ventures paid enough to support his wife's perfume habit.

"What do you want?" Cerevin's face went from blustering red to desert-bleached white. His voice dwindled to a simpering whine. "Money? A contract? Longer terms on your loan? I'll give you whatever you want. Anything you want. Just don't hurt my son."

Dhani released a slow breath. She had no intention of hurting the child. Truth be told, the blade in her hand was a ceremonial dagger made to impress the gods and the gullible. It didn't even possess a sharpened edge. Theatrics were everything, however. *A hooded stranger dressed head-to-toe in black, appears in your bedroom in the dead of night holding a knife to your youngest child's throat.* Most people didn't have the balls or the wits to deal with that kind of conundrum when roused from a deep sleep.

"One question. One answer," she hissed.

The woman gasped, knuckles whitening as she clutched the bedclothes. Her eyes hadn't left the blade pressed to her son's neck. She swallowed loudly. The little boy began to cry. Dhani tried not to curl her lip. She hated sniveling kids.

"Anything," Cerevin said. "Please don't hurt him."

"Who is Scythe?"

Cerevin blinked. He stared at the knife pressed to his son's throat and nothing else. A trickle of perspiration dribbled down his cheek. His throat tightened and released. "I've never heard of anyone called Scythe."

There was no hesitation in the man's word, no darting eyes, not even a flicker. As far as Dhani could tell, it was the truth; Jursek Cerevin simply didn't know the name. She shifted her attention to the woman. "You?"

"Never heard of any *Scythe*." The woman fussed with the sheets. She glanced at her husband and back to Dhani.

"Milej Tarovik might know. She's a *librarian*. She collects information and passes it on for a fee."

"*Where?*"

"Balta Lane. A compound with a red door." The woman's eyes were round and pleading. "Please, let him go. He's only a child."

Without another word, Dhani withdrew the knife from the quivering child's throat. She pushed the boy forward hard enough that he went sprawling onto his parents' bed with a high-pitched squeak. The sound reminded her of Cerevin's whining voice.

She was gone from the house long before Cerevin thumped to the floor, swearing and stumbling down the hallway with all the grace of an inebriated, overweight cow.

—

Balta Lane and the red door weren't hard to find. Even in the small hours of the morning, in this part of Izurum, Dhani could rely on crossing paths with someone wandering the streets—someone usually engaged in something illegal, immoral, shameful, or all three.

Several streets on from Jursek Cerevin's house, she encountered two women dressed in long black skirts and hooded cloaks carrying a pair of suspiciously squawking, angry hessian sacks. They were only too glad to offer directions to Milej Tarovik's red door. Especially when she grabbed the heavier of the pair from behind and pressed the bone knife to the woman's trachea. The woman froze, corpse still. She smelled faintly of mud, cornmeal, and stale beer. Her breath hissed through her teeth like the slow creak of an arthritic knee joint. Her companion's eyes bulged as they took in Dhani's hooded, leather-clad form, as if a giant's hand had grasped her neck and squeezed.

"Milej Tarovik's house?" Dhani rattled in a low, guttural whisper. "Is where?"

"Over there. Go to Hudial Street and look for Dagormet's Bakery. Balta is the third lane after that," the woman with the knife at her throat croaked. Whatever was in the sack gave a disgruntled honk and flapped its wings. Dhani's lips thinned. A goose, by the sound of it. One mean-arse, butt-angry, furious goose. The creature flapped and struggled so much the woman suddenly lost her grip and the sack fell to the ground. The goose thrashed about inside the bag, kicking up dust.

"*Ayee! No, you bastard bird! No! Ayee!*" the woman shrieked. She shunted forward, pressing against the knife. Dhani released her and she staggered, immediately diving for the sack. "*No, you bloody don't.*"

Dhani slipped away as the goose broke out of the bag in a cloud of feathers, indignant hisses, and honks. When she looked back, both women were chasing after it, more concerned about the bird than having a knife pressed to their throats.

—

Milej Tarovik lived in an adobe-walled compound as depressing and derelict as any other family compound in this part of Izurum, save for the heavy door set within an ached portico fronting onto Balta Lane. At night, and hidden in shadow, Dhani couldn't tell if the door was red, purple, or eye-watering yellow with black spots. The metal name plate beside the door, however, said *Tarovik*. Business hours were listed as *noon to sunset, strictly by appointment*. Obviously, there was enough money selling *information* to warrant an engraved brass sign and be choosy about business hours.

Dhani retreated along the lane a little way, crouched in the shadows, and waited. The next ten minutes passed slowly, watching the red door and listening for signs of guards or dogs within the compound. She planned to do to Milej Tarovik what she'd just done to Jursek Cerevin and his wife—a tactic she'd used many times before.

What niggled was going in blind.

Most of Izurum's family compounds contained lodgings for several families, all related, whose two story, blockish homes were grouped about a central courtyard and a well. Milej Tarovik could be in any of the adjoining buildings—or nowhere at all. Worse, she had no idea what Milej Tarovik looked like. For all she knew, Tarovik could be a gap-mouthed crone, sucking on a hookah and dribbling nonsense, or a sixteen-year-old vixen screwing men in return for their dirty little secrets. Which left her with no choice but break into one of the houses, find someone, wake them, and hope they'd lead her to the librarian. Every blade-sharp, assassin's instinct screamed *no, find another way.* Time, however, wasn't on her side. If Milej Tarovik knew even a tattered half-whisper about Scythe, the risk would be worth it.

Dhani ran her gaze over the three-metre-high adobe wall and estimated a takeoff point. She made a calculated leap, slapped her fingers down on the top of the wall and hauled herself up. As soon as her toes found purchase in a crack, she levered herself over the wall.

The moment she dropped into the Tarovik compound, she knew she'd made a mistake.

Two huge dogs launched themselves from the courtyard's deepest shadows like snarling, furred cannonballs. It happened so quickly, there was scarcely time to register them, much less to note the sudden, metallic taste of adrenaline in her mouth.

She bunched her muscles and sprung upwards again, grasping the flaking adobe atop the compound wall and heaving herself back up the way she'd come. The hellhounds' jaws gnashed at empty space just centimetres below her boots. She scraped at the crumbling render, struggling to find purchase. The dogs threw themselves at the wall, barking and snarling and scrabbling with their claws, fangs, and hot breath gnashing at her heels.

An instant later, one of the dogs backed away, took a run-up and tried to launch itself over the wall. Dhani swore, pulled herself up with all her strength and hurled herself into the lane below.

She landed off-balance and stumbled on some unseen object, partly twisting her left ankle.

A jab of agony shot upwards from her heel, but there was no time to dwell on the pain or the extent of the injury. A snarling canine mouth appeared above the wall for an instant, hovered mid-air, then fell away. Less than a second later, another snapping maw appeared. Claws scraped on brick. Teeth gnashed and clicked. *Creator Above!* She drew her curved dagger from its sheath.

Bastard dogs. Another leap like that and they'd clear the fence.

She gritted her teeth and prepared to run. Her ankle sent a shaft of pain spiralling upwards, but she shut the discomfort down. *No emotion. No weakness. No retreat.* It wouldn't be the first or the last time she'd needed to ignore a sprain.

Two steps on and a burly human shadow peeled out of an alcove, materialising before her. At the last moment, Dhani caught sight of the right hook coming her way, turned, and blocked, but the man anticipated the move and countered as well.

His other fist slammed into her ribs, stunning her and sending an explosion of agony across her chest.

Her reaction was instinctive. A decision she wasn't aware of making between one heartbeat and the next. A response honed from years of being a Flame-mute Jhiriyan working on a continent populated by Deenjin. *Kill them first.*

She lunged, sinking the dagger into the man's chest, angled upwards between his ribs. A hot wash of liquid gushed over her gloved hand. The metallic stink of warm, fresh blood filled the air, rich and deep.

The man choked. His eyes goggled and his mouth opened, revealing a tongue poised mid-air, ready to ask a stunned last question, *Why?*

She wrenched the dagger from his chest and pushed the man away. He staggered back and collided with a wall, clutching at the wound. A long, rattling groan broke from his lips. Behind her and far too close for her liking, the hellhounds snarled, clawed and pawed at the wall. Further down the lane, other dogs barked and snapped, joining the fray.

Inside the compound, a man's voice called an urgent command. Several voices answered.

Dhani wiped the blade on the dying man's tunic and shuffled off into the darkness, wincing every step.

CHAPTER TEN

Geraktin's clock tower, built at the western end of its long, rectangular souk, chimed the quarter hour. Dhani limped past the lounge on the first-floor landing of the safe house, just before four bells. The newspaper was exactly where she'd left it, the lounge invited her to sit and linger. She ignored both, setting her jaw and grimacing as her ankle twinged.

Her own fault.

For the entire hour-and-a-half she'd taken to change out of her assassin's garb and then hobble back to Geraktin and the Ha'filu safe house, she'd cursed her own impatience. She'd gone over Milej Tarovik's walled fence like some novice cocksure-hothead, unprepared and undisciplined.

Stupid, careless, dumb fool. Her own haste could well have cost her life.

And for what?

She set her jaw against a jagged spear of pain, this one from her battered ribs. Answers to a question a few dironi could have paid for at a civilised hour, probably over a cup of strong, sweet kaffai and home-baked baklava? She swore again in Erissi, Tizraki and finally in Massayalam, the Continent's common tongue.

Was this what six months of suspension and shuffling papers around a desk rewarded her with? Was this what she'd become after a decade of training, broken bones, strained muscles, and hours spent planning and rehearsing missions? *Carelessness. Impatience.* A beginner's mistake, and one which could have been fatal. Given the hounds of hell lurking in the compound and the Shadowman in the alcove, she'd been damned lucky to get away with only a jarred ankle and some bruised ribs.

Some assassin.

Still fuming, she hobbled along the hall to Parvan Gorshayik's room, knocked and waited.

There was no answer.

Damn him. She balled a hand into a fist and released it. *Why was she even bothering?* Knowing her luck, *dear* Captain Gorshayik was tucked up in a whore's bed elsewhere, snoring out his lungs with a belly full of food after a pleasant night of hot and sweaty sex.

She turned stiffly, ready to leave, when a cough sounded inside the room. She knocked again and waited.

Again, there was no reply.

"Open up," she hissed through the door. "I know you're in there."

There was a long pause, and for a moment, it seemed unlikely she'd receive a reply.

Then came a muffled, "*Go away.*"

Her hand made another fist. "Open up. We need to talk."

No response save a faint creaking of bedsprings.

Dhani ground her teeth. She checked the hall and narrowed her eyes.

Yes, it was early. Truth be told, the birds hadn't even started carolling the dawn chorus. However, they were one day down and no closer to finding Scythe than they had been in Bethsehal Shalamir's office the previous morning. She was tired, hungry, sore and completely—*utterly*—out of patience.

She flattened her lips and listened again. Perhaps Gorshayik had someone with him? *Very well.* She'd let herself in. If he had company, she'd kick the woman out.

She slipped the lock pick and rake from her brassiere and picked the lock. After less than a minute, the door swung open.

The scent of soap, freshly laundered clothing and, faintly, almonds, were the first things she inhaled. As her eyes adjusted to the lamplight, she registered Parvan Gorshayik alone, sitting on the bed.

He was dressed in the nightshirt she'd seen folded on the pillow hours before, knees poking out beneath its dark blue hem. His hair stuck up in several cock's combs, whilst dark trenches ringed his eyes—eyes that were puffy and red. The photograph frame lay beside him, face down on the bed.

A surge of guilt warmed her cheeks. Dhani looked away. *Other people's emotions* had always been high on the list of reasons not to work with a partner—especially when that partner suffered from a *condition*. For several seconds, she listened to the yawning silence, its passage marked by the rush of blood in her ears.

"Are you...unwell?" she managed, finally.

"*Go away.*" Gorshayik stared at her with a corpse's blank stare. Then, his gaze dropped to the floor. She made a quick check of his head wound. Clearly, he'd found a healer and a good one at that. All that was left of the cut from the wooden baton was a faint, pink line. The lump, too, was gone.

"How is your head?" She slipped the lock pick and rake into her brassiere and closed the door. "The wound looks almost healed."

"I saw a *drukpa*."

"You found a *Yargan* healer?" She cocked an eyebrow. "Must have cost you a fortune. Those wool-haired mountain bastards don't come cheap."

Gorshayik didn't reply. He continued to stare at the rug on the floor, expression glazed.

"Look, I'm sorry about the intrusion, but we really do need to talk." That she *wasn't* sorry at all was something he didn't need to know. In his condition, he wasn't likely to notice, anyway. "My room was ransacked yesterday," she said, more matter of fact than it should have been. She pulled the folded note from a pocket. "They left me a note. It says, *Next time, we come for you.*"

He didn't respond. Not so much as a shrug.

"Did you hear what I said, Captain? My room was ransacked." She tapped her boot on the bare floorboards. The sound echoed about the spartan room but Gorshayik gave no indication he was listening. He stared at the rug as if it were the most interesting thing in the universe. *As if his mind had skipped out of his head and left behind a note saying, 'gone out for dinner, not coming back anytime soon.'* "We were followed yesterday, we were attacked, my room was ransacked and I was left a threatening note. Something isn't right here."

A long pause, then he said, "Go away."

She fought the urge to roll her eyes so hard she'd probably sprain both optic nerves, and lost, turning them skywards. "Gods above, is that *all* you can say? I'm looking for some assistance here, Captain. You know, a bit of adulting, doing your job, playing the role the Imperium pays you to do…that kind of thing?"

Gorshayik returned a glare so scorching, it was a wonder the air between them didn't burst into flame. "Go away, Karim."

"We have two days to find Scythe, Captain." She thrust the note at him, rustling the paper. "I will not go away."

Several seconds passed. A long way away, a door closed. Muted voices floated in from outside. A hand pump clanked as someone drew water from a well.

"Find Scythe yourself. I don't care what they do to me." He sighed, curled his fingers and stared at the floor again. His shoulders slumped. "Now, please. Go away."

Dhani didn't move. She cycled through three slow breaths, repeating the nonsense mantra she'd been given in Ta'Hafiq training to focus her mind. Then, she stared at the slouched form sitting on the bed.

Melancholy, the physicians called it. The General called it *a condition*. She called it *weakness*, and part of her wanted to kick Parvan Gorshayik in the shins until he bled.

Another part warned he was well beyond the kind of assistance kicking might give.

"Have you spoken to anyone about your...*condition?*" She refolded the note and tucked it away. "It might help. Your drukpa, for instance? I've heard Yargans are good with those kinds—"

He jerked his head her way and glowered. His hands bunched into fists so tight, his knuckles whitened the skin.

"Did you break in before, Karim?" he demanded, imperious. "Someone touched..." His eyes slid sideways, landing on the photograph.

Dhani chewed on the inside of her cheek. There was no use denying what she'd done, especially when she could justify her actions with Ha'filu protocol. "I was worried about your head injury. When you didn't answer, I thought you might have been in here, unconscious or dead. So I thought I'd best check. There's something in Service manual about partners looking out for each other, isn't there?"

Gorshayik didn't reply. Instead, he lowered his gaze, burying it on the floor whilst his shoulders slowly rose and fell. The scar on his cheek twitched. Outside, the hand pump continued to clank.

"I know..." She continued, stumbling over her words. *Why was she persisting?* She was wasting time here, time she didn't have. And it wasn't as if anything she said to him would matter, anyway. She'd have better luck giving instructions to a rock wall. "I know it can be hard to talk about how you're feeling, but—"

He stiffened, nostrils flaring. He drew a loud breath, then exploded, "*What the hell would you know?* You're an assassin. *A killer.* You don't have feelings. You don't show any emotion at all."

Fury coiled in Dhani's belly, a hot, iron-hard fist. No feelings? *Really?* He had no idea. None at all. And he'd just sliced open a wound that hadn't fully healed.

She glared back at him. A wave of memory crested within, of a time when she'd had a family, another name, a life of petty crime in the grimy backstreets of a sweltering tropical city. Of a man she'd killed in self-defence at age seventeen after rushing to the aid of a woman being raped. *Of another time her trust had been betrayed.* Her pulse raced, her cheeks burned, but when she spoke, her voice was wound tight as a coil of wire, as controlled as the arc of a well-thrown blade.

"My parents were murdered in their beds when I was eighteen. Six months later, my twin brother was flayed alive whilst I listened to him scream." She thrust a finger to the east where Jhiriyah lay, half a continent and an ocean away, a home to which she could never return. "*They* even killed and skinned my cat. I had to change my name and *leave* Jhiriyah to keep myself safe. Don't tell me what I do and don't know about feelings or grief, Captain. You know nothing about me."

The big Tizraki's gaze swung about, landing on her with such force she took a step back. He watched her for moment, eyes drilling into her skin. Finally, he rasped, "What else did you touch?"

"Nothing," she snapped. "Just the bloody picture."

He stood up, his shadow smothering her like a dark, impenetrable cloud. A tug beneath her ribs warned of him drawing the Flames. He took two steps forward and clenched a fist. "We're done, Karim. *Finished*. I never want to see you again. Now, get out before I do something I regret."

"And what about Scythe? What about the mission?"

"Get out!"

Dhani raised her chin defiantly. *Fine*. If that was the way he wanted it, she'd be happy to oblige. Happy to serve it up on a silver platter replete with the Emperor's finest bone china and a golden teaspoon...*if that was what he wanted.* She spun on her heel and stalked across the room with as much lurching indignation as a jarred ankle permitted.

When she reached the door, she turned back and glared. "I'll find Scythe myself, Captain. Don't fool yourself into thinking I ever needed your help."

Gorshayik didn't react. Didn't so much as blink at the statement. Infuriated, she slammed the door behind her, not caring what he thought, not caring when someone in another room yelled at her, *Take it somewhere else, you dumb bitch.*

She hobbled back along the hall, heart beating as hard as if she'd been sprinting. *Screw him. Screw him sideways in the head with a rusty nail.* She passed the alcove with its comfortable lounge and still-opened newspaper, but scarcely registered them. *Screw Parvan Gorshayik, screw Bethsehal Shalamir, screw this fractured farce of a mission all the way to the Ninth Tizraki Hell.*

It was time to do things her way, the way she should have done it all along.

Time to work the mission *alone.*

CHAPTER ELEVEN

Dawn's blazing patchwork of fiery oranges and reds crowned the sky as Dhani limped towards the shanty she'd been looking for: a rusting iron shack nestled in a row of four similarly patch-worked iron shacks, just to the north of Koyulerin's heartland on the sprawling plain outside the city's walls.

It had been a lurching, hour-long journey on a sprained ankle through Izurum's streets and out of its southern-most gate. A journey painful enough to drain most of her anger away, but a journey that strengthened her resolve to find Scythe and the semi-literate, third-rate thieves who'd ransacked her room. As for Parvan Gorshayik...*he* could go burn in the fires of hell.

At a street name scrawled in chalk on an iron wall, she took a left turn and entered a tiny laneway—little more than a single-width foot track between fences. A few strides on, she stopped at a chest-high gate made from a flattened oil drum and surveyed her surrounds.

Ahead, a rat scuttled into a discarded wooden box. In

the distance, an infant wailed and a dog barked. The cool, still air hung with thick spices and early morning cooking smells, with acrid, burning refuse and, faintly, human waste.

Dhani wrinkled her nose. The Imperium *could* have leaned on the Majapayit to do something for Koyulerin's residents. Open drains and public wells at the very least, piped sewage if the Majapayit was feeling benevolent. Perhaps a school or two to give children a glimmer a hope and a subtle hand up? That was what Shaliaat had to do *by law* in Jhiriyah—provide the basics for each province's people, no matter what caste they were.

But there was no help for those who lived in Koyulerin or any other shantytown she'd visited in Tizrak Yirda. No help save for that the poorest of poor made for themselves.

And always the smell.

She lingered, closing her eyes and inhaling cloves, fresh laundry, onions, night soil, frying meat, decaying raffia, rusting iron and dirt. Remembering similar scents during the year she'd spent eking out a living on Dassien City's poorest streets, on the run after she'd killed a man in self-defence. A seventeen-year-old of the Gishatriya caste, the lowest of Jhiriyah's low—and for a time she'd been the most wanted criminal in the province. *She'd killed a noble. A member of the Shaliaat.* At the time, she hadn't known who he was. He'd been just another lowlife, party to the rape of some hapless woman in a lane, a woman she'd rushed in to help.

With a shake of the head, Dhani pushed the memory aside and focussed on quietly opening the gate.

Beyond lay a small, neat yard, filled with rows of pots

and planters sprouting a crop of vegetables and herbs. A hand pump stood in one corner flanked by a wooden bucket. Last time she'd visited, there'd been no garden nor had there been a well. A fleeting smile crossed her lips. *Five dironi a month meant a lot to the poorest of poor.* Her life on the streets of Dassien City bore testament to that.

She waited in the yard until she heard stirrings inside the house; a few clangs and groans, whispered words, a man's cough as he cleared his throat, a woman's musical laugh, then she knocked on the shanty's back door. Though it wasn't much to look at, by Koyulerin standards the modest shack was a shanty towner's mansion with its iron roof and walls, its windows with glass panes, its scavenged blue door with splintering wood and peeling paint. The shantytown's less fortunate pieced together homes of woven raffia, wood scraps, and if they were desperate, cardboard.

After she'd knocked a second time, the door cracked open. A sturdy Tizraki woman blinked into the pre-dawn gloom, dark eyes wide and wary. Her hair was pulled back in a single braid, her face careworn and lined for someone just shy of fifty years. She held a cast iron frying pan in one hand. Her other was flared, ready to hurl Deenjah.

"Who is it?" the woman whispered, fear giving her voice a suspicious edge.

"*Yelanda,*" Dhani said. It was the name she'd used on every occasion she'd worked in Izurum previously. An uppity name, one which the Homeland's bureaucratic caste—the Kishaat—had lost their hot and sweaty minds over thirty years before. There was no need to change it now or to burden Esmille and Fikret Beriktiin—the shanty's owners—with her real identity. As far as they knew, Yelanda Sarif was an agent working for the Office of Revenue who visited Izurum from time-to-time, chasing down bad debts. Best it stayed that way.

"Yelanda?" Esmille's worn face found a smile that bloomed like roses in spring. The cast iron pan disappeared and the door opened wide. "It *is* you! Mother Yamir be blessed! Quickly, come inside. Fikret! Hai, husband, put some kaffai on. Yelanda is here."

Dhani ducked her head and slipped into the iron shanty. Esmille made a point of looking both ways along the lane beyond their yard before closing the door. She locked it and smoothed her hands on a plain dark blue tunic, bound at the waist with a sash of dark grey cloth and worn over loose black, bell-bottom pants. The clothes were worn but serviceable, whilst the door and the lock were shiny and new, the benefit, Dhani suspected, of the five dironi she sent the family every month.

"When did you arrive?" Esmille planted a kiss on each cheek. Dhani returned the gesture before lowering her head shyly to Fikret.

"A couple of days ago." She adjusted the pack slung over her shoulder and chewed at her lip. "My apologies for the intrusion at this early hour. I should have sent word I was coming. Everything was a little rushed…"

"No intrusion at all. You're just in time for breakfast," Fikret said, smiling broadly and taking her hands in his. "It's good to see you, Yelanda. Here." He released her and turned back to the stove top, lifting a cast iron kettle. "Come in and sit down. I'll put the kaffai on."

A half hour later, Dhani sat with Fikret and Esmille

around their table, inhaling the scents of bitter kaffai and sweet barley porridge. Like the well and vegetable crop outside, the room she sat in bespoke a small but significant change in the family's fortunes since her last visit.

In place of raffia mats, worn rugs now carpeted the floor. An ancient but serviceable blue couch took pride of place where there'd previously been a set of butt-numbing wooden crates. A flimsy plywood wall now separated the dining-cum-lounge room from a small kitchen, whilst the rest of the shanty had been divided into two bedrooms, both of which boasted wooden doors.

"You're investigating someone powerful, you say?" Fikret said, dribbling honey into his porridge. A man as sturdy and careworn as his wife, the frown on his sun-lined brow didn't quite fit. He had a broad, earnest face, the kind made for laughter and tossing small, giggling children into the air. It matched his solid build and caring demeanour.

"Aye, someone powerful," Dhani lied. She'd come up with a story on her way to Koyulerin—investigating unpaid tax from someone close to the Majapayit. Fikret and Esmille knew better than to ask more than that. "Which is why I'd prefer to stay somewhere inconspicuous like Koyulerin. If it's any trouble, just let me know. I wouldn't like to be an inconvenience."

Fikret's expression darkened on the plain jute cloth covering the table, clearly searching for an appropriate reply. Before he could speak, however, Esmille squeezed his arm and beamed. "Nonsense Yelanda! You're staying here and we won't hear any more about it." She shoved

Fikret in the side. He winced. "Tell her, husband. Tell her the good news."

Whatever had been bothering Fikret slipped away. A smile bloomed on his bearded face, warm and bright as a summer sunrise. He lowered his gaze to the table as any polite Tizraki man would in the presence of a foreign benefactor. "With the money you've sent us, Yelanda, I was able to secure a job at Gruycik quarry last spring. It's not much, but I have three shifts every five-day, crushing and hauling rock."

"Tell her the rest!" Esmille elbowed him, shaking her head. She clapped her hands together, looking like she might well burst. "Tell her the *other* news."

"The overseer on my shift gave me a reference and…" Fikret's cautious smile returned to his face. "We've been accepted onto a waiting list to rent a small apartment in Tergayit."

A surge of warmth flooded Dhani's chest. She sipped her kaffai, keeping her gaze lowered as Tizraki custom required.

Such a small thing.

With just a little extra money, Fikret had been able to pay a *promise price*—essentially a bribe—to secure a job. No doubt he'd paid a second bribe to some grimy, money-grubbing overseer to get his name on a waiting list for the apartment as well. In the Homeland, it was called *corruption* and came with a jail sentence or a public flogging, but in many places on the Continent, this kind of bribery was part of life. And—bribery or not—a move out of Koyulerin and into the city's walls meant a better life for Esmille, Fikret and their two surviving children, Abil and

Rivek. She picked up her spoon, making a mental note to ask for the overseer's name and see if there was any way to lean on him to make sure their names jumped to the top of the list.

"That's wonderful news," she said, dipping her head to the pair of brass hearth gods set on a crate converted into a home altar. "The Gods have smiled on you."

"*Akhajelem*," both Fikret and Esmille murmured, a word meaning *blessed be the Gods*. The moment passed, Fikret scooped porridge into his mouth, the faint frown returning to his brow.

"There's something you should know, Yelanda," he said after a few moments, his voice wary and low. Esmille hissed under her breath and shook her head, but he waved her away. "I don't know if you've heard, but there's been trouble here in Koyulerin. Religious trouble. You'll need to be careful coming and going from the city."

Dhani stiffened. *Religious trouble?* She spooned porridge into her mouth, savouring its honey sweetness even as her mouth soured. Tizraki were a peaceful people, a nation of farmers here in the south, whilst around the Osmancik Sea in the north, they were fisher folk, olive growers and winemakers. Only once had she seen *trouble* connected with religion in Tizrak Yirda—along with a deadly wave of uncustomary violence fuelled by nationalist, anti-Jhiriyan sentiment.

"What kind of religious trouble?"

Esmille scowled, staring at the children's bedroom. "Husband, you should not—"

"Hush, wife. Yelanda needs to know for her own safety." He curled a loose fist. "The rumours say the *Bapa*," he whispered, eyeing the closed door where Rivek and Abil slept, "have come to Koyulerin."

"The Bapa?" Dhani repeated. "As in *Yevengik cu Bapa?* The nationalist cult whose followers blew up two passenger ships in Istanakhand harbour and massacred over a hundred people in the Odesstra Souk last year?"

"Yes, *that* Yevengik cu Bapa." Fikret nodded, tongue flicking nervously about his lips. Esmille smoothed her apron again and touched at Mother Yamir's cow horn amulet worn about her neck. "Right here in Koyulerin if you can believe it. They come at night, always in hoods, sometimes with weapons. They ask you to join or to leave Koyulerin. Sometimes they offer money, but mostly, it's a beating." His fingers tightened about the spoon. "A few who've refused have disappeared."

"You're *certain* it's Yevengik cu Bapa?" She frowned, unable to keep the concern from her face. *What were the odds?* A year earlier, she'd been part of a team of assassins sent to hunt down the sect's leaders in Odesstra, the nation's second largest city. The operation had taken six weeks, had been bloody, brutal, and thorough, sending the organisation's leaders and adherents to early graves. As far as she knew, Yevengik cu Bapa, which translated as *People and Fatherland*, had been all but wiped out. "I thought they'd been executed by the Imperium, right to the last man," she paused, gesturing to the north with her chin. "At least, that's what I've heard in Istanakhand."

"Well…" Fikret exchanged a worried glance with Esmille. "People are saying—"

"It's a rumour, husband. Nothing more." Esmille cut

him off, her cheeks flushing red. "And we shouldn't be troubling Yelanda with it."

"Ai! Esmille, I've a right to warn her." Dhani felt his eyes sweep over her, coming to rest on her ash blonde braid. "She's not *Deen*—"

"Fikret! Enough." Esmille slammed a hand down on the table. "You're insulting a *guest.*"

In the uncomfortable silence that followed, Dhani dropped her gaze to the bowl. *She's not Deenjin* had been what Fikret had been about to say. Which was the entire point; she was not only a foreigner, she was *different*, a member of a race able to sense but unable to raise Deenjah. A descendant of the *Tjiri-tjiri*, a race bred as slaves to serve the long-vanished Aretellian Empire. And, to the followers of Yevengik cu Bapa, she was both godless infidel and oppressor, a native of the regime who stole Tizrak Yirda's wealth and subverted its culture. Whilst the *wealth* part was certainly true—the whole point of Jhiriyah taking colonies was to extract profit from them—the Imperium was hands-off when it came to culture and religion.

A cart rattled past in the street, a child's voice and a bell announcing *susa-susa-susa*, or milk, over and over again. Dhani leaned forward a little, nodding at Fikret. "So Yevengik cu Bapa want people to join them or to *leave* Koyulerin? Do you know why?"

Fikret stared at his chipped mug. The child's voice faded away, replaced by the warbling of a Jackdaw. "No one really knows why. One rumour is that someone wants to buy the land Koyulerin is built on." He shrugged, scratching at his beard. "Another rumour says the

Majapayit thinks Koyulerin is a disgrace and wants us gone."

"But the Majapayit isn't a nationalist," Dhani said. "He's a staunch imperialist from what I've heard."

"Aye, but frightened people believe anything." Fikret drained his cup. "All I know is that someone is trying to bully people into leaving."

"And where would we go anyway?" Esmille held up her hands. "Koyulerin might not be much, but it's home to those who live here. Most people have no family elsewhere, or they're like us…born here. Our grandparents came in from the edgelands when the Loy started raiding and burned their farms. Most people are too poor to find housing inside the city walls and the farmers who own the land up near the river don't want us moving in."

"What's the Majapayit doing about this?" Dhani asked. "You'd think he'd do something."

Fikret laughed, a hollow, mocking sound. "Yelanda! It's *Koyulerin*. We're outside the city walls on land the Majapayit doesn't own, so he has no responsibility to us. We're slum dwellers. A tiny pimple on the rump of a fat, wallowing pig."

"*Shanty towners*," Esmille finished.

Dhani tilted her head. *The Majapayit didn't own the land?* That came as a surprise. "The Majapayit isn't your landlord? Then who is?"

"The Huyurgal family own most of the land Koyulerin is built on." Fikret's calloused hands curled into loose fists. "Not that they care a half-peshak about anyone here. Long as they collect their rent…"

Dhani sat up so quickly Fikret raised an eyebrow at the

sudden movement. She stared at him, mouth slightly ajar. *The Huyurgal family owned the land.* Temek Huyurgal's nervous tick and missing finger flashed through her mind. *Was it the same family?* Huyurgal wasn't an uncommon Tizraki surname—but it seemed too uncanny to be a mere coincidence.

"Has anyone been to see the Huyurgal family and talk to them about the gangs?"

"Not us," Esmille whispered. Her gaze shifted toward the children's room.

"Aye, not us." Fikret's lips thinned. "Asking questions only brings trouble for people like us. Best we say nothing."

Dhani scooped the last of the porridge into her mouth and set the bowl aside. Her scalp prickled. *She'd need to get word to the General and alert him to the rumours about Yevengik cu Bapa.* She'd also need to find out if Temek Huyurgal owned any land out here in Koyulerin. There'd be records, surely. Tax records, land title records—land ownership in Tizrak Yirda had been well documented by the Imperium's obsessive ink-and-triplicate-loving clerks. For the moment, however, she'd let the subject go. Asking Esmille and Fikret too many questions would be both suspicious and rude—especially when she was a guest.

"How are Abil and Rivek?" she began anew.

Esmille and Fikret glanced at each other, fear evaporating from their faces. Fikret nodded at his wife, and Esmille leaned forward, sitting straight and proud in her chair. Again she clapped her hands. "We hope you don't mind, but some of the money you sent...well, we paid the Temple to take Abil as an apprentice scribe. He's learned to read and write, Yelanda. *Ai!* We're so proud."

"Ai! I never thought a child of mine would learn to scribe, much less to read." Fikret beamed, the smile bursting across his face. "Abil's read the entire *Ambituryan* cover to cover."

The Ambituryan was a dense and torturous book of religious scripture, the main text of Father Ulgan's Temple. It wasn't an easy read or an enjoyable one. And, outside of the nation's northern cities and wealthier classes, few could read more than numbers and their own names. There simply wasn't the need.

Dhani smiled. "Impressive. How old is he now?"

"Twelve," Esmille said, sitting even prouder in her chair. "Oh, he'd be so ashamed if he were here, listening to us talk about him. Turn bright red like one of those light-skinned Guldar merchants when they go out in the midday sun." She tapped her nose. "He's a little *shy*, you see."

"I still don't know how we made such a shy child, my wife." Fikret stood, frowning at a pocket watch. He began to collect the breakfast plates. "You sure he's not Habi the baker's?"

"Ai! He came from my womb, husband, and he has your nose and eyes." Esmille waggled her eyebrows then turned back to Dhani. Fikret chuckled. "Abil stays at the Temple several nights each week, so he's not here right now. He'll be home this afternoon, though."

Dhani glanced at the pair of bronze hearth gods, one a breed of longhorn cow common to inland areas, the other a rearing stallion prancing on a cloud. An offering plate bearing grain, raisins and almonds sat before them, alongside a pair of copper half-peshak coins. She wondered if Abil knew Papat Yenidogat, the priest whose name had been on the list Bethsehal Shalamir had given her. Later, she'd ask.

Fikret collected her empty plate and disappeared into the tiny kitchen. When he returned a few minutes later, he'd donned a plain brown tunic and clutched a pair of thick leather gloves in one hand. He bent to kiss Esmille then, straightening, matched Dhani's gaze. His expression sobered.

"I'd best be off. Old Martikan and his quarry cart won't wait." He scratched at his beard. "Be careful, Yelanda. I mean it. Cover your head and don't walk around alone. If the Bapa really are here, and you're Jhiriyan… Well, I'm sure you know what that means."

With a last purposeful glance, Fikret kissed Esmille on the lips then strode out the front door, whistling a tune.

CHAPTER TWELVE

The stuffy, shoebox sized office was exactly as she'd left it the previous day, red smears of desert dust on every surface, the desiccated cockroach on the desk corner, Parvan Gorshayik's notes in neat, flowing Tizraki calligraphy on the lined but heat-yellowed pad.

Dhani set a pot of strong kaffai on the desk, pulled the drapes open as wide as they'd go and instantly regretted it. The rust-coloured curtains emitted a sandstorm of shimmering dust, suggesting they hadn't been cleaned in the better part of ten years. She scowled and wrinkled her nose, fighting the urge to sneeze.

After unlocking the drawer, she pulled out each of Jursek Cerevin's files and stacked them on the desk. She yawned, poured herself a cup of kaffai and yawned again.

A shake of her head and a roll of her neck failed to relieve the tension in her upper back or the scratchy tiredness behind her eyelids. As an assassin, forgoing sleep had been part of life—along with sweating, shivering, hunger pains, long hours of training and memorising details, bruises, scars, broken bones and occasionally, near-debilitating thirst. Right now, however, she felt like she'd been hit in the head with a sack of rocks. She picked up the chipped mug, inhaled the kaffai's bitter aroma and cursed. *Suck it up, sweetheart. Six months of suspension and you're getting weak. You're better than this.*

Which was true.

After all, she'd had an entire *four hours* of sleep—Creator be praised!—tucked up on a mattress in a corner of Esmille's front room. She'd had time to wash, bind her sprained ankle and examine the storm-coloured bruises covering the left side of her chest. After that, she'd been able to don a plain, dark blue Tizraki tunic and bell-bottoms, cover her head and hobble back into the city. Along the way to Ha'filu Regional Command, she'd found time to catch a cab up to Temek Huyurgal's workshop in Mursik and then another down to the Zidurat Temple where Papat Yenidogat presided over the faithful. Huyurgal—conveniently—was out until the late afternoon, and the Papat's secretary had given her an appointment for later in the day.

And she'd ditched her unreliable, unpredictable, imperious, boat-anchor of a partner. She drummed her fingers on the mug. Working alone was a victory in itself.

Today would be a *good* day.

The kaffai was strong enough to stand a spoon in, and she sipped it, holding it her in mouth for a moment and savouring its bitter-sweet taste. Then, she flicked once more through Cerevin's files—looking for what, though, she couldn't say. The files contained the same details of his various misdemeanours she'd read yesterday: names of people he'd loaned money to, names of stall or shop owners who'd fallen for his protection racket and other information about his grimy little liquor distillery but little else that might help her find Scythe.

After a few minutes of fruitless searching, she sat back and frowned. Her appointment to see Papat Yenidogat wasn't until four bells, and she'd already decided to wait until evening before paying jumpy Temek Huyurgal another visit. There were a couple of old contacts she could chase up, and after Fikret's comments, she wanted to head over to the Izurum Land Titles Office and find out exactly who owned the land Koyulerin was on. First, however, she needed to make a trip to the government Signals Office and send word to the General about Yevengik cu Bapa. It wasn't Ha'filu protocol—Bethsehal Shalamir should have been told first—but as far as she was concerned, protocol could hold Shalamir's hand and take a flying leap off a high cliff.

She grabbed the notepad, scanned Gorshayik's notes and found nothing of interest. Instead, she flipped over a page and wrote out the coded message to the General instead.

When the communique, which took the form of a grocery list, was complete, she drained her second cup of kaffai, rolled her shoulders again and stifled her six hundredth yawn. Her eyes fell on Cerevin's files and another thought occurred to her

Before she headed over to the Signals Office, it was probably a good idea to return Jursek's files and see there if there was anything on Milej Tarovik as well. Surely a *librarian*—Tizraki street slang for a rumour monger—

would have a file? Whilst she was there, she'd could ask the Registrar to check for a file on the Huyurgal family and to double-check whether the cordwain's file had been issued to another agent—like the *senior operative* Bethsehal Shalamir had mentioned. As much as she hated to admit it, Parvan Gorshayik was right. As a businessman of note, Temek Huyurgal should have had a file.

With a last glance at the cockroach and its upturned legs, she tore the coded message off the pad, tucked it into a pocket and set off for the Service Archive.

A few minutes later, she stood at the long, wooden counter in the Service archive's foyer, Jursek Cerevin's files in hand. This morning, the Registrar on duty was a sturdy, middle-aged Tizraki woman whose rod-straight posture and stern, unsmiling face suggested someone who took their job—and life in general—seriously. The woman gave a murmur of thanks as she took the files, marked them off as *returned* in the register, then looked up with an expectant, slightly unnerving gaze. The woman's right eye squinted.

"Would you be able to check for a file on a woman named Milej Tarovik and anything on the Huyurgal family of Mursik?" Dhani said.

The woman frowned, opening and closing her mouth as if the request was completely out of order and she'd been asked to fetch a woolly mammoth from the arctic tundra or summon her firstborn's soul. From beneath the counter she produced a small book with a grey cover, which she opened with a series of precise, clockwork movements. "Fill in a requisition slip. One for each name."

The Registrar passed over the requisition book. It was a

small pad, roughly the size of a banknote, lined—of course —with carbon paper. Dhani pursed her lips. As usual, everything the Imperium's hand touched had to be in triplicate.

When she'd filled in a slip for each request, she handed the book back to the Registrar. The woman frowned again, an expression of momentary confusion crossing her face, then immediately returned the book. "*You* must tear out the requisition slips, keep them and hand them back when the files are retrieved."

"I see…" Dhani tore out the slips. Clearly the woman had some hot and sweaty carnal affair going on with Imperial process. "Would you also be able to see if a file for Temek Huyurgal has been checked out to anyone else?"

The woman's lips flattened. "Fill in *this* form." She handed over a third book with a green cover in a set of precise, jerky movements. "In triplicate."

"Triplicate. Of course." Dhani filled in the form, this time tearing out the slip *before* returning the book.

"Tarovik, Milej and the Huyurgal family, recently of Mursik," the woman said, staring at the book as if seeing the names for the first time. "And check for a file for Huyurgal, Temek, previously requisitioned. Wait here."

The Registrar took Jursek Cerevin's files and fumbled with a keyring she drew from a pocket. She unlocked the Registry door and slipped into the archives beyond. Dhani caught a glimpse of row upon row of shelves extending into the gloom, accompanied by an overpowering whiff of old paper. Then the door swung shut, the lock tumblers clicking into place as the Registrar locked the door. She smiled thinly. *Couldn't be too careful.*

Or too officious, as this strange, clockwork-powered woman seemed to be.

She waited, staring down at the leather-bound register. The woman had—predictably—closed the book, and she studied the title on the front cover, embossed in gold print. Parvan Gorshayik's words flashed through her mind. *A man like Temek Huyurgal should have a file…*

Her pulse kicked up several beats. Surely that was the case, and Temek Huyurgal's file had been borrowed by someone else. And, if the Huyurgal family owned most of the land on which Koyulerin was built, they'd *have* to have a file, even one as slim and purely biographical as the priest's.

The sound of the keys clanking in the door snapped her back to the present. The Tizraki woman opened the door, cradling two files in her arms.

"Tarovik, Milej is known," the Registrar said, in her stilted, mechanical tone. "Two files. I am unable to give you any information on the Huyurgal family, recently of Mursik, nor for Huyurgal, Temek."

Unable to give you any information? Dhani ignored both the woman's awkwardness and the strange, backwards arrangement of names. The hair on her neck prickled. *Just what did that mean?* That the files were classified or there were no files? Given the Registrar had some kind of weird personality tic that made her seem more cog-and-spring automaton than human, it was impossible to be certain. Dhani's eyes settled on the leather-bound Register again. The answer, no doubt, lay in there.

The Registrar set Milej Tarovik's files on the counter, opened the register, and began writing details in painfully neat Tizraki calligraphy. By the time she looked up, Dhani had a plan.

"Will there be anything else, Operative Karim?" the woman asked, once she'd handed Tarovik's files across and taken back the requisition slips.

"Ahh, yes." Dhani flashed a smile. "I've just remembered two other names I'd like you to check for: Imril Saludin and Yussif Loviktil. Could you see if either of them have files?"

The woman's right eye twitched. Her mouth formed a firm, flat line again. "You could have asked before."

"It's just a hunch." Dhani shrugged. "I doubt you'll find anything, but…" She gave an apologetic tilt of her head.

"Fill in the requisition book." The Registrar slid the narrow pad across the counter again. Dhani scrawled out the names of people whose names she'd plucked out of thin air and this time, tore off and kept the slips.

"Wait here," the woman said, right eye still squinting.

Dhani counted off twenty seconds after the woman had locked the door, then dashed behind the desk.

Heart thudding, she opened the register to the previous day and scanned the entries, searching for Temek Huyurgal's name. *Nothing.* She went back another day and the one before that, but found nothing, either.

Amongst entries on the third day prior—the same day she'd arrived in Izurum—she struck gold. *Temek Huyurgal* was entered on a line with two words alongside: *Restricted Section.* She swallowed, listened for the Registrar's footsteps padding off behind the door and glanced out into the courtyard, praying to the Creator no one chose *now* to make a visit to the Archive. Pulse racing, she thumbed to the tab at the back of the register marked *Restricted.*

Her breath snagged the instant she opened the page. The second entry down was marked *Temek Huyurgal.* The third line contained another entry: *Huyurgal Family Trust.* Both files had been checked out by the rat-faced adjutant, Ziraat Olucik, to none other than Bethsehal Shalamir herself.

The muffled sound of jangling keys warned of the Registrar's imminent return. Dhani closed the book and scooted around the other side of the counter just as the heavy door creaked open. She made a show of studying the requisition slips as if they were sacred texts, whilst her blood raced in her ears.

The Registrar emerged from the room, expression slate blank, a single file cradled her arms. She closed the door in a series of stiff, jerking movements. Her right eye still twitched.

"Saludin, Imril is not known," the woman said in a mechanical tone. She placed the file on the counter, alongside Milej Tarovik's. "Loviktil, Yussif is known."

Dhani stared at Loviktil's age-yellowed file, scarcely listening. Her mind turned circles, reeling from what she'd seen. *Had she been wrong and Bethsehal Shalamir* was *involved in this...*whatever *this was?* It seemed unlikely. There could be a dozen reasons for Shalamir to requisition the file and not want anyone to know about it, all of them perfectly reasonable. Even so, the niggling sensation in the pit of her gut suggested something was amiss—as if a piece of information lay hidden behind a curtain she couldn't quite pull back.

"…Operative Karim?" The Registrar blinked at her, waiting for some kind of response. Between them, the leather-bound register lay open, a writing nib set on a neat diagonal on the page, waiting for Dhani's signature.

She nodded an apology. "Oh, of course. Sorry, I was elsewhere."

The Registrar's eye squinted. "If you make any amendments to the files, please inform the duty Registrar upon their return."

"Of course." Dhani scrawled her name in the book, scooped the files up—including the file for Yussif Loviktil, whomever he was—and hurried out of the building.

The afternoon heat hit her like a wall as she stepped out from the building, the air so parched, a single spark might well set it aflame. She wrapped a scarf over her head and limped towards a shady, trellised walkway, this one covered in white bougainvillea. Her ankle sent a jab of pain up her calf, but she scarcely felt it.

There *had* to be a connection between her ransacked lodgings, Temek Huyurgal's obvious lies, the gangs in Koyulerin and Yevengik cu Bapa. *Had to be.* Of that, she was as certain as the bougainvillea growing on the trellis or that she'd turn up at the Signals Office and fill in five more pointless forms, all in triplicate. What she needed was another set of eyes to sift through the facts she'd gathered. *Experienced eyes honed from a lifetime in Secret Service.*

There was only one person to whom she could turn to for assistance, the only person she truly trusted.

General Behzad El'Meshid.

—

The Imperial Signals Office—*A'Jhaliyya Waktil Khamaar* in Jhiriyan—was a typical colonial building: symmetrical, imposing, hewn from pink sandstone, and topped by three copper domes and a series of pennants which hung despondent in the unyielding afternoon heat. After sending the communique to the General, Dhani stood in the cool shade of the building's verandah, eyeing a descent which involved thirty-two ankle-crunching, tendon-mashing steps.

Before her, people came and went, ascending the steps from the jacaranda and cedar-lined plaza below to carry out their business with the Imperium, their faces red and glistening under the fiery inland sun. She rewrapped her scarf about her head and scanned the heat haze shimmering over the city, her gaze lingering on the black-topped minaret of Father Ulgan's temple where her four o'clock appointment with Papat Yenidogat awaited.

She blew out a breath. *No use delaying.* The clerk in the Signals Office, a Homelander woman wearing a spotless royal blue uniform with a typically Jhiriyan high-necked collar, assured her that signals took six to eight hours to reach Istanakhand. By her calculation, it would tomorrow afternoon at the earliest before she received a reply from Behzad El'Meshid.

With one last, longing glance at the shaded verandah, she began to make her way down the steps, wincing as she went.

One-third of the way down, she saw him: Parvan Gorshayik mincing up the steps, his attention fixed on her with the murderous intent of a sniper taking aim.

Despite the invading-army stride, Gorshayik looked remarkably *normal*—well, as normal as a bear with a smouldering firecracker shoved up its arse could get—an entire continent away from the dishevelled, undressed, incoherent man she'd slammed the door on earlier that day. His beard and hair shone, washed and freshly trimmed, his boots held a gleaming polish, the creases of his fine blue tunic looked sharp enough to cut paper. A black silk turban sat on his head, glistening under the sun's rays, contrasting with the embroidered silver thread on his tunic's hems and cuffs. In his hand, he clutched a folded paper sheet.

So intense was his gaze, Dhani struggled to keep her face blank, see-sawing between a derisive snort and an insane cackle. In the end, the only thing she could do to *not* laugh involved pursing her lips like a chicken's sphincter and studying the careful placement of her boots every dusty step.

Two steps on, she still wasn't sure of the best course of action. *Ignore Gorshayik completely or simply turn and run?* Not that her ankle in its current state would thank her for sprinting up the stairs. Most likely, she'd end up inelegantly slipping and falling head over tit into the street below.

She'd decided to ignore Gorshayik when, at the last moment, he came to a sudden, jarring halt and blocked her way. He stuffed the note in his hand swiftly into the depths of his tunic pocket. Ten dironi down, he was headed to the Signals Office to send a message to the General.

"Nice day, isn't it?" she said with as much venom as she could muster and *not* smile at the storm-cloud expression on his face. He looked so positively angry, it was little wonder his head didn't explode.

"What are you doing here?" His tone matched his glare. The deep, diagonal scar on his left cheek twitched.

"Well, Captain Gorshayik…" Dhani tilted her head towards the doors of the Signals Office, taking her time to reply.

"Well *what?*"

"What am I doing here? Oh, let's see." She tapped her chin. Several Homelanders passed by, frowning as they were forced to avoid both her and Parvan Gorshayik midway up the steps. "Option one: I've just declined an invitation to the Emperor's one-hundred and fifteenth birthday celebrations. Option two: I received a telegram informing me that my long-lost Great-Aunt Saldarinel died and left me a diamond mine in Kaltesh. Or for two dironi, you could try option three: *I'm working.* Your choice." She shrugged and sidestepped him. "Excuse me."

He stepped to the right immediately, blocking her way. "I asked you a question, Karim. I expect an answer."

"Captain." Dhani forced a smile, raising her hands defensively. A Tizraki man climbing the stairs noticed the gesture and swung his head her way, checking to see whether she was being harassed. "I seem to recall your last words to me were something like, *I never want to see you again.* Now, if you'll excuse me, I have an appointment to attend."

Again, he stepped in front of her. The Tizraki man began to angle towards them, taking two steps at a time, brows furrowed.

Gorshayik reached out a hand. He seemed to remember himself at the last moment and stopped just short of grabbing her. "*Answer me.*"

"Let me pass, Captain Gorshayik." Dhani nodded at the advancing Tizraki man. "You're making a scene."

Gorshayik's attention swept from the approaching man to the pair of Homelanders ascending the stairs, then returned to her face. Some emotion she couldn't name flashed through his eyes so quickly, if she hadn't been toe-to-toe with him, she would have missed it altogether. *Regret? Embarrassment? Guilt?* Whatever it was, she didn't care. There was nothing more to say.

She took her chance and brushed past him, deliberately bumping his right side as she did. Pure opportunism and a good measure of spite saw her slip three fingers into his pocket and relieve him of the note.

Then, she was past him, lumbering down the steps.

The Tizraki man who'd been on his way over held up a questioning hand. Dhani replied with a curt *I'm fine* nod. The Homelanders, as expected, looked away.

"*Karim.*" Gorshayik's voice followed her down the stairs, tone low and hoarse. Almost...*desperate.* She stuffed his note deep inside her own pocket. In truth, she didn't care what it said, and he'd figure out soon enough what had happened. The theft had hardly been subtle; she'd simply done it to piss him off.

"Dhani," he began again, softer. "Please don't—"

She silenced him with a backwards glare. "I have nothing more to say to you."

She hobbled down the remaining steps and straight to a waiting cab, a small two-seater sulky drawn by a tall bay gelding whose clean, neat lines suggested more than a touch of desert warmblood. Not once did she look back.

"Father Ulgan's temple in Zidurat," she said to the sulky's driver. "Hurry."

"Yes, ma'am," the man said, and *hooshed* the bay with a gentle shake of the reins. The horse swished its tail and moved off at once.

Dhani blew out a breath and eased into the padded leather seat. She slipped Gorshayik's note from her pocket and unfolded it.

It was no surprise to discover a coded communique to the General, similar to her own, disguised as an order for five bolts of dark blue linen. As she studied it, relying on memory to untangle the cypher, her brows beetled.

Decoded, the message comprised three lines—three lines which made sense, yet made *no sense* at all:

The group have been located; thus I must act. No time to complete the assassin's training. I tender my resignation from the Service and will continue alone.

126

CHAPTER THIRTEEN

The journey to the temple took ten minutes. Dhani spent the entirety of the time reading and re-reading Parvan Gorshayik's note hoping the Tizraki gods, the Creator or even the stinging mid-afternoon sun might inspire some understanding of its content beyond *sorry General, I quit*—and what it might mean for her fast-sinking career.

She was still pondering this ten minutes later as she lowered herself into a chair opposite Papat Kyvil Yenidogat, straightened the scarf on her head and attempted to look as demure and respectful as a member of a conquering empire ever could. The explanation of why she'd come to see the priest tumbled out of her mouth, droll, dry, and one hundred percent sweet-smelling, certifiable bullshit.

A large, fatherly man in late middle age, Yenidogat listened with only half an ear. He pawed through the sea of paper strewn across his desk as she spoke, looking for something, though Dhani had no idea what. His four or five *hundred* chins wobbled, his cow-sized girth nudged the desk and—predictably—his chest-length, salt-and-pepper beard hung like a cheap and dirty curtain over a stained black cassock. Given he'd just admitted to running not one but *two* temples dedicated to Father Ulgan—one here in Zidurat and the other in Koyulerin of all places—the priest's face wore the kind of harried scowl that said, *terminally busy, please come back later, maybe when I'm dead.*

"What did you say the man's name was again?" The Papat paused, peering under a large accounts ledger covered in an untidy stack of papers. "Was it Jamir? *Samir?* Oh, no, no no…"

All at once, a slew of loose sheets fell from the ledger to the floor, fanning out across the tiles like errant doves flying the coop. Most of them came to a stop at the base of a nearby stand holding Yenidogat's bejewelled black and gold temple headdress.

The priest heaved a sigh and cast a helpless glance at a painting depicting a scene from the Ambituryan—a fierce and over-fed Father Ulgan riding in a golden chariot pulled by a lion and a bear. Then, he sighed again and heaved himself up, and began lumbering about to gather up the pages.

Dhani scanned the office as the priest huffed and puffed around like an asthmatic cow. Two more paintings of Father Ulgan adorned the walls alongside Yenidogat's decree of ordination. The room's furniture comprised several overstuffed rosewood bookcases, two matching rosewood cupboards, a daybed (rosewood, of course) covered in yet more paper, and a small window. The must of old paper, the faintest trace of sandalwood incense and stale sweat hung in the air.

"Now, what *was* the name again?" Yenidogat said. The springs groaned and the upholstery creaked as he flopped back into his chair. His beard hung askew and a cock's comb of steely grey hair now stuck up just above his left ear. "Zamuryek?"

"*Scythe* is the man's name." There was not the faintest flicker of recognition in the priest's face as she spoke the name. She could well have said *the Emperor's anus* or *green donkey balls* and received the same non-reaction. "Scythe isn't his real name of course. Unfortunately, it's all the information we have."

"*Scythe...*" Yenidogat scratched at his beard. A chunky gold ring on his middle finger snagged in his whiskers. "Perhaps I've heard of him, perhaps I haven't. I hear so many names, *Izn*...?" He scratched his beard again. This time, the ring didn't catch. "Forgive me, Izn, but your name has completely slipped my mind."

"*Sarif.* Yelanda Sarif," Dhani said. *Izn* was one of a handful of Jhiriyan words most Tizraki knew. It meant *honourable woman* and had a male equivalent, *Izni*.

"My apologies, Izn Sarif." Yenidogat chuckled. "I'll forget your name five minutes after you've left. Don't take it personally. I forget everyone's name." Another chortle and he stopped completely. His deep-set brown eyes narrowed on an open book. In a move surprisingly swift for someone of his size, he swiped the book aside and triumphantly seized a writing nib in his pudgy, ink-stained fingers. "*There you are...*" he whispered.

Satisfied with his conquest, the Papat's attention fell

upon the letter of introduction from the Office of Colonial Revenue she'd given him when she'd first entered the room.

"What exactly has this *Scythe* done to attract the attention of the Office of..." He squinted at the page. "Colonial Revenue?"

"Money laundering," she said. "The Office has traced a considerable amount of revenue from an import business based in Odesstra to Izurum, channelled through several third parties." Dhani shrugged. "I've been tasked with asking at all of Izurum's temples. All part of a routine investigation."

"Money laundering. I see."

The Papat hauled another book from under a stack of paper and opened it, making a note on a greased-smeared page. Dhani leaned forward, studying the text. The page was filled with scrawled lists of things which needed doing like, *have PYT send account for cotton, APK needs thirty peshak, DJY MUST FIX!* Only a handful were crossed out.

"*Scythe.*" Yenidogat wrote the name carefully, making a note to *ask PYT, TJK* alongside. He raised his eyebrows. "Strange name. Like someone wanting to be important or play at being a spy." He chortled again. "I'd think I *would* recall a name like that, but…" He sighed, waving a hand over the unchecked list. "One's mind has more holes in it nowadays than a leaky bucket."

"I imagine you are a very busy man, Papat." Though it was tempting to smile, she kept the same bureaucratic poker face she'd maintained since entering the room. Colonial Revenue officials generally weren't known for their pleasant demeanour. "I would be grateful for anything you or your staff may know about this man."

"I'll ask around. I can't promise anything..." A sudden tap at the door sounded. The priest patted his girth and murmured a weary, "*Come in.*"

The door opened, admitting a boy wearing a dark blue apprentice's robe carrying a tray laden with a pot of kaffai, a lone glass, and a hill-sized mound of sweet-scented baklava triangles on a plate. On the cusp of puberty, the boy was all gangling arms and legs topped by a child's puppy-round face. His eyes widened on Dhani for an instant before reaffixing upon the tray. His olive cheeks flushed bright crimson.

The boy set the tray down, bowed, and backed out of the room. Yenidogat reached for the baklava mountain like a starving man, remembered himself and offered her the plate. Dhani declined with a shake of the head. In all truth, the priest should have done the same. He resembled a walking cardiac arrest.

"I'd offer you kaffai, Izn Sarif, but I really must deal with some paperwork." He gestured at the ledger. "Accounts to prepare for the Hierophant in Talmakhan."

"Of course." She inclined her head. "One last question before I leave, Papat."

"Yes, Izn?"

"You mentioned the Koyulerin temple. Is there someone there I could speak with about this matter?"

The priest's brow caught a tiny, irritated wrinkle. His hand stopped midair, holding his second baklava. After the shortest of short pauses, he said, "I'll have someone ask the Recip about this Scythe fellow, Izn Sarif."

"I'm happy to go there myself, Papat. What's the Recip's name?" It was no surprise to hear a *Recip* rather than the Papat oversaw the Koyulerin temple. A Recip was a junior priest commonly sent to lesser temples in poorer or more obscure places—like shantytowns outside walled cities.

"No need for you to sully yourself in Koyulerin. It's not safe. I'll have someone ask the Recip for you." The baklava disappeared into Yenidogat's mouth. The wrinkle in his brow remained, even as he picked up the pot and poured strong black kaffai into a glass. "Now, I'm sorry to sound impolite, Izn, but I really *do* need to do my accounts."

"Of course, Papat." Dhani rose from the chair. The skin on her neck prickled. *Yenidogat didn't want her near the Koyulerin temple.* Interesting. Perhaps he'd heard of the *religious* trouble in the shantytown and was trying to keep her safe? Then again, perhaps he didn't want her prying. Whatever the reason, she filed it away for her report to Shalamir. Instead, she clasped her hands in the traditional Tizraki prayer pose—palms pressed together, thumbs touching the forehead. "Thank you for your time, Your Grace."

"Not at all." Yenidogat's fatherly smile returned. "Forgive my impatience, Izn. I'll ask around about this Scythe. Come back at midday tomorrow. Who knows? Father Ulgan may favour us with some information."

She left the priest's office and made her way toward the temple gates, footsteps echoing on the tiles as she strolled along a cool, shaded verandah flanked by dazzling white, onion-arched porticos. To her left lay a walled courtyard containing a well-tended medic garden where fever-bush, yellow-flowered Saint's Blessing, and other plants she couldn't name wilted under the blazing afternoon sun. Her ankle ached, her head throbbed faintly from lack of sleep, and an errant bead of sweat dribbled down her back.

Tick that one off the list. Dhani rolled her shoulders, easing the tension from her muscles. Kyvil Yenidogat had been the final name of the four Bethsehal Shalamir had given her and her now *former* partner as leads to investigate. With the exception of the warning about Koyulerin, she couldn't say she'd learned anything useful here. And, though it was tempting to return and ask the Papat what he knew about the trouble in the shantytown, that would be far too suspicious for someone purportedly from the Office of Revenue. All she could do was wait until tomorrow and hope that he or his minions turned up something about the mysterious Scythe.

Of course, she'd need to make a note of everything she'd learned and pass it on to Bethsehal Shalamir—the thought of which sent her gut plummeting through her boots and into the terracotta tiles beneath.

What did she do now Gorshayik was gone?

His role as captain meant only *he* was authorised to liaise with their superiors, as well as being tasked with guiding her in regards to the expected contents of reports. She'd have no choice but to read the damned Internal Affairs manual, write up the report—explaining what had happened to dear *Captain* Gorshayik—and then hand it to the Regional Controller Chisel-Face herself.

Dhani puffed out a breath, sidestepping a broken tile with a boot-catching edge. Truth be told, she'd rather chew off her own arm than ever speak to rule-worshipping, hot-for-a-deposed-emperor Bethsehal Shalamir at all. *Correction*, she'd rather chew off her own arm *and then* feed it to rats than speak to that brown-nosing Shaliaat bitch.

A boot scrape behind drew her attention. Her hand clutched at the dagger hidden beneath her tunic. She cast a glance over her shoulder, heart beating unnecessarily loud.

For an instant, the boy who'd brought the tray to Kyvil Yenidogat's room peered out from behind one of the porticos, cheeks blooming red as their eyes locked. He licked his lips and brushed a lock of floppy raven hair from his eyes. Then, he turned and hurried off in the opposite direction, sandals slapping the terracotta tiles as he went.

Recognition came as his steps faded away. Dhani smiled to herself. *Well, at least that made sense.*

The boy had been Abil Beriktiin, Esmille and Fikret's son.

—

Dhani arrived at the Izurum Land Titles Office fifteen minutes before closing, filled in a form (triplicate, of course) requesting information on the owners of Koyulerin's land. She was told to return the following day, preferably after midday. Then, she caught a cab down to the Ha'filu compound, located a service manual from a nearby office, and wrote up a report as the guidelines recommended.

It was close to six bells by the time she arrived at adjutant's desk where she'd stood the previous morning, clutching her regulation-prescribed report in a sealed brown, regulation-prescribed envelope. It was here that the Creator or one of the lesser manifestations of Father Ulgan decided to play a divinely twisted and insidiously cruel joke. Instead of the rat-faced adjutant and his tapping nib, Bethsehal Shalamir herself hovered over the desk, scowling her best scowl at a stack of correspondence whilst resting a finger on her perfectly proportioned, boat-rudder nose.

"Report for you, ma'am," Dhani said. She thrust the envelope at the woman as if it were burning her hand.

Shalamir glared at the envelope, then at Dhani, and then beyond into the evening's gathering gloom. "Where is Captain Gorshayik?"

"Indisposed. The report explains it all."

The woman's nostrils flared. She took the envelope. Her other hand brushed the white silk scarf bearing House Shalamir's pudgy, leaping antelope standard. "This is highly improper, Operative Karim."

Dhani was tempted to say, *Oh, tell me about it*, but held her tongue. Instead, she replied, "I know this isn't our brief, ma'am, but I've been told about possible trouble in Koyulerin twice today. Religious trouble linked to Yevengik cu Bapa."

The Regional Controller's left brow arched. Even with Bethsehal Shalamir peering down her nose with the full force of the Mawat—Jhiriyah's oppressive and discriminatory caste system—a thrill of satisfaction coursed through Dhani's veins. Not only had she surprised Shalamir with the news, but she'd also irritated her as well. *And* she was also taller than the chisel-faced sow by half a head.

The victory lasted less than a second.

"The issue in Koyulerin is none of your concern, Operative Karim," Shalamir said in a voice as cold and hard as ice. "Finding Scythe is. Make sure that you do as your time is running out."

With that, Shalamir turned on her heel and strode back towards her office, slamming the door behind her.

CHAPTER FOURTEEN

Dhani arrived at the rear of Temek Huyurgal's workshop and took up position in the shadows of an adjacent building just after seven bells had chimed out across the city. Overhead, the sky was clear and moonless, the air warm and pleasant on her skin and here, scented with a faint hint of cinnamon, leather, and machinery oil. Inside the workshop, the lights winked out one by one. As far as she could see most of the workers had gone, which left only the clanking of doors and locks as Temek Huyurgal and his overseers closed up.

The last person to leave the building was a well-built man with a dark coat slung over his shoulder. He whistled a jaunty tune even as he wrestled with the workshop's heavy rear doors, sliding them into place. A sphere of bluish white Deenjah appeared above the man's head as he began to fumble about his clothing, searching for something.

Dhani squinted and blinked, adjusting to the sudden

light. *Ai, Creator's bright shiny balls!* Unless he'd suddenly lost thirty years, fifty pounds and grown a full head taller since last evening, the person shutting up shop was most certainly *not* Temek Huyurgal. With a determined bump of the shoulder, the man shoved the doors together and snapped a series of heavy locks into place. His actions were fluid and economic, undertaken with the grace of someone who'd performed the ritual a hundred times before.

She pushed out of the shadows, clearing her throat to let the man know he wasn't alone. *Might as well ask where the elusive Huyurgal was.* A niggling suspicion told her the cordwain was purposely avoiding her. Even so, she hadn't hurried up here to Mursik for nothing, paying twice as much for a cab to ensure it didn't pick up anyone else.

"Excuse me," she began, walking towards him. "I'm sorry to trouble you…"

The man jumped, dropping his keys and reaching for a long knife tucked into his belt. The sphere of light dimmed momentarily before flaring with renewed vigour, growing twice as large and twice as bright.

Upon sighting her, the man's shoulders relaxed. His hand fell away from the knife. Clearly, Jhiriyan women weren't on his list of potential thieves or assailants.

"My apologies, I didn't mean to startle you." Dhani lowered her head. "I'm looking for Temek Huyurgal."

The man's gaze swept over her, first assessing her footwear then slowly travelling upwards to the scarf on her head. He was a few years older than her and typically Tizraki: obsidian beard, thick, raven hair, a broad, honest face framed by a slightly heavy brow. The sparkle in his eyes hadn't yet been dulled by years of hardship or cynicism, and his full lips parted in an easy, welcoming smile. All in all, it wasn't an *unpleasant* arrangement of features if you were looking to make conversation about the weather or purchase custom-made leather boots.

"Ahh, Izn, I'm sorry, he's not here," the man's voice was rich and deep, unhurried, as if he had all night to stand and chat. "Uncle Temek left just after six bells. He had some business in Geraktin Souk to attend. He'll be in early tomorrow." His smile widened. The spark in his eyes caught alight, probably at the prospect of selling an expensive pair of boots to a foreigner with copper skin and a fat purse. "I'm Imril, his nephew. You came by earlier today didn't you?"

"I did."

"If it's about some custom boots, I'd be happy to help." Imril's smile flashed again. Earnest. *Hopeful.* Dhani flattened her lips, fighting a smile of her own and failing. Yes, of course, Imril-nephew-of-Temek wanted to sell her some overpriced, handmade boots. *Overpriced* because anything sold by a Tizraki to a *Jhiryaktaan* was inflated by at least a third. Which made what he said next almost as predictable as the moon rising in the east. "Perhaps we could discuss designs over a glass of wine? There's a cantina just around the corner. Very good food, too."

Dhani shook her head. "Thank you, but no. I've got a friend waiting for me at the Souk."

"Oh." Imril's face fell. His cheeks reddened. "Of course, forgive me for being impolite."

As the light in his eyes extinguished, she realised she'd misread his intentions—misread them by half a continent's width. Her face flushed with sudden heat. *The invitation hadn't been all leather boots and business.* Imril-nephew-of-Temek had just invited her out. An oddly pleasant tingle, a feeling dead since the blood-drenched night in Casa-del-Toro eight moons earlier, stirred within.

"Many thanks, Imril. I'll come by tomorrow and see your Uncle Temek. And perhaps…" She inclined her head, cheeks still burning. *What in the Creator's name was she doing?* The words, like the stirring low in her belly, escaped before she had time to stuff them back in. "Perhaps we can have that glass of wine then?"

Imril looked up, eyes shining as if she'd just ordered custom-made boots for the entire Imperial Navy. "Izn? Oh, yes, Izn. Wine. Tomorrow. Perhaps?"

He then simultaneously kicked the keys he'd dropped *and* tripped over his coat.

"Tomorrow." She inclined her head, turned, and left.

When she looked back, Imril was fishing his keys out of the dirt, whistling again. The smile on his face was as big as the moon, perhaps even bigger.

The corners of her own mouth kinked up. At least she'd made *somebody's* night.

—

Dhani found a cab just down the street from the cordwain's workshop and headed over to Geraktin Souk in search of Temek Huyurgal and his business there. For the entire journey she tapped her fingers on the leather armrest, trying not to think too much about Imril's bright eyes and let-me-kiss-you smile. Her pulse banged in her ears, jangling in time with her nerves and the sulky's bone-jarring suspension.

Imril aside, she was running out of time.

A day and a half gone, and with the exception of a jumpy cordwain who didn't want to be found, a pair of turbaned tails, a ransacked room, and a threatening note, she had nothing to show for it. Unless of course, you counted a sprained ankle, bruised ribs, and sore feet. As much as she hated to admit it, this case was proving to be harder than taking out a foreign noble in a guarded fortress.

Of course, *if* she'd had Huyurgal's home address—something which would have been on his file—she'd have simply gone there and waited for him. His file, however, was safely locked up in Bethsehal Shalamir's office.

Which left her undertaking what would surely be a fruitless search of the city's most popular souk in the hour after evening prayer when Tizraki indulged in their most holy and favoured past times of all: eating and drinking. The chance of spotting a man she'd met just once before amongst the crowds was slightly less than firing a bullet at the sun and hoping it would hit. *Maybe even less.*

Still, she had to try.

Just as she'd feared, Geratkin Souk was stuffed full of people stuffing their faces when she arrived. A rectangular space about four hundred metres long and two hundred wide, the Souk was identical to every other in Tizrak Yirda she'd ever visited: flanked by shops, emporiums, cantinas and the occasional ashishqa den, all gathered under wide verandas formed by a long procession of arched, lime-washed porticos. By day, the cool, shady spaces behind the porticos were filled with stalls hawking fresh produce, food, clothing, pots, utensils, and every other item you could sell; by night, it was tables, chairs, benches and crates, food, wine, ale and of course, the cloying, sweet fumes of ashishqa smoked in elegant glass hookahs.

She worked her way along the Souk's eastern edge first, noting a cross-section peoples from Soolaith and beyond: raven haired, wiry Erissi with bright blue or jewel green eyes seated alongside their heavier-set, broader faced Tizraki neighbours. Dark-skinned Sindari rubbed shoulders with narrow-eyed Mylokki and Tolmin from the Continent's west; a handful of fearsome Yargans with their dark curls and athletic grace downed jugs of millet beer. There were even groups of Jhiriyan Homelanders like herself, willowy, golden-haired, and copper-skinned, taller than any other race. Of Temek Huyurgal, however, there was no sign.

Dhani reached the southern end of the Souk, a gloomier area housing several open-air cantinas and paused. The cantinas' entrepreneurial owners had set tables and chairs out beneath the arched porticos and most of these were filled with eager patrons. Her stomach rumbled as she inhaled the rich aromas of spiced meat, onion, garlic, and cardamom. She tried to recall when she'd last eaten and came up with *midday* and *kofte* before all thought of food vanished. At a nearby table she spied an unusually tall, impressively built Tizraki man hauling out a chair and taking a seat. On the opposite side of the table a figure in a cloak sat waiting, hood drawn over its head.

Her gut knotted in on itself.

Parvan Gorshayik.

She melted back into the shadows, the skin on her neck prickling.

Well, this was *interesting.* The content of Gorshayik's stolen note flashed through her mind. Was he here to eat, meet a friend or for another reason—like finding the group he'd mentioned in the missive to the General? Her gaze switched to Parvan Gorshayik's companion, an indeterminate human shape. Her mouth kinked into an ironic half-smile. Who in the Ninth Tizraki hell wore a woollen cloak and a hood on a summer night in Izurum? Either they were insane or trying to scream *Hello! I'm not half suspicious!* at the top of their lungs.

And, though she had no right to pry, much less care what Parvan Gorshayik did in his own time, she couldn't help but peer around the pillar and watch what unfolded.

In truth, not a lot happened.

Gorshayik's mood had improved as much as one could expect of a bear with a nest of hornets jammed up its rear end. Although he didn't smile at his hooded companion, the way he canted his body towards them suggested the person was no stranger. In response, the Hood nodded, gestured in the manner of someone speaking to a friend then nodded again. Gorshayik frowned and stared at the table before burying his head in his hands. The Hood asked a question, to which he responded with a shake of the head.

The exchange continued for several minutes. Then, the

mysterious person stood up and left Parvan Gorshayik alone, burning holes in the table with his surly glare.

Dhani watched the Hood for as long as she dared, tracking the person's movements as they wound through the crowd and into the gloom at the Souk's southern end. Whether they'd been male or female was impossible to say, just as she couldn't guess the person's race—though the utter confidence of the person's stride and the fact that several people darted aside as the Hood approached, offered a clue, even if it made little sense.

When she returned her attention to the table, Parvan Gorshayik sat with his head still clutched in his hands. He stayed that way until a serving girl from the cantina buzzed past and wheedled an order from him.

Dhani exhaled and pressed her back into the pillar. Several nearby diners gave her a quizzical glance, and she decided to move on.

Who could say what she'd seen?

Really, it was none of her business. Gorshayik had been Secret Service for a decade. Before that, he'd worked as a historian amongst the dusty scrolls, parchments and rotting papers of Tizrak Yirda's only university in Istanakhand. For all she knew, he had friends and contacts everywhere. His meeting with someone foolish enough to wear a hood on a warm night could mean a hundred things. Had he been meeting with a whore perhaps and she'd turned him down? Although, she'd never heard of a *Yargan* whore before. Perhaps he'd been seeing his healer?

She was about to step out from the pillar and leave Parvan Gorshayik boring holes in the table with his glare, when Temek Huyurgal passed by, less than a metre in front of her.

She stopped dead in her tracks.

The cordwain, dressed in an unassuming dark blue tunic, slowed, scanned the tables and drew a deep breath. He sawed on his lip, hesitated, then moved on.

When he made his way to Parvan Gorshayik's table, Dhani's jaw almost hit the ground.

Obviously Gorshayik had been expecting Temek Huyurgal. The big Tizraki looked up, not a moment of surprise on his face, and offered Huyurgal the seat vacated by the mysterious and possibly Yargan Hood. A nervous Temek Huyurgal surveyed the crowd, chewed on his lip some more and then sat.

Four Winds! What was this?

Dhani moved forward, winding her way out from one arched pillar to the next. Her mind raced. *Was Gorshayik working the case himself?* Did this mean he'd had a change of heart and *not* resigned from the Service? Or did he simply *not* want to work with her? At the third pillar along, she pressed her back to the smooth, cool stone, hoped no one was taking too much notice, and settled in to watch.

What followed were several minutes of discussion, Temek Huyurgal doing most of the talking, Gorshayik listening with his paw-sized hands clasped before him. The serving girl brought two glasses of red wine and a plate of dolmades. Gorshayik paid and she left.

At length, Huyurgal's posture and arms went rigid, as if he were uncomfortable or afraid. He leaned forward suddenly and slid something across the table, opening his hands in a pleading gesture.

Parvan Gorshayik sat back, staring at the table, brows lifted. *Coin.* The cordwain had just pushed a small pile of glittering peshak across the table. Dhani's breath hitched in her throat.

Gorshayik wavered, the scar on his cheek twitching, studying the coins as if they were barrels of gunpowder with a short fuse attached. Temek Huyurgal cupped his palms together, pleading.

Several seconds passed and Gorshayik came to a decision. He offered the cordwain a curt nod and palmed the coins with a single hand. The cordwain's shoulders slumped in apparent relief.

Dhani's breath hissed through her lips. *Had she just witnessed an operative taking a bribe?* Though she hardly knew Parvan Gorshayik, nothing in his record suggested he was the type to take bribes. Quite the opposite, in fact. Had his *condition* changed him? Clouded his judgement, perhaps? Or was this something else again? Temek Huyurgal seemed like a frightened man—and Gorshayik had been genuinely surprised by the coin. Was Huyurgal *paying* Parvan Gorshayik to deal with whatever it was that troubled him?

Whatever it was, she intended to find out.

She sucked on a cheek and came to a decision. She'd follow Temek Huyurgal when he left and convince him to discuss the matter of Scythe with her. After that, she'd pay *Captain* Gorshayik a visit. Whether he liked it or not, they were going to have a cosy chat about what she'd just witnessed—probably with a knife to his throat, just to make sure his hornet-up-the-arse attitude didn't cloud his judgement.

"Izn," a woman's voice said. "Izn?"

Dhani jumped, turning to see a Tizraki woman in an apron gesturing at a vacant seat. "Would you care for a meal? We have lamb kebab, felafel or kofte. Our house wine is—"

A loud *pop! pop! pop!* drowned out anything else the woman said. Dhani whirled about, instinctively pulling a blade from her thigh. Her gaze tore across the souk. There was a scream, followed by several flashes and more loud pops—the sharp reports of a pistol.

Then, an entire chorus of screams.

"Take cover," she hissed to the woman in the apron and shoved her behind the pillar.

A surge—a tidal wave of frightened, panicked humanity—poured out from the middle of the souk. More gunfire rang out, alongside more terrified screams.

Not far from the centre of souk, a space yawned.

Dhani caught sight of several bodies sprawled in the dirt, unmoving or crawling away. A golden-haired Homelander sat on the ground, cradling a man in her arms. Her wailing rose and fell, a howling, primal sound.

He's got a gun! someone screamed.

Run! They're insane! another voice shrieked.

Dhani found the cause of the ruckus, a pair of Tizraki men waving revolvers in the air not far from the pair of stricken Jhiriyans. Standing back-to-back, both men held a gun in each hand. The one nearest to her had two more pistols tucked in his belt.

Death to the Imperium! one of the men yelled. *Freedom for Tizrak Yirda!*

Death to the Imperium! his companion echoed. Then, he took aim and shot the Jhiriyan woman at point-blank range. The woman's head blew apart in a spray of gore. She slumped to the ground.

There were yet more screams, and now a dangerous crush of humanity at every one of souk's exits as people fled the men and their guns as a seething, frightened mass.

Almost everyone that was.

Most Deenjin—Tizraki included—could do little against bullets. Certainly, they'd be able to kill the men with a well-placed bolt of the killing Flame, but that meant taking their chance against a pistol *and* getting close enough to hurl Deenjah with sufficient force to cause a fatal injury.

Yargans, however, had no such problem.

From the eastern side of the souk, a group of Yargan caravan guards advanced on the armed men. Like a pack of stalking wolves, they closed in. Two peeled off to the right and two to the left, mingling with the fleeing crowd, attempting to flank the men. With their shimmering red shields, they had nothing to fear from a pistol. Any bullet fired at a Yargan's shield would be swiftly turned to metal slag.

Several more Yargans appeared from the northern end of the souk and began to openly stride towards the gunmen, intent on reaching them. They moved with utter certainty, a relentless, unshakable cadence, the same way they'd once surged down from their mountain homes far to the south and conquered Tizrak Yirda all the way to Talmakhan.

The pair of gunmen, however, ignored them.

Instead, they changed tactic and began shooting indiscriminately at the unprotected crowd milling at the nearest exit, one of the men shouting *Death to the Imperium!* over and again.

Dhani pressed her back to the pillar, the hot sting of adrenaline flooding her veins. *She had to do something.* The Yargans would kill the men without a second thought, of that she had no doubt. Somehow, she had to intercept them, convince them knock the pair of men senseless rather than burning them to smouldering ash. The Empire needed to know who the men were and why they were shooting innocent people.

She ducked out from the pillar in time to see a wall of wide-eyed, white-knuckled humanity surging towards her.

In seconds they reached her, a torrent of arms, legs, torsos fighting each other to get past and forcing her back. Bodies, chairs, tables, wine bottles flew everywhere. People fell and screamed. A bullet hit a pillar, spraying chips of razor-sharp stone into the air.

Dhani resisted the crowd for three hot and sweaty seconds, scrambling behind the pillar to stay afoot. An elbow smashed into her ribs. A boot heel slammed down on her toes. Something struck her thigh. She craned her neck, fighting to see where Temek Huyurgal was—and sighted the cordwain alongside Parvan Gorshayik, being shunted by the crowd towards the Souk's southern end.

Then, someone slammed her in the chest hard, knocking the wind from her lungs.

A voice screamed *run!* so loud, her ears rang. She tripped over a chair, was hauled to her feet by an unseen hand. Swept up in the confusion and noise, she had no choice but to let herself be pushed forward, inexorably towards the souk's nearest exit and out into the street beyond.

CHAPTER FIFTEEN

A half hour later, Dhani stood in the shadows outside
Bethsehal Shalamir's office window, flexing her
fingers, aching and bruised after escaping the crush in the
souk. For the third time in a minute, she counted the
screws in the window's insect screen then counted them
again, purposely ignoring the fist-sized knot in her gut.

She drew a long breath and mentally rechecked her
plan. *Scanned the office layout, re-counted the screws in the
insect screen. Estimated the force needed to push open the large
sash window. Stared at the desk's bottom drawer, the likeliest
place to find the file.* Breaking into the Regional
Commander's office probably carried a death sentence, but
after Parvan Gorshayik's cosy little transaction with the
cordwain in the Souk and then shooting, there really was
no other choice. Temek Huyurgal's file held information
she needed. Information she should have had yesterday.

Information she'd been denied.

On the other side of the glass, Shalamir barked orders
to an underling and sent them on their way. The office

door clicked shut, only to open again to admit another visitor. Dhani tugged on a pair of black leather gloves and drew a small screwdriver from her pocket. A pair of moths batted at the wire insect screen, drawn to the oily light seeping out from the room. In the garden behind her, crickets chirped.

Through the open window conversation began anew. The gauzy curtain blurred the Regional Controller's outline, sitting rod straight as she faced a Homelander man standing to attention on the opposite side of the desk. The desk's left side was perpendicular to the large window, two strides away from where Dhani waited, temptingly close.

"…I don't care what they say, Tanjil," Shalamir's voice cracked in clipped, hacking upper-caste Jhiriyan. "I'm ordering you to detain them until we wring every last detail from their lips."

"Ma'am." Tanjil's boots shuffled uncomfortably on wooden boards. "We have no authority to detain Yargan citizens without just cause. They've already quoted sections of Imperial law to me."

"*Killing* people in Geraktin Souk constitutes murder under Imperial law."

"Ma'am. Nine people are dead. There'd be more if they hadn't intervened, and it could be argued they were acting in self-defence—"

"Self-defence my arse, Agent Tanjil. They're bloody *Yargans* bred by an ancient empire as ruthless killers. Arrest them for loitering, and if you can't do that, find something trivial to hold them over, a spelling mistake on their travel papers…anything, I don't care." Shalamir's fist thumped on the desk. "Just keep them here until they agree to answer our questions. That's all I'm asking."

Agent Tanjil was the fifth visitor to the Regional Controller's room in as many minutes. Dhani couldn't make out the expression on his face, but a heavy sigh conveyed his feelings. The pair of crazed gunmen in Geraktin Souk were now charred bone and ash, courtesy of several mountain-dwelling, over-educated Yargan demon-spawn. Attempts to question them, however, weren't going to plan.

"With due respect, ma'am, we can't hold them and they know it. These aren't illiterate villagers we're dealing with. As you say, they're Yargans. They can probably quote subsections of the law I've never even heard of."

"Then pay them."

Tanjil spluttered. "*Bribe* them, ma'am? We can't—"

"No, you fool. Pay them for their time. Offer to compensate them as contractors." She drummed her fingers on the desk. "Preempt their arguments by having someone raise invoices and issue payments on their behalf."

Dhani arched an eyebrow. For every problem someone dragged through her door, Bethsehal Shalamir offered at least one solution. From belligerent Yargans quoting obscure sections of Imperial law to slack jawed Homelanders stumbling over their third and fourth syllables at the sight of *Jhiriyans* with their heads blown apart, the Regional Controller offered calm and unflappable advice. If the woman hadn't been such a gold-plated, rusted-on, upper-caste cliche, she would have been impressed.

A brisk rap sounded at the office door. Shalamir barked a prompt, *"Come in."*

"Ma'am," a Tizraki voice began. Dhani stiffened, recognising the visitor as Ziraat Olucik, the rat-faced adjutant. "The Majapayit's Under-Seneschal is here to see you. She says it's urgent."

"Under-Seneschal? The Majapayit has such a thing?" Shalamir's reply was more statement than question. "Very well, Olucik. I'll see her now."

"Shall I bring her in?"

"Creator, no. Keep her in the foyer." Shalamir snapped to her feet, rod stiff as if she did indeed have a pole inserted in her rectum. "Tanjil, whatever are you waiting for? Go and deal with the Yargans. You're dismissed."

Agent Tanjil about-faced and left, Shalamir right on his heels. The door snicked shut but the light wasn't extinguished. Dhani's knuckles tightened on the screwdriver. Shalamir obviously didn't intend to be gone for long. She'd need to work fast on the screen.

After a swift check of the garden for anyone who might be approaching, she began to unfasten the screws holding window's the insect screen in place. She had the third screw of eight in hand when the office door opened. She eased back from the window, taking cover in the shadows cast by the parted drapes.

The slight, dark-haired form of Ziraat Olucik entered the room. He closed the door behind him, beelining across the office and darting behind Shalamir's desk. He glanced once at the door as if he were a rodent avoiding a trap, before rummaging about in a trouser pocket. A tarnished metal key appeared in his hand and he dropped to a crouch, inserted the key, and unlocked the desk's large bottom drawer.

With the drawer open, the adjutant rifled through its contents—which largely seemed to be files— with all the finesse of a rat scurrying up a drainpipe to evade a cat. He plucked out several files, locked the drawer and shot to his feet. He'd made it halfway across the room when the door opened and Bethsehal Shalamir re-entered.

For a moment, the Regional Controller stood granite-still, staring at the adjutant. Though Dhani couldn't make out the woman's face clearly, the upsweep of her chin suggested she was less than impressed at finding the adjutant alone in her office.

Before she could speak, however, Ziraat stumbled out, "Ma'am, I'm…I'm returning a few of the files you asked me to—"

"Never mind the files, Ziraat. They can wait. The Majapayit is on his way. I need you to head over to West Block and prepare the reception room right now for a party of ten."

The adjutant bowed his head. "The reception room, of course, ma'am."

He sidestepped Shalamir, scrambling for the door so fast, he stumbled. The Regional Controller cleared her throat. Ziraat stopped.

"Olucik, the files in your possession?" she said. "Leave them here, please."

The adjutant's cheeks flushed deep crimson. "Ahh, yes, ma'am. Sorry." He scurried back across the room, dropped the files on the desk, nodded again, then hastily left.

As soon as the door clicked shut, Shalamir made a

snort of disgust. She swept up the files from the desk, frowned at their titles and tilted her head as if confused by what she held in her hand. Dhani leaned in, watching closely. Something about those particular files bothered the Regional Controller enough that, instead of placing them in her bottom drawer, she slipped them into her top drawer and locked it.

With a flick of her wrist, Shalamir snatched up her noble's white silk scarf from her chair and draped it around her neck. She picked up a leather-bound notebook, her gold writing nib, switched off the light and left, locking the door behind her.

Dhani blew out a thankful breath. A dribble of perspiration ran down her back, leaving an itch in its wake. She returned to work, removing the last five screws from the insect screen's frame, pulling it free of the window and placing it carefully on the tiled verandah.

After slipping the screwdriver into her pack, she set both hands on the sash window and pushed. The frame slipped upwards with a smooth and almost noiseless *shish*. Her shoulders dropped as she exhaled, relieved.

Thirty seconds later, she stood behind Bethsehal Shalamir's desk, lock picks in hand, a silver flint lighter ready on the desk. Though the bottom drawer certainly contained more files and a simple latch-lock, it was the files Shalamir had frowned over and stashed in her top drawer Dhani wanted to look at first.

In the darkness, she toggled the tiny picks inside the lock's cylinder, working at the tumblers and pins. Her heart thumped, slow, controlled beats. Five clicks later, the drawer slid open. Lighter in hand, she flipped the cover and spun a thumb across a tiny brass wheel. A small, blue-white flame sputtered to life, a tiny spark of Deenjah powered by a miniature deenjili rod inside the device.

The light was enough to show two of the files were Temek Huyurgal's, whilst the other belonged to someone named *Yakobi Jartik*. Dhani swore softly, clenching a fist. *Ai, Creator's bright, shiny balls!* Sure, she'd found Huyurgal's files but to remove them when they were two of only three in the drawer would be far too suspicious. She'd have to settle for sifting through and pulling out the pages she needed.

Outside the window, the steady cadence of footsteps alerted her to someone's approach. She extinguished the light and froze, holding her breath.

The person walked by the window without pause, their passage soon fading into the distance.

Dhani counted off thirty thumping heartbeats, then re-struck the lighter. She opened the first of Huyurgal's files, flicked through and unfastened the soft metal clip securing the pages in place. The first five pages of a file were usually enough to provide the kind of overview she'd need, but she removed ten, just to be safe. Folding file pages was probably against Ha'filu protocol, but right here and now, the rules could go skewer themselves on a rusty pike and die a long and painful death.

Satisfied, she reassembled the file, slipped it into the drawer, relocked the drawer and slid back out through the window. Finally, she pulled the window into place, leaving the gap exactly as she'd found it.

She'd replaced four of the eight screws in the insect screen when voices and footsteps warned of company.

Dhani slipped the remaining screws into a pocket, shouldered her pack, and began to walk with casual purpose towards the blockhouse's front door.

She turned a corner onto the blockhouse's front verandah and walked straight into Bethsehal Shalamir and a female companion. Her pulse shot forward in her veins. There hadn't been time to remove her gloves, and she doubted it would go unnoticed. From what she'd seen so far, Shalamir was the kind of woman attuned to details.

"Shulim Regional Controller," Dhani said quickly, recovering and lowering her head. "I heard about the shootings in the Souk. I'm here to report for duty, ma'am."

Shalamir seemed a little surprised—a slight twitch of an eyebrow, a tiny tilt of her chin. Her companion, a tall Homerlander woman whose face resembled a series of sharp edges cut with a ruler and blade, raised both brows. Two sets of eyes travelled from Dhani's gloved hands to her face, to her tunic sleeve and back.

"Your service will not be required, Karim." Shalamir drew herself upright. "Several hours ago, I believe I told you to concentrate on finding Scythe. Did I not make myself quite clear?"

The angular woman at Shalamir's side twitched her head to the side just enough that her *Oh, you're THAT person* thought played across her face like a lighthouse's beam in a fog. Dhani ignored it. She had no idea who the woman was and didn't care.

"Has Captain Gorshayik spoken with you, ma'am?" she asked instead.

The Regional Controller's mouth thinned. "You'll report to Captain Khasain in Block North 2 tomorrow morning at nine bells, Karim. He will be your direct report for the time being."

Dhani offered a curt nod. Shalamir's reply was as close to, *Yes, Captain Gorshayik has tendered his resignation* as she was likely to get. *And Khasain.* It was tempting to shrug indifference, screw up her nose or flip Shalamir her middle finger. She'd been placed with a Homelander, Vashistriya caste by the sound of the name. Some other hapless, lower-caste sod Shalamir probably hated as far back as his genealogy could be traced.

"Captain Khasain, nine o'clock, Block North 2." Dhani tapped her temple and flashed a smile. "Got it, ma'am. If you will excuse me, then."

Shalamir's gaze lingered on her right sleeve just a little longer than it should have, before finally returning to her gloved hands and face. The Regional Controller's companion made an impressive show of studying the verandah tiles as if they were the most interesting thing in the world.

"Before you leave, Karim." Shalamir raised a finger. "I should remind you to advise Personnel of your current domicile. Your report mentioned you'd moved out of the lodgings in Faissa."

Dhani's gut tightened. It was an odd question, one she didn't like at all. She sucked on a cheek, thinking through options. Best to offer a vague but plausible answer. "I'm not sure where I'm staying tonight, ma'am. When I find suitable lodgings, I'll advise the Personnel Office immediately."

Shalamir's mouth puckered as though she'd just bitten

into an especially sour lemon. "Make sure that you do, Karim."

Then, the Regional Controller and her knife-faced, anonymous companion swept past, vanishing around the corner—a path that would lead directly past the office window she'd not long exited.

Dhani passed the blockhouse's door and turned onto a footpath leading beneath a Bougainvillea-covered arbor. The skin on her neck prickled. Something about the conversation had been *off*, as though she'd been listening to a violin with one string ever-so-slightly out of tune. She picked up her pace, heart suddenly thudding.

When she glanced down at her right sleeve two strides on, her blood turned to ice.

A fine, dark green thread clung to her sleeve, no longer than her hand. The kind of fine, fragile cotton someone might leave on a windowsill to alert them to tampering; a tiny detail most thieves would overlook.

And Shalamir had seen it. Not only seen it—the chisel-faced bitch had ogled her gloves as well.

By her calculations, she had exactly thirty seconds before someone as sharp as Bethsehal Shalamir added *green thread* to *gloves* and *missing screws in the insect screen* and came up with a solution called *execution via firing squad.*

Fuck. Fuck. Fuck! Dhani slapped a hand to her thigh. Some small creature scurried through the bougainvillea's leaves, the distant howl of a dog reached her ears. Elsewhere in the compound, the constant hubbub of voices.

Her fingers curled into a fist, her pulse knocked at her veins. She needed to leave and leave *yesterday*.

A scan of the courtyard delivered a handful of exits: the obvious footpath leading beneath the arbor, a mad dash along the verandah and back inside the blockhouse, and a pair of two-metre high, flaking adobe courtyard walls. She chose the wall on the right, dappled in shadow and clothed in some thick, spiky climbing plant she couldn't name and would probably regret. Prickles aside, it was half-reasonable escape route and she dived into the garden.

At the base of the wall, Dhani crouched and sprung upwards, vaulting over the crumbling adobe and sliding down the other side. Her ankle twinged as she landed in another garden, this one filled with orange trees laden with unripe green fruits.

A muffled voice in the courtyard behind her shouted, *"Karim!"*

Dhani didn't look back. There was no need. Shalamir had found the missing screws in the insect screen.

In spite of her sprained ankle, she began to run.

CHAPTER SIXTEEN

D hani reached the Service Compound's main gate sucking air like a whipped pony after a limping sprint across the facility via the shortest route she could find. She arrived just as His Grace Duyjarit Lurgak, the current Majapayit of Izurum, also arrived, replete with a platoon-sized entourage of guards, advisors, scribes, two of his three wives and his own private photographer.

If she'd been in less of a hurry to leave, she'd have knelt down and kissed Lurgak's well-padded, pony-sized arse. A portly man bedecked in a tunic boasting more colours than a peacock's tail, Duyjarit Lurgak stepped inside the gate in a cloud of perfume, stared down the stone-faced security detail and demanded to see Bethsehal Shalamir at once. Mid-sentence, the Majapayit paused, turned to his photographer, and asked if this was his *best angle*.

In the confusion, Dhani shouldered her way through the crush of tunics, ample bellies and eye-watering cologne and slipped out the gate. The photographer's flash strobed once and then again, leaving a starburst of colour on her retinas as she checked over her shoulder for signs of pursuit.

She caught a cab up to Mursik and hobbled about in a circuitous, meandering route for an hour. Finally, certain no one was following, she wandered into a small, well-kept bar called *The Last Sow*, found a vacant table near the back door, and ordered not one but two fingers of Diresh whiskey, each in its own tumbler.

The chair's upholstery accepted her tired behind like a well-worn pair of shoes, and she settled into a wary slouch, nursing her whiskey whilst scanning the crowd for anyone suspicious. She found no one. The *Last Sow's* patrons ignored her for games of taroch, private conversations or problems shared only with their drinks.

After a moment, she scanned her body, mentally checking her injuries. Her ankle throbbed, several cuts from the crush in the Souk stung, her heart knocked at still-tender ribs. Her eyes were gritty and worn from lack of sleep. Yet, all of those were fleeting discomforts, forgotten as the storm of consequence dumped a hot torrent of complete and utter *fuckery* down on her head.

Of all the fucked-sideways-in-the-head-fuckups, this was the fuck-up beyond all fucked-up fuckups.

Even if she personally delivered Scythe, butt-naked and trussed with gold ribbons to Bethsehal Shalamir's door, it wouldn't matter. Her goose was not only cooked, it had been sectioned off and devoured by wolves. Along with the dead goose, any chance of rejoining the Ta'Hafiq had just plunged off a cliff and died on the jagged, metaphorical rocks below. Shalamir would send her to the firing squad or worse—of that she was sure.

She lifted the tumbler to her lips and downed the first finger of whiskey in one mouthful. The alcohol burned, leaving a faintly smokey, cinnamon taste in her mouth. It didn't help. Not one bit. She'd need half a bottle or more to silence the spectre of death grinning at her from the not-too-distant future. And even then, as her father had often said, one bottle was never enough to dull the pain.

What to do? She picked up the second tumbler and studied it, brows notched.

If she'd been Ta'Hafiq, her superiors would have simply shrugged her actions off. As an assassin, she'd had licence to do whatever was necessary to complete a mission, be it burglaries, bribes, killings, or beatings. In the Ha'filu, however, as a lowly unranked operative, she'd be sneered at, told she should have worked harder to find Temek Huyurgal's address and punished. Which left her alone, fifteen hundred keloms from any kind of real help, squatting on the wrong side of a mountain of Imperial law and a universe of don't-argue-with-me Ha'filu protocol penned in damning black ink.

Her finger traced a circle on the glass's polished surface. She massaged her neck, working out a knot with grimy fingertips.

Whilst it was tempting to flee the city and make her way back up to Istanakhand, running away wouldn't bring her any closer to clearing her name. In fact, running away would do little more than place a bounty on her head, and, ironically, gain her all the Ta'Hafiq attention she'd ever dreamed of. Two weeks at the most, and she'd be feeding the worms, courtesy of one of her own superbly trained, single-minded former colleagues.

She took another sip of whiskey and held the liquor in her mouth until it burned. She stared into the honey-coloured liquor, hoping for inspiration. Nothing came. Somehow, she had to turn this continent-sized clusterfuck around and make it work to her own advantage.

The sound of clinking glass drew her attention. A serving girl stood behind the bar polishing wine glasses with a tea-towel, a far-away expression on her face. Dhani studied her for a moment, then returned to doom-staring into her drink.

No emotion. No weakness. No retreat.

No use burying her hands in her head. No use feeling sorry for herself. She had to outthink, outplay, out-manoeuvre Bethsehal Shalamir as if this were a Ta'Hafiq mission.

She needed to find Scythe.

If she could do that, she could anonymously tip off another Ha'filu operative to his whereabouts then get the hell up to Talmakhan and send a signal to the General. If she could at least get Behzad El'Meshid to listen to reason, maybe her breach of protocol—and Imperial law—would be overlooked. And Talmakhan, the regional capital, was four times the size of Izurum. Not only would it be easier to disappear, she had contacts there, powerful people who owed her favours.

Several patrons left the bar, banging the door behind them. An older, harried serving girl bustled past with a tray full of glasses and a bottle of wine. A drunk woman demanded more ale. Her male companion shook his head and ordered two mugs of kaffai instead.

Dhani sipped the whiskey, thoughts scuttling about like roaches on a floor. The furrow in her brows deepened. *Temek Huyurgal. Yevengik cu Bapa. The men in turbans who'd followed her. Her ransacked room. Scythe.* A group of disparate events and people. The niggling in her gut said otherwise. There was a connection to be found—of that she was certain—if only she could figure it out.

Find Temek Huyurgal; find Scythe. The cordwain seemed to be the key. She needed to wring whatever he knew about Scythe out of his slippery-eel lips. She nudged her backpack with a boot where it rested on the floor at her feet. At least now, she had his home address.

Her fingers curled about the straps of her pack, burrowed inside, found the pages she'd taken from Huyurgal's file and drew them out.

In the dim light of the bar, she began to read.

—

Temek Huyurgal lived in a modest, well-kept family compound surrounded by other modest, well-kept family compounds in the refuse-free, clean-swept, modest streets of east Geraktin.

The compound's adobe had been recently re-rendered and whitewashed, and the front door freshly painted in striking turquoise bright enough to stand out in yellow lamplight. A pair of terracotta hearth gods, one female, one male, sat guard on either side of the stoop. Dhani couldn't name either of them, though she suspected they'd be avatars of Mother Yamir, from whom craftspeople such as Huyurgal would surely seek favour.

Before approaching the house, she'd spent a half hour checking nearby streets for operatives or anyone who looked out of place. She found no one, deemed it safe and walked straight up to the compound's front door. She inhaled, wrinkled her nose at the lungful of fresh paint, knocked, and waited.

As she did so, she mentally sifted through the information in Temek Huyurgal's file.

Not only did the file contain his address, but the pages she'd stolen held a great deal of very interesting information. The first five pages comprised a file note documenting a number of threats against the cordwain, along with a record of his various requests to the city constables for protection. The file note confirmed that Huyurgal did indeed own most of the land on which the shantytown of Koyulerin was built, and also stated that last spring, Papat Yenidogat's temple tried to buy the land. He'd declined the priest's offer and heard nothing more about it. Dhani's skin prickled as she'd read the words, wondering if this was the reason the priest hadn't wanted her to pry too much at his Koyulerin temple.

Even more interesting than the revelation about Kyvil Yenidogat though was the information that just two moons ago, someone named Golan Fiyuret made an offer to buy the land, not once but twice. After Huyurgal refused the second time, Fiyuret threatened him. A day later, the cordwain was beaten up, his workshop burgled, and he received two threatening notes telling him to sell his land or his workshop would be burned down. Once more, he reported the incidents to the city constables, who investigated but found no trace of anyone named Golan Fiyuret. The city constables had, as a matter of protocol, passed the notes to the Ha'filu, marking the case as *suspicious* and requesting further investigation.

The sound of footsteps padding down the hall behind the freshly painted door drew Dhani's attention. She checked her tunic, smoothing it down, sniffing her armpits and wrinkling her nose. Hopefully, Huyurgal wouldn't notice her less than perfect grooming.

"*Temek?*" a woman's quavering voice whispered through the door. It was a tired voice, one frayed and worn ragged at the edges.

"No, ma'am," Dhani said. "Ha'filu. I'd like a word with your husband."

The door cracked open, releasing a pleasant waft of lemons, pastry, and cinnamon. A handsome woman wearing a plain blue tunic and the kind of black bellbottom pants favoured by most Tizraki women peered through the gap. She stared up at Dhani, dark eyes round with fear. Midnight visits from Imperial Secret Service operatives probably weren't what most people expected.

"Ha'filu?" The woman's shoulders slumped as Dhani produced papers to confirm her identity. "Temek's not here. He was due home hours ago. I heard there were a pair of madmen in the Souk and they shot nine people. Please…" The woman's knuckles whitened as she grasped at her tunic, bunching the fabric. "Please tell me he's not dead."

Damn. It was tempting to kick the step in frustration, but Dhani kept her face pleasantly blank. "No, ma'am. I was in the Souk when the gunman was there. Your husband left as soon as the shooting began."

The woman's expression widened in hope then collapsed again. She looked Dhani up and down, wrung her tunic and peered into the street. "Is this about...*the threats?*"

"Yes, it is." Dhani's pulse kicked up a notch. *So the wife knew about the threats.* Perhaps she knew something about Scythe as well? It wouldn't hurt to ask. "I visited your husband at his workshop yesterday. There's something I need to ask him. Something which can't wait."

Temek's wife wrung her tunic again. Her tongue made a circuit about her lips. "I don't know where he is. He's never been late before without sending me word. He's a good husband and father. Something's wrong."

Every hair on Dhani's body prickled. *Yes, something was wrong.* She glanced over her shoulder, also checking the street. Quiet and orderly. Nothing out of place.

"I'll make some enquires, ma'am," she said. "I'm sure he'll turn up." She pursed her lips, studying the careworn creases around the woman's eyes thoughtfully. "Ma'am, you may be able to help me. Would you be able to answer a couple of questions? They might help me find your husband."

The woman frowned. "I'll try."

"Did your husband ever mention a man called Scythe?

"No, never."

"Did your husband ever describe the man who made the threats against him?"

"The man who threatened us?" The woman's knuckles whitened once more, squeezing her tunic like a wet rag.

169

"Temek said he was young and slender. Well-dressed, educated, but there was something shifty about him. He wouldn't look my husband in the eye."

"Tizraki?"

Temek Huyurgal's wife nodded. "Yes. He didn't beat Temek, though. He brought other men with him who did that." Her mouth twisted and she pointed with her chin toward the south. "Thugs from Koyulerin or Tergayit. Temek said he'd never seen them before. We don't associate with *those* kinds of people."

The image of Temek Huyurgal handing Parvan Gorshayik coin across the table in the Souk flashed through Dhani's mind. The cordwain might not like associating with *those* kinds of people, but he wasn't above bribing former Secret Service operatives when desperate. She thinned her lips. *If* it had indeed been a bribe that she'd seen.

Temek Huyurgal's wife scraped her boots on the tiles. Her knuckles turned white as she twisted tunic again. "You're sure you saw him in the Souk, Izn Karim?"

"I'm sure." Dhani nodded. "I was looking for him. It was just bad luck that the shooting began and we all had to run for our lives."

"If you find him…" The pain in the woman's voice left a lump in Dhani's throat. Despite whatever mess Temek Huyurgal was mixed up in, his wife loved him dearly. And she knew only too well how much it hurt to lose a person you loved.

In the end, there was little more she could do but nod and thank Temek's wife for her assistance. She promised to keep looking for the cordwain and left.

Thirty seconds later, she turned a corner just down from the compound and began to pick up her pace. Temek Huyurgal's wife might not know where he was, but she suspected someone else did. *Parvan Gorshayik*, possibly tucked up in his too-tidy room in the nearby Geraktin safe house. She picked up her pace, ignoring a stab of pain from her ankle.

It was time for her and her former Ha'filu partner to have an insightful and cosy late night chat.

CHAPTER SEVENTEEN

Midnight had come and gone by the time Dhani switched her serviceable blue tunic for her assassin's close-fitting black pullover, found a building near the safe house with an external staircase and climbed onto the roof. From there she made two painful, ankle-straining jumps and landed on the safe house roof.

She spent a half hour creeping about the roof top, searching for operatives watching the building.

It didn't take long to find two operatives watching the building from below, one slouched in a nearby doorway, pretending to be drunk or asleep, the other crouching in an alley, changing his posture every so often as his knees no doubt began to ache. Certain these were the only two, she picked the lock on the access door, left the door open for a quick getaway, and slipped down a set of narrow stairs, headed for Parvan Gorshayik's room.

She cracked open the door at the first-floor landing and listened. Inside the building, a calm silence greeted her. Her heart beat out a slow, easy rhythm and she rolled her shoulders, easing tension from her back. The scent of cinnamon cigarillos, bitter kaffai and mint tea flavoured the air, water pipes and wooden joists creaked as the building cooled. Ten minutes passed, her ears straining for signs of footsteps or snoring inside the rooms surrounding Parvan Gorshayik's.

She heard nothing.

Satisfied no armed operatives awaited her, she crept to the big Tizraki's door and stopped. She didn't bother knocking. Her lock pick and rake were already in her hand. If Gorshayik said anything, she'd direct his concerns to the nearest orifice and recommend in the strongest of terms he firmly jam them there.

When she tested the door handle, however, it became obvious there would be no jamming of *anything* into *any* bodily orifice whatsoever. The lock's tongue gave up a definitive metal click. The door handle swung down without resistance. Her breath latched in her throat.

The room was unlocked.

An unlocked door could have meant a dozen things— Parvan Gorshayik being lazy, forgetful, distracted—but the sudden chill of gooseflesh down her arms suggested something amiss.

She dropped the lock pick and rake into a pocket and drew a knife. Then, she eased the door open.

It swung inwards effortlessly, gliding away from her touch.

The *stench* hit her at once: an overpowering cocktail of blood, raw meat, the stink of an opened bowel or gut. A scent she knew well—*too* well. The scent of someone or something gutted and left for dead.

"Captain Gorshayik?" she whispered.

No answer.

She turned sideways, stepping into the room blade first.

An upended chair greeted her just inside the door. Across the room, boots, trousers, nightshirts, books, and papers were strewn about, scattered as if there'd been a struggle. A darker, all-too-human shape lay on the far side of the room, slumped against the wall.

She exhaled loud enough that the sound echoed in the spartan room. *Had Parvan Gorshayik been murdered?*

After closing the door, she hurried to the window and pulled the drapes shut. Groping about, she found the deenjili lamp on the floor, dialled the brightness down as far as it could go and still offer light, then flicked the switch to ignite it.

The light-emitting rod snapped to life, throwing out a dim white light. Lamp in hand, she made her way across the room, studying the grim scene before her.

The body slumped against the wall was not Parvan Gorshayik's.

Instead, she stared at the lifeless corpse of slipperier-than-an-eel cordwain, Temek Huyurgal. She didn't need to check for a pulse. Huyurgal's belly had been sliced open like a prize fish, his gut spewing pink, ropey intestine sausages that looped out and rested in his lap. T he man's face was bluish white, his jaw slack, his eyes half-open slits, a blood slick covered the floor beneath him. Of Parvan Gorshayik, however, there was no sign.

Dhani blew out a breath and made a slow scan of the room.

There'd been a struggle. The slew of clothing, the upturned chair, the scattered books, and furniture told the story. She knelt down, staring at a craze of bloody footprints and drag-marks on the once ice-white cotton bedsheets which had been dragged off the bed, trailed across the floor and stomped on. Huyurgal looked to have been sliced open on or near the bed, struggled, and then pushed—or staggered of his own volition—to the wall where he drew his final breath.

But where was Parvan Gorshayik?

She squinted in the dim light, searching the room for answers.

Under the bed lay Captain Gorshayik's battered suitcase, intact and unopened. Off to the left were the books she'd seen the previous day, now scattered across the floorboards. The wedding photograph lay facedown alongside the upturned bedside table. On the floor next to a belt, Gorshayik's brass pocket watch ticked out the passing seconds.

What in the name of the Four Winds had happened? Dhani studied the patterns of bloody footprints, positions of clothing, the way the sheets had been ripped off the bed. Had Gorshayik and someone else had an argument with cordwain and killed him? *And why so viciously?* Unless Huyurgal had attacked Gorshayik first, it made no sense.

Her gaze returned to the photograph and the pocket watch. Both held significance for the big Tizraki captain, the kind of sentimental objects no one would leave behind even if they *were* fleeing the scene of a murder.

She frowned at the upturned photograph, studying the play of shadow and light across the brass frame. No matter how screwed in the head he seemed, she couldn't believe for a moment Parvan Gorshayik would kill someone in cold blood, unprovoked.

Something else had happened here.

And whatever it was, it took no gravity-defying mental leap to imagine her dedicated, protocol-worshipping Ha'filu colleagues adding *newly resigned operative Parvan Gorshayik* and *disgraced former assassin Dhani Karim* to *Temek Huyurgal's gutted corpse* and reaching the conclusion: *death by firing squad.*

She slapped the blade against her thigh. *Clusterfuck of fucked-up clusterfucks!* She'd landed feet, torso and headfirst in so much trouble, it required its own volume of Imperial law. Hell, they'd probably need a second volume as well, just for the case notes.

Dhani pushed to her feet, raising the lamp to shine its frail light over the confusion of bloody footprints on the wooden floor. *So where was dear Captain Gorshayik?* Three sets trailed towards the door, two sets of near identical sized boots and a larger pair that had to be Gorshayik's. By the look of the zig-zagging scuff marks and diagonal scrapes, he'd left the room unwillingly.

Somewhere outside, a door closed suddenly—a muffled but sudden *bang*.

Dhani jumped and held her breath.

Boots thumped up an internal staircase, their rhythm urgent and swift. Two people in a hurry for something, taking two steps at a time. The thudding pulse in her ears joined flood of metallic adrenaline to her mouth. She didn't need to be a mind-reader to know that something was *her.*

She tossed the lamp onto the bed, swiped Gorshayik's pocket watch and wedding photograph from the floor and tucked both in her pack. A parting glance at the cordwain —and a gut-twist of remorse for his widow and nephew, Imril—she shot out the door.

She made the narrow staircase leading back to the roof just as an unfamiliar man's voice shouted,

"Karim! Stop! You're under arrest!"

Dhani slammed the door behind her, locked it and bounded up the darkened staircase, heading for the roof.

Moments later, the warm night air rushed past her face as she leapt the gap between buildings. She landed hard, took three jarring steps to regain her balance, then sprinted into a small forest of freshly laundered bedsheets hanging from a crisscross of rooftop lines.

Behind her, the sounds of pursuit followed: four solid thuds and a splintering of wood as the safe house's rooftop door burst open. Dhani chanced a look over her shoulder.

Two shadowy figures rushed onto the safe house's roof, paused, and made a beeline for the roof she was currently sprinting across. Both were men judging by their height, both wiry, copper-skinned, blond-haired Homelanders like herself. Their economy of movement and swift reactions told her everything she needed to know. Her tails were a pair of well-trained Ha'filu operatives. Losing them wouldn't be easy. Worse, they'd both be armed with pistols.

Clusterfuck indeed. She batted the bedsheets aside and focussed on crossing the roof. The sickle moon offered just enough light to map a path to the next roof and the one after that. *Two flat roofs, and then a third with a pitched roof*

and terracotta tiles. The wall looming ahead at least looked to be thigh-high, an easy jump.

Which meant an easy jump for those chasing her, too.

She shortened her strides, cinched her belly, and took a flying leap over the wall.

The black-as-pitch gap between the buildings flickered past beneath her. She cleared the second building's short wall and landed with a grunt. After two steps to steady herself, she lurched forward again, scanning her surroundings.

Dark rectangular shapes set across the roof at neat intervals suggested coops and pens for chickens or turkeys. The smell of straw, manure and a faint clucking confirmed the owners of this building kept their poultry on the roof. Other slightly larger boxes grew vegetables and fragrant herbs.

It took a half-second to pick a way through the confusion of pens, cages, and crops. Behind her, two solid thuds and the sound of booted footsteps warned the pair of tails had jumped onto the roof she'd just left and began sprinting through the forest of sheets.

"*Stop, Karim!*" a voice shouted. The man's rounded vowels suggested a South Jhiriyan accent. The brusque, huffing tone said he didn't much care for midnight chases across rooftops. "Give yourself up."

A spear of pain shot the length of her lower leg. Her ankle gave way, and she stumbled, righted herself and jumped a vegetable plot, intent on the next roof.

Halfway across the rooftop, a dog burst out from the shadows, snarling, barking, and gnashing its teeth. It made a lunge at her and caught hold, clamping down on her boot leather at calf-height.

Dhani kicked at the mutt once and then again, but its jaws remained clamped on her boot. Though nowhere near as large as the pair of demon-spawn who'd chased her in Milej Tarovik's compound, she'd give the animal credit. It held on with a tenacious, bear-like grip, growling and thrashing its head from side to side as if its life depended on tearing her boot to shreds.

Harming animals was something she tried to avoid, but she had little choice save to dislodge the dog using force. Drawing her dagger, she spun the blade and slammed the balled pommel down on the dog's head.

The mutt yelped and let go. She kicked hard at the animal's rump, sending it skating across the roof's adobe floor and smashing into a wooden pen. Squawks erupted, a sudden cacophony of disgruntled, frightened poultry. Dhani ground her teeth and hurried on. *So much for being quiet.*

At the far side of the roof, she slid to a stop. The next building lay a good three metres away, its roofline steep-pitched and covered in uneven terracotta tiles that shimmered in the pale moonlight.

Behind her, the dog began snarling, its claws scraping on the roof's surface as it came after her again. The pair of tails thudded onto the roof and began to pick their way through the chicken coops and vegetable plots. She ran her tongue about her mouth, tasting blood. Her pulse drummed at her neck. Five seconds and they'd be on her.

She measured the distance between this building and next. Uninjured, it would be a simple jump. With her ankle now screaming five different kinds of pain, failing a jump like this could very well mean a broken neck.

But what choice did she have? If they caught her, it would be the firing squad.

Dhani backed up, inhaled, and took off at a sprint. She bounded up over the building's low wall, sailed across the gap and landed awkwardly on the sloping terracotta tiles with a jarring *clank*. She winced, took a moment to regain her balance, then scampered upwards, the tiles shifting and clinking beneath her boots.

"Karim! Stop or I'll shoot!"

"Bite my arse!" Without looking back, she flipped the man a middle finger, zagged left, then right.

A crack sounded and a bullet zipped past her ear.

Bastards! She zagged left again then launched herself over the roof's apex. The second bullet buzzed past as she topped the room and half-slid, half plunged down the roof's sloping western side on her behind. A third shot hit a roof tile, sending a spray of terracotta fragments into the air. Either the man needed more time on the shooting range, or he'd purposely missed.

The Creator smiled on her then, as the dog chose that exact moment to make its reappearance, barking and snarling with renewed vigour. A man's voice cursed the animal in hard, hacking Jhiriyan. Clearly, the dog had found a new best friend to clamp its jaws on—and she'd gained a decisive few seconds.

At the bottom of the roofline, she clambered to a stop. Her breath rasped in her ears as she took in what lay ahead. A roof tile teetered beneath her boot.

A gap of five or six metres separated her from the next

building and its high-pitched, tiled roof. Her shoulders sagged. *Of all the butt-cursed, maggot-infested bad luck!* Unless she grew wings or the ability to levitate, she had not a chance in this life or the next of making the distance from a dead stop. Even with a decent run-up, a gap like that would be a risk. She'd have to find another way down.

She scanned the darkness for an escape route. Below lay a narrow lane filled with soupy shadows and an unknown number of bone-breaking obstacles littered across the ground. There was nowhere else to go.

Her heart thudded in her chest. She clenched a fist so hard, her knuckles popped. No matter what might lay in the lane below, she'd have to chance it.

The building's height suggested the drop into the lane would be five metres, reduced to three and a bit if she lowered herself down from the roof and let go. She massaged her lower leg and winced. Her ankle wasn't going to be delighted by the abuse.

A clattering *thud* and clink of tiles sounded behind her as one of the operatives landed on the roof. She scooted to the left, found a window ledge wide enough to grant her a brief, steadying foothold and swung over the roof's guttering.

She hung for a moment, feet dangling mid-air, clenching her stomach and thighs against the inevitable hard landing, and let go.

A jolt of raw pain blazed through her ankle as she landed and something important—a bone or a tendon— crunched. Dhani ignored the flare of agony scorching up her leg. She took one limping step, then a second. If nothing else, she could hobble along at a fast walk. As the sound of clattering roof tiles grew loud, she moved soundlessly into the lane's gloom.

Ten paces on, she found an alley rich with the peculiar tang of rotting citrus and slipped along it, following it to its end where it turned into another laneway. She curled her lip as her boots crushed something soft and squelching and the eye-watering stink of decaying fruit festered in her nostrils. After two right turns, the laneway opened into a small courtyard housing a well.

Dhani slowed her pace, willing her frantic pulse to slow. The soothing scents of damp earth, water and potted mint replaced rotting citrus. The moon's faint light revealed three lanes exiting the courtyard and its low, circular well.

She exhaled a sigh of relief and hobbled towards the right-hand lane. In the darkness, and with so many twists and turns now separating them, not even a pair of well-trained Secret Service operatives would find an assassin.

As she reached the lane, she adjusted her pack and set her jaw against the grinding pain in her lower leg.

Ahead lay a long, slow painful hobble—and the distinct and life-ending possibility that Bethsehal Shalamir had operatives waiting for her at every city gate.

CHAPTER EIGHTEEN

The staccato peel of clocktowers clanged out across the city, marking the first hour after midnight. Dhani pressed her back into an alcove, waiting for the single-horse cab that had delivered her to the city's southern wall to disappear from sight. The knot in her gut had an each-way bet on the grizzled cab driver reporting her to the city constables—or *not* reporting her, given the generous three peshak tip she'd given him. She winced at constant pain in her ankle, and shrugged, favouring the latter.

In the end, she'd had to take the risk.

After giving the pair of Ha'filu operatives the slip, her ankle collapsed three times, a sure sign she'd abused the injury to the limits of reasonable bodily tolerance, even for a pain-denying assassin. Either she found a cab or found somewhere to rest for the night. She'd been just about to search for a dark corner to curl up in when luck delivered her not only a cab, but a cab with a driver willing to take her to Atoulibba, in Izurum's south, without the flicker of an eyelid.

Generally, people avoided Atoulibba unless they had business there. She didn't blame them. Filled with tanneries, slaughterhouses and cavernous, open-ended grain stores, the air in Atoulibba's streets hung with a fetid mist of pigeon shit, cow piss and chemical leather dyes. If that wasn't enough to cave in one's nasal cavities, the stench of rotting innards and offal added enthusiasm to the nose-crushing mix. In other circumstances, she would have avoided the area altogether.

The Creator, as usual, offered her no such option.

Atoulibba possessed a number of gates, all of them directly adjoining Koyulerin. The insignificant gate she'd chosen to leave Izurum by bore the uninspiring moniker *'number five gate'*. At this time of night, and with her ankle threatening to take a leave-of-absence from her body, number five gate was as good as any.

First, however, she had to be certain the area wasn't being watched by over-friendly Ha'filu operatives on after-hours double-pay.

From the alcove, she slid through the street's gloom, stopping in the dense shadows offered by a tannery whose astringent blend of stale piss and chemicals smelled so bad, her tears cried tears of their own. After five minutes or so, the worst of the stench faded and her eyes ceased stinging. The next ten passed without anything more than a rat and a stub-tailed, one-eared cat fighting to the death over a hand-sized portion of blackened meat.

As the pair of animals rolled, hissed, and spat, she moved on from the tannery's wall, scouting the gate's surrounds and keeping an eye on its pair of taroch-playing sentries—two men dressed in the camel-brown jodhpurs and wide waistbands of the Tizraki Territorial Militia— better known as the *Camelskins*. Her earlier flush of luck held. After a half hour surveying the area, she found no Secret Service operatives lurking in the shadows, ready to arrest her and bitch about working past ten bells.

When one of the sentries stood up, stretched, and strode off to relieve himself against a wall, Dhani blew out a breath. *No time like the present.* She sauntered up to the remaining man as best as one could saunter with a pronounced limp and offered the remaining sentry a gold dironi to keep his mouth shut.

As any underpaid, overworked Camelskin conscript would, the man happily obliged, and she hobbled through the gate and out into Koyulerin, unchallenged.

It took several minutes to get her bearings. The sickle moon hung too low on the western horizon to be of any real assistance, and unlike the city with its oil and deenjili lamps, the shantytown's streets boasted no external lighting and few signs. She found a dusty, uneven lane heading in roughly the right direction, and made her way along it, inhaling rose and musk incense as she went.

About her, Koyulerin lay quiet and still, as if the entire place had sucked down one long in-breath and held it. Not a dog's howl, not a child's cry. Not even a hissing cat with half an ear disturbed the silence. Save for the slow thud of her own heart and the *step-step-pause, step-step-stop* of her uneven gait, no sound marked her passage towards Fikret and Esmille's dwelling.

At least she had time to think. Her ankle needed to be

bound, and, if she wanted to walk on it anytime soon, it required a morning trip to a healer. Then, she had to figure out what to do next given the universe of shit-fuckery she'd dived head-first into. She turned into a second lane flanked by high corrugated iron fences, avoiding a rusting metal drum and a stack of wooden crates. The night enveloped her, a heavy blanket of skin-prickling stillness.

No doubt she'd be accused of murdering Temek Huyurgal, and of all places, inside a Ha'filu safe house. Whilst she'd eventually prove her innocence, instinct screamed it wouldn't be easy. Then, there was Parvan Gorshayik. Though the big Tizraki's hornet-up-the-arse attitude was hardly endearing *and* he'd as much as told her to launch herself into a spike-filled bottomless pit, the pang of guilt over his fate nagged like a bothersome toddler.

Most likely, he'd been taken by the same people who'd killed Huyurgal, either as ransom or because he possessed something his captors needed. The nagging toddler argued the latter, then had the audacity to suggest she should try to find him.

Problem was, she had no idea where to start looking or if, indeed, he still drew breath.

Her ankle gave way without warning and she stumbled, throwing a hand against an iron fence to steady herself with a loud *bang!* Pain shot from her heel to calf, spiralling upwards like a butcher had taken a cleaver to flesh. She sucked in a sharp breath and shook off a wave of head-spinning dizziness.

"You shouldn't be out here alone, Izn."

The low, gritty voice came from nowhere. Dhani spun about, hand swiping for a blade.

In the darkness behind her loomed a pair of beefy Tizraki men, both dressed in dark tunics. Just where they'd *loomed* from took another half-second to ascertain: a rectangle of inky darkness that hadn't been there ten seconds before, an open gate in a nearby fence. Shadows masked their faces, but the hard set of their shoulders and the pace at which they approached said they weren't exactly here to enquire after her health.

Her ankle flexed and threatened to drop her into the dirt. She ground her teeth. *Of all the butt-cursed luck!* There was no way to outrun the pair, and in a narrow lane surrounded by fences, nowhere to casually slip away. Instead, she snicked the metal baton from her belt and cinched her belly. Balanced her weight as evenly as she could and focussed on the pair of fast-advancing adversaries.

No emotion. No weakness. No retreat. And an entire cartload of *kill them first.*

The men split, attempting to flank her. The man on the right dived forward, coming at her with something held in his hand. *A weapon*, she guessed, likely a blade.

She waited until the last split-second, where the whites of his eyes became a glassy blur, then she hurled the metal baton. Either the man hadn't noticed the weapon at all or he was slow to react. The steel bar smacked him hard across the bridge of the nose. He grunted once and hit the dirt like a sack of lead. The baton clanged as it fell to the ground and rolled to a stop.

The second man lunged, his hand now shimmering

with the red glow of Deenjah. She had a second—perhaps less—to disable him.

She ducked to the left, ignoring the agony searing through her ankle, and punched the blade into the man's solar plexus with all the desperate strength she could muster. The man let out a surprised *oomph*.

Then, she dived and rolled, coming to a jarring stop on one knee. The first man was out cold or dead on the ground—it was too dark to tell. The second man stumbled about, eyes goggling at the blade protruding from his gut. The red glow of the Flames had vanished, replaced with the stink of blood and sweat.

She drew her curved dagger from its sheath and climbed to her feet, breath rasping in her ears.

The man reefed the short throwing blade from his middle with a small *yelp*. Wild-eyed, he turned and charged at her, slashing the air with an arc so predictable, a blind crone could have seen the blow coming the previous year.

Dhani jumped back, blocking the man's thrust with a jarring swipe of the forearm. With the man's momentum, she whirled him about, snapping his wrist upwards whilst pulling him in and jamming the dagger under his sternum. Up close, she inhaled almonds from his hair, sweet soap and freshly baked bread from his clothes.

A wet, sucking sound burst from the man's lips, but there was no scream. He struggled for a moment, flinging his weight backwards, trying to dislodge her, but his strength failed and his body went limp.

Dhani released him, letting him fall to the ground. She

heaved out a breath and placed her hands on her thighs, surveying the scene.

The lane was empty and still. A cat yowled in the distance. A dog snarled and yipped in reply. The man she'd downed with the baton still twitched. *Alive then.* He'd have an Imperial-sized headache when he awoke—*if,* indeed, he awoke at all. She stooped to recover her dagger and throwing knife from the man she'd killed, wiping them clean on his baked-bread and lemon soap-scented tunic. Several painful strides brought her to the baton. She snatched it up, dusted it off and replaced it on her belt.

As she passed the first man again, still twitching in the dirt, something small and shiny on his wrist caught her eye. A closer look revealed a small devotional bracelet, silver with an oval icon. Something about the locket's design nagged at her consciousness; devotional lockets and necklaces were common, but the icon was not. She tugged the bracelet hard, broke the chain and held it up, squinting.

The dim light was just enough to reveal the design. She sucked in a double-sharp breath.

A silver serpent coiled around Father Ulgan's black stallion.

The same symbol tattooed on the turbaned man she'd killed in the lane the previous day. The same symbol Ziraat Olucik had on his desk in Bethsehal Shalamir's foyer. Her mind spun with questions and conclusions, formed connections she probably shouldn't have been making.

What if…?

A backdoor creaked open behind a fence less than five strides away. A man's voice—followed by a woman's— whispered several frantic questions. Dhani closed her fist about the silver icon and began to hobble along the lane as quickly as she could.

It was time to find out exactly what the serpent coiled about the rearing stallion meant—and she knew just *where* she might be able to find out.

CHAPTER NINETEEN

I n the smokey morning light of Esmille's front room, the icon looked much the same as it had in the gloom. Chunky pewter, caste from a mould rather than handmade by a smith, the design showed a snub-nosed serpent coiled about a rearing stallion with a slightly bowed back leg. Dhani frowned at the icon, turning it over and over in her hand as she sat at the table with her ankle propped up on a crate. Both Esmille and Fikret had shaken their heads at the symbol. Their guess—not unusual for Tizraki—was it belonged to a hearth god from Talmakhan or some other distant city.

"Are you sure you don't want us to call a drukilyi in, Yelanda?" Esmille worried at her apron, one hand in a pocket, the other holding a needle and thread. "It's no trouble, really."

"Just give me names and directions and I'll find my way there." She flashed a watery smile and yawned. "Honest, Esmille. I can see you're busy."

"Don't argue, girl," Fikret said, poking his head in from the kitchen. "That ankle needs seeing to."

Dhani stared at the toes of her left foot, visible above the line of bandage strapping her ankle. The sprain was slightly better, the benefit of six hours' rest, but a long way from being healed. She'd need to find a drukilyi—a Deenjin healer—and waste more time she didn't have.

After fleeing her attackers in the lane, she'd limped to Esmille and Fikret's as quickly as she could. By two bells, her ankle was bound and elevated, and the bedroll spread across the lounge room floor. Exhaustion claimed her the moment her head hit the pillow. Eight bells had come and gone, and she'd slept right through the household's early morning activity. Though she couldn't really afford the hours of rest, she'd at least awoken with a clearer head.

"It's a little better this morning, but you're right." A spear of pain shot up her calf as she flexed her foot. She winced. "I do need to see a drukilyi."

"You do," Esmille agreed. She'd returned from her room carrying a fine, royal blue tunic embroidered with gold thread on the cuffs, collar, and hems. With a satisfied smile, she laid the tunic out on the lounge and pursed her lips, inspecting the material for creases and tears. The scent of Fikret's flatbread and couscous cooking in the tiny kitchen beyond the divider filled the entire shack. Dhani's mouth watered.

"I'd recommend the drukilyi just down the street here, but…" Esmille shrugged. "Truth is Yelanda, I'm sure you can afford better than old Maritja. Her mind's not what it used to be these days."

"She's one hundred and twenty-seven, what do you

expect?" Fikret said from the kitchen nook. "I hope I'm half as spry as Maritja, if Mother Yamir lets me reach that age."

"You burn the bread and *I* won't let you reach fifty-seven, husband," Esmille teased. "I don't want our wedding clothes to smell like they were scorched by the Flames."

Fikret's bemused snort was followed by the clanging of a cast-iron pan and the clatter of crockery. He retreated and began to hum a tune Dhani recognised as a wedding dance.

"Wedding clothes?" Dhani turned back to the royal blue tunic Esmille had taken to with her needle and thread, repairing a small tear in a side seam. "Are these yours?"

"Oh, no, no." Esmille laughed. "We had to borrow our wedding clothes and *pay* to borrow them, too. We're going to a wedding at the temple just after midday. These are our best clothes."

Fikret came out of the nook carrying a steaming plate of flatbread and a large bowl of couscous. He set both on the table and turned towards the closed door sealing off the children's room. "Abil, Rivek! Breakfast."

The door opened and a sleepy, tousle-haired Rivek toddled out, beaming a smile only a three-year old could beam. Abil followed more cautiously, already dressed in his temple robe—a simple blue tunic which fell to his shins over loose black pants. The tunic's round-necked collar was embroidered with a black and white filigree, a student's white cotton belt bound it to his waist. When his gaze met Dhani's, he immediately looked away, cheeks suffusing with pink.

"Manners, children! Rivek! Abil, we have a guest. Say good morning to Yelanda."

Rivek warbled a bright, *"Good morning, Izn Yelanda,"* but Abil scuffed his feet.

After a pause, he peered through his eyelashes and offered a bashful, "Good morning." He sat down at the table and immediately began heaping couscous onto bread. Fikret frowned at his son, unhappy with his impolite behaviour, and tutted. The boy's cheeks turned blood red.

Fikret and Esmille sat and began to eat, Rivek climbing onto her father's lap as there wasn't a spare seat. Dhani scooped couscous onto the bread and ate in silence. Yesterday, she'd handed Fikret five peshak for food, and the knobs of butter melting in the couscous suggested he'd put the money to good use. Butter, which needed to be chilled in Izurum's warm climate, was fare for those with cellars, ice rooms, or able to afford rare and expensive cold chests powered by deenjili rods. In a place like Koyulerin, butter was reserved for celebrations and honoured guests.

Conversation soon turned to the wedding at the temple, a young couple named Harmit and Tulki, then the shooting in Geraktin Souk and, finally, to Abil's studies at the Bisantrik, the religious school attached to the temple. Dhani listened but didn't offer any comment unless asked. When breakfast was done, Fikret and Abil gathered up the dishes, and Esmille returned to preparing her and Fikret's wedding outfits.

After a time, Abil returned to the table with several

books, a quill, and a bottle of ink. He glanced once at Dhani, opened a textbook and began to laboriously write notes. He ignored her with a force so hard, she could sense it pushing at her seat.

Something was bothering the boy. Dhani counted three long seconds where Abil's quill hovered over the same space without making a mark. Was it the encounter in Kyvil Yenidogat's office the previous day? Or something else, like sitting at the table with a foreign stranger? Her thoughts turned to the devotional bracelet tucked in her pocket and she closed her fingers around its cool edges. *Would Abil know what it was?* Perhaps she could break the ice by asking him about it—and save herself a trip to the Koyulerin temple and a meeting with an unwilling recip?

"Abil," she began, and drew the bracelet from her pocket. "I found this on the street not far from the number five gate." She laid it on the table. "It looks like a devotional bracelet. Do you know if it belongs to a local hearth god?"

The boy sucked in a too-quick breath. "No. No, I'm sorry, Izn Yelanda." He shook his head. "I do not know what that is."

"Here, have a closer look." Dhani offered him the bracelet. His hand trembled as he took the piece. Abil might have been quick to learn reading and writing, but when it came to dissembling, he had no skill at all. Clearly, he *had* seen the icon before, knew what it was—and wanted *nothing* to do with.

"I haven't seen it before." His tongue traced a nervous line about his lips and he handed it back, almost as if the symbol burned to touch. "Maybe it's a hearth god from Talmakhan or Burukalin?"

Dhani shrugged. "Perhaps. I was thinking about asking the Recip or the scholars at Koyulerin's temple this morning."

Abil stilled for a moment, pressing his lips together in a thin, hard line. Then, his quill resumed its journey across the page. "You visited the Ziddurat temple yesterday." He licked his lips again. "What was that about?"

"Revenue Office business. Enquiries about a man who owes Tizrak Yirda a lot of tax. Apparently he visits the temple from time to time. Papat Yenidogat said he'd ask around for me and see if anyone knew the man." The boy nodded and resumed writing, matters of internal revenue as uninteresting to him as they would be to most twelve-year-olds. Dhani studied him closely. This time, he did a much more convincing job of feigning disinterest, a frown gathering between his brows, his eyes fixing on the mathematical problem he was working on. "Well," she said, easing back in the chair. "I won't disturb you anymore."

The boy didn't reply. She rose and hobbled past the room divider, to where Fikret stood humming and washing dishes.

"I'll help," she said.

"Ayee! No you won't, girl." Fikret chased her away with a soapy flick of the hand. "You go and sit back down. Put that leg up and rest. Do some of that fine embroidery I saw you doing yesterday."

Chastised, she returned to the living space and huffed back into the chair at the table, setting her ankle on the crate again. In the few moments she'd been gone, Abil had slipped away, leaving his textbook open on the table.

A folded piece of paper caught her eye, protruding from beneath the book's cover.

Yelanda was written in the neat Dewari lettering used for the Continent's common tongue, Massayalam, rather than in flowing, right-to-left Tizraki calligraphy. Not that it mattered. Neither Esmille nor Fikret could read much more than their own names, the shops they visited and of course, the numbers on coin and bank notes.

She took the folded paper and opened it. The page contained a rough drawing of the bracelet's mysterious icon, a clumsy rendering of Father Ulgan's rearing stallion and the serpent coiled around it. Alongside the design in Massayalam were the words, *Papat* and *cu Bapu,* followed by, *don't speak of this to Mama and Papa.*

Dhani's heart skipped a beat. She looked up and straight at Abil's raven head where he'd appeared in the doorway of the room he shared with his sister. His brows beetled together. He pressed a finger to his lips and shook his head. Had he scrawled *say nothing!* across the walls in his own blood, the message couldn't have been any clearer.

She sucked in on a cheek, her mouth suddenly dry and stale. *Did this mean Kyvil Yenidogat was connected to Yevengik cu Bapa? Or was it Abil's way of telling her to show the bracelet to the Papat and ask for his help?* An overweight, absent-minded, harassed priest with no recorded political sentiment seemed an unlikely candidate to be a member of a violent nationalist cult, but stranger things had happened. She folded the note and tucked it into her pocket before Esmille looked up from her sewing and noticed. Abil slipped away, retreating into his room.

Whatever the warning meant, one thing was clear. After she'd visited a healer, she would be paying Kyvil Yenidogat an unexpected and somewhat less than cordial visit.

CHAPTER TWENTY

The onion-shaped domes and minarets of Father Ulgan's temple in Zidurat glared down at Dhani, their black tiles shimmering in the afternoon heat. From the tallest minaret's balcony, a bell rang out over and over again, the same *blah-BLANG, blah-BLANG* rhythm heard the length and breadth of Tizrak Yirda, calling the faithful to zenith prayer. After a final glance over her shoulder, she passed into the temple's walls and eased out a tiny breath.

No Secret Service tails. At least none she could see.

But who knew what awaited inside? She adjusted the dark blue scarf covering her hair, smoothed down a matching and equally nondescript tunic and cowed her posture as best she could to blend in. Was it sheer dumb luck no operatives had turned out to greet her? Or were they more concerned about the shooting in the Souk?

She'd taken several hours to make to the journey to the temple from Esmille's, sticking to back lanes and tiny alleys, slipping into shadows when anyone drew near, or squeezing onto crowded *tuchek* wagons with twenty other people and keeping her head covered with the temple scarf. Along the way, she'd found a drukilyi who'd done a reasonable job of healing the sprain, and she could at least walk pain-free again. But the nagging sensation of being watched, a creeping, itch on the back of her neck, wouldn't go away.

Inside the temple's towering main wall, she joined a shuffling throng of worshippers, a sweaty tide of black and dark blue covered heads streaming towards the main prayer hall. The crowds were larger today, no doubt the result of the Geraktin Souk shooting, yet also quiet and sombre.

As the throng slowly moved towards the prayer halls, Dhani's pulse thudded like a drum, drowning out the peeling bell and scuffling of feet on tiles. A quick scan of the temple's courtyard, its arched porticos, and the sparse greenery around its trio of fountains revealed nothing out of place. Even the pair of black-robed recips were depressingly predictable, wafting clouds of myrrh and rose incense from brass censors whilst mumbling sonorous blessings on those who'd come to pray, all in the hope of adding coin into woven baskets at their feet. Neither gave Dhani a second glance as she passed.

She climbed a set of polished marble steps then skived off from the crowd, hurrying inside the temple's cool shade and along an echoing stone passage leading to an administrative area at the rear of the complex.

For the next half hour as the zenith prayers were held, Dhani sat in an alcove just off the administrative main chamber, studying a vaulted ceiling tiled in blue, white and black mosaics, patterns, and calligraphy quoting sections of the Ambituryan. She wasted time admiring the workmanship and rehearsing what she'd say to Yenidogat in the privacy of his rooms. In her pocket, her fingers worried over the silver icon, turning it over again and again.

As soon as the prayer service finished, she hurried towards the cluster of offices at the rear of the space, a close-spaced grab-bag of wooden doors and archways. A blue-robed cleric attended a counter of aged rosewood, the man's craggy brows and shock of white hair suggesting he was older than the temple itself.

"Is Papat Yenidogat in?" Dhani asked the cleric.

The man blinked at her, leaned nearer—blinked again —registered she was Jhiriyan, and slowly shook his head. "No, Izn. He's out at the Koyulerin temple, officiating at a wedding."

Dhani stared back at the man's nut-brown, rheumy eyes and straggle of errant eyebrow hair. She cursed silently. *Why was Yenidogat at Koyulerin when there was a recip to officiate?* Her hand clamped down on the pewter icon, its angles biting into her palm. The hair on her neck shivered. She checked behind her, but no one else had entered this section of the building.

"Do you know what time he'll be back?" she said, keeping her face blank. "I came to see him yesterday. He asked me to return this afternoon."

The cleric's gaze flickered to a wall clock. "Half four, most likely. He usually stays and partakes in the feast with the guests."

Of course he partakes. That Yenidogat might have decided to officiate simply in order to attend the wedding feast required no mental gymnastics at all. She thinned her lips, chewing over what to say next.

"I see." She offered a polite smile. "Would you be so kind to let him know Yelanda Sarif came to see him? I'll come back at five bells."

The clerk clasped his hands in prayer and lowered his head. "Of course, Izn Sarif."

A group of chattering children and their parents, visitors to Izurum judging by their knee-length city tunics and the women's bejewelled silk scarves, entered the hall. Dhani turned and cut a path for the rear door, casually tilting her chin upwards as if admiring the mosaics as she passed. One of the children whispered, *Metalskin* in Tizraki. A man's voice snapped an instant, *Don't be rude, Erdogan.*

She moved past the group, not looking back. *Curse Yenidogat's bovine-sized arse!* If she'd known he'd been officiating at the wedding, she could have stayed in Koyulerin. Could have caught up on a few hours' sleep or lazed about in Esmille's lounge working on an embroidery and thinking about how best to get a message to the General.

Head down, she stepped out from the hall and onto its tiled external verandah, peering out from the porticos across manicured physic and vegetable gardens. A handful of older boys wearing plain Besantrik tunics like Abil's tended plants or raked crushed stone pathways. Dhani paused, checking over her shoulder before turning back to the gardens again.

Whilst it was tempting to look for Abil and quiz him further about the cryptic note he'd left, fear of repercussion made that a last resort. Her gut—and Abil's note—said Yenidogat was the key. She needed to catch the man alone and off guard. A wedding feast was as good a place as any to do that.

And if Yenidogat identified the icon as belonging to Yevengik cu Bapa? What then?

A man's voice behind her, a soft tenor arguing a brain-shrivelling theological conundrum about the first humans *not* possessing navels became the cue to move. Dhani walked on with an unhurried gait, pretending to admire the gardens, before turning a corner and stealing away towards the compound's rear exit.

If Yenidogat knew something useful, something connecting the icon to Yevengik cu Bapa, then she'd have only one choice: re-enter the city, risk arrest and court-martial and attempt to send a signal to General Behzad El'Meshid.

—

The long, dusty street leading to Koyulerin's temple was lined with makeshift canvas market stalls, their awnings hanging lifeless and flaccid in the blanketing midday heat. As far as Dhani could see, the market's only patrons comprised four old women congregated about a pottery stall and a little further on, a pair of young men wearing expressions as flat and dull as the hard-packed desert dirt beneath their feet. In the distance, the jaunty strains of wedding music—traditional strings, reedy woodwinds, and thumping tambourines—stirred the listless air.

The vague sense of being watched sent spidery shivers up her spine, but another check over her shoulder and she shrugged it off as nerves. *Locate the priest, figure out what the icon was—or was not—then decide what to do next.* At least Yenidogat would be easy to find. With the music confirming the wedding ceremony had finished, the cow-sized priest had no doubt wedged his cow-sized arse into a seat at the buffet table and was likely filling his cow-sized belly with food at the expense of the bridegroom's family.

"Dates, Izn?" a stall holder said, beaming. "Local grown."

"Kofte and naan, kofte and naan," another called, a man who stood up as she passed, tapping his fingers hopefully on his cooking pans.

Dhani politely smiled and gave a shake of her head. The man placed a melodramatic hand on his heart, pretending to be shattered. A clucking white chicken crossed her path, chasing an errant cockroach. A scrawny cat hissed at the pair from beneath a cart laden with dried figs. She fought off the urge to pet the frightened tabby and settled her gaze on the temple's lone black minaret instead.

Unlike the artisan-tiled domes of the Zidurat temple, Koyulerin's dome had been made from black-painted, hastily beaten iron sheets whilst its lone balcony appeared to be constructed of *please-wear-a-safety-harness* rickety timber planks. The walls surrounding the compound were plain mud brick with a slap of whitewashed render, thin and peeling in several places. She bit back a wry smile. Here, in Koyulerin, it seemed it was the thought that counted, with only a lazy wave of the church's hand of in the direction of money.

"*Karim!*"

A sudden harsh, hacking Jhiriyan voice rang out behind her, spearing the torpid air like a bolt of electrified steel. Dhani jumped, adrenaline drying her mouth, swiping for her metal baton.

A single glance over her shoulder and she picked him at once: a tall, blond, clean-cut man jogging after her, dressed in an immaculate and wholly unsuitable Homelander long shirt and jacket. The shirt even possessed a predictable royal blue Mandarin, neck-squeezing collar. Just where he'd come from was anyone's guess. Not that it mattered—she didn't intend to stay long enough to ask.

"Karim! Wait up."

She had time to scan the street ahead, locate a convenient lane off to the left—then she was face-to-face with a second operative, a man some years younger than herself who stepped out from a gap between a pair of iron shanties boasting garish red doors. He also wore a body-broiling, charcoal grey Homelander suit. Everything about him, from his sweaty, narrow forehead and icy glare to the knife-slash of his lips screamed *Ha'filu operative* in metre-high, official black ink.

Before she'd taken her next step, the man grabbed her upper arm and hauled her to a stop. His other hand pushed back a coat flap, making a purposeful and definitive display of the revolver holstered on his hip.

"Don't make this harder than it has to be, Karim." His grip tightened, matching the iron in his voice. Like his partner, he was Jhiriyan, an unsmiling, rod-thin man whose light brown eyebrows framed steel blue eyes and a fine, straight nose. His educated, central Jhiriyan accent and fine clothing screamed *upper caste*. "You're in enough trouble already."

Every stall holder and patron on the street turned to watch. A pair of old women packing up a fruit stall canted their heads together, whispering. One of the bored young men frowned, clearly deliberating whether to intervene. The jolly, thumping wedding music came to an abrupt end.

Dhani's pulse surged in her veins. She sucked in hot, dry air mixed with dust and cooking spices. The operative tugged her forward, ignoring the stares of those around them, fingers blushing coppery-white where they bit into her sleeve and skin. She resisted, pulling back against his grasp. There were perhaps five seconds before the second operative arrived.

Which made her decision to act simple.

The calculations weren't difficult: *two against one.* Both operatives would have at least some basic hand-to-hand combat training. If they were sticklers for protocol—a Jhiriyan obsession—they'd both be carrying guns, handcuffs, identification papers and nothing else. She'd bet her last fifty dironi *and* her very best hand of blades neither of them, however, had ever been Ta'Hafiq.

"Look," she said, opening her hands. She slouched her shoulders and hung her head. "I can explain everything."

"Save it for the interrogators." The man shoved her back the way she'd just come, past the kofte stand. "I'm not interested."

She dug her heels in, refusing to move. The thin man did exactly as she'd anticipated: hauled her about by the arm so savagely, the old women at the fruit stall gasped and the kofte seller took a backward step.

The second operative arrived, a man several decades older than his partner, a pair of handcuffs already swinging in one hand. Dhani waited until he'd slowed to a stop before screaming over her shoulder in Tizraki at the pair of bored young men, "*Thieves! Rapists! Help me!*"

It had the desired effect: a disbelieving misstep and double take from the thin man clasping her arm. She took the chance and rammed her elbow into his solar plexus so hard, a great *oomph* burst from his throat, followed by a wheezing gasp as he tried to inhale. A single sweep of her right leg sent him sprawling backside first into the dirt.

Without pause, she spun and hooked an uppercut to the jaw of the second operative and then smashed her other fist into the space just behind his temple. He toppled like a pillar of loose brick, spinning about and falling to the ground. The cuffs flew from his grip and clattered against a nearby shanty wall.

Then, she turned and began to run. Ahead, the young Tizraki men hurried towards her, expressions hovering between shock and anger.

"Are you alright, Izn?" the first man said as she reached him. He put a hand on her shoulder, slowing her down.

"They tried to rob me!" she panted, hoping she sounded shaken. A backwards glance revealed the thin operative clutching at his middle, still obviously winded but trying to stand. Handcuffs had rolled over, expression muddled as he clutched at the side of his head. "Please, I'm frightened. I just want to get away."

"Excellent right hook," the second Tizraki said, teeth flashing an approving smile through his beard.

"Was it?" She made her voice high and breathless. "I was so scared, I just hit them as best I could. Ai, Creator! They're coming after me."

"You go," the first man said. "We'll take care of them."

Dhani clasped her hands together in a gesture of prayer. "Mother Yamir's blessing on you both."

She broke into a jog, fixing her eyes on the temple's flaking whitewashed walls. Hopefully, she'd just bought enough time to get inside and find Yenidogat.

A few seconds later, a cheer went up from the old women behind her, followed by clapping and laughing.

Dhani chanced a peek over her shoulder. The pair of not-so-bored-Tizraki men and several stall holders stood over the thin man and Handcuffs, fists clenched and voices raised, threatening violence for picking on women.

CHAPTER TWENTY-ONE

Dhani entered the temple courtyard via a side gate, slipped inside, and pressed her back to a lime-washed wall. The courtyard held pretty much what she expected to see in a shantytown's temple courtyard. A lone, rectangular fountain emitting a piddle of water, flanked by a handful of gardens and a few timber walkways grown over with—*what else?*—five different shades of bougainvillea. A paved path ran from the fountain to the temple steps, but the remainder of the space was hard-packed earth.

The wedding feast and its attendant crowd lay beyond the fountain, clustered around a single, large canvas marquee. The structure was far from adequate for what seemed to be a hundred-strong gathering of family and friends, many of them spilling out into the baking afternoon sun. If nothing else, the marquee's sides were rolled up, allowing people and air to circulate.

A quick search of the crowd revealed no sign of Yenidogat's substantial form amidst the dancing bodies and groups of conversing guests. She tapped a fist against her thigh. With so many people glued to the marquee's shade, she'd need to get close to even catch a glimpse of the priest.

She ducked along a bougainvillea-covered walkway, heading for the crowded marquee. To her right, the temple's main gates stood open to invite the faithful in. Her aching knuckles gave up a subtle warning throb. She'd give Handcuffs and the Thin Man five minutes—ten at a generous stretch—to flash their credentials and convince the small but incensed market crowd to let them go. Then, no doubt, they'd be on their way to the temple.

Which didn't leave much time to find Kyvil Yenidogat and question him—wherever the forgetful lard-slab might be.

She drew level with the fountain and a pair of garden beds planted with marigold and fragrant white sage. A flicker of movement inside the temple caught her eye and she peered past the building's ogee-shaped porticos, into the dim coolness beyond.

A group of dark-robed figures flitted between columns deep inside the main chamber. *Clerics? Adepts?* She couldn't be sure—most of Father Ulgan's attendants wore black. The wedding band began to play a popular tune. A cheer went up from the crowd. Dhani shrugged and hurried on.

Beyond the bougainvillea-covered walkway, the newlywed couple began a foot-stomping traditional dance on the dusty ground just outside the marquee. At one end, a small band played a tune on fiddles, five-stringed *bhuzuks*, tambourines and reedy woodwind instruments.

Opposite, a long buffet table stood piled high with platters. Spiced kofte, bhugal, roast lamb, marinated goat, and mint tea mixed with the dust kicked up by dancing feet. Her stomach growled, and she blew out a frustrated breath. Less than thirty strides separated her from the marquee and Kyvil Yenidogat was still nowhere to be seen.

The tune the band played came to an end, sending up a collective groan from the guests. Someone called out the name of another song, the flute player nodded and counted to four. The music and dancing resumed. In the crowd, she picked out Esmille and Fikret dressed in the fine tunics Esmille had prepared this morning. They laughed, rushing hand-in-hand to join the dance beneath an archway made of red and gold ribbons. Fikret took Esmille in his arms, his smile likely recalling their own wedding, then began to whirl her about in an enthusiastic dance.

Abil was notably absent—perhaps the boy was at school or running errands at the Zidurat temple—but nearby, little Rivek sat in the lap of a snowy haired matron with a time-wrinkled face. The old woman bounced the little girl on her knee. Rivek clapped her hands in time with the band. Dhani thinned her lips. *Happy, happy families.* Too bad she'd never had one.

As she reached the end of the covered walkway, Kyvil Yenidogat finally made an appearance, waddling out from inside the temple's sanctum and into the baking afternoon sun. She froze, pulling back into the arbor's filtered shade.

The priest stopped beneath the temple's ogee arches and rested his hands on his girth. He still wore his official robe and headdress, the twin tufts of his tall, black biretta arcing about as his head made a slow sweep of the courtyard. He stroked his salt and pepper beard, his gaze coming to rest on the buffet table and its dishes. For some reason known only to himself, he didn't descend.

Dhani narrowed her eyes, peering through papery pink bougainvillea blooms. *What was he waiting for?* Assistance to make his way down the steps? A formal invitation from Father Ulgan himself?

A sudden gust of air sent the fountain's mist her way, a brief wash of cool on her skin, gone in an instant. At that exact moment, an attendant appeared beside Yenidogat and the priest took his first teetering step.

Five steps led from the temple's promenade down to the courtyard's level. Yenidogat completed the first but didn't make the second.

No one expected a group of dark figures to burst out from the temple's bone-white walls, revolvers in hand— shiny new pieces, gun-metal grey, oiled and glistening.

After all, no one expected to die at a wedding.

Certainly not the priest, suddenly standing cheek-to-jowl with two black-clad, pistol-wielding men, nor his attendant as he was thrown head-first down the steps. More men streamed out from the temple's cloying darkness, others stormed in through the compound gates. The priest's mouth opened—a horrified, round-lipped gasp.

For a gut-squeezing moment, Dhani stared through the heat shimmer watching the scene unfold. The band stopped playing. A long way away, like an out-of-tune fiddle in the far distance, her mind added the words *nationalist cult* to *wedding* and came up with *massacre*.

Then, the shooting began.

Wedding guests scattered from under the marquee, cried out, fell. Chairs flew sideways, a platter piled with naan and a jug of wine wobbled and shattered on the ground. Beyond the dribbling fountain, Fikret grabbed Esmille and scanned the crowd for little Rivek. His shoulders sagged in anguish. The child was nowhere to be found.

A woman shrieked, "*Yevengik cu Bapa!*" and then, *RUN!*

After that, the hiss and sizzle of people hurling the killing Flame at their attackers turned the afternoon fiery red.

A bullet smashed into the wooden arbor a hand's breadth from Dhani's ear. Splinters and crimson bougainvillea stung her cheek, blood blistered on her skin. A bolt of scarlet flame scorched the air just metres away, close enough it tugged at her solar plexus. Her knuckles blazed white as she reefed a blade from its holster.

Now would have been a good time to develop the ability to hurl Deenjah or some other kind of magic. *Creator above!* She'd settle for tossing sparkly pink fairies if it gave her an advantage. She stole a glance at her olive-copper skin.

Nope. Not going to happen. Still a Jhiriyan Homelander. Still mute to the Flames. Blades and batons would have to do.

She crouched low and ran, retracing her steps beneath the bougainvillea-covered walkway. A bullet whizzed past. A man screamed and cried out to the Gods. Burned hair and charred skin choked her nose, making her gag. Sweat stung her bleeding cheek.

At the end of the walkway, she made a hard right, angling for the temple's western steps. A desperate flanking move, sure, but one that might—*might*—just save lives.

Especially if she could get her hands on a gun.

On the temple balcony, Papat Yenidogat had somehow fallen over. His ample form lay prostrate on the tiles, his legs peddling frantic circles in the air. Slowly—somewhere around the speed of waterlogged continental drift—he rolled onto his belly and began to elbow his bulk towards the temple's main chamber.

As people scattered, an old man and a small boy, both wedding guests, stumbled and fell, blocking her path to the temple steps. A ginger cat tumbled out of the child's arms and onto the dirt. It froze, arching its back and hissing.

A hooded man rushed in to cut off the pair's escape, wielding a pistol. Dhani swerved to a halt.

Time *could* have slowed if the Creator, Father Ulgan, Mother Yamir—heck, even a long-forgotten, one-eyed tortoise god with foot fungus—had even the slightest sense of compassion.

Time didn't slow. It zeroed in for a direct collision, delivered to the gut with a bull camel's kick.

The hooded man wheeled, aiming the pistol at the old man's head.

The small boy bounced to his feet, screaming for his *Bopa*—his great-grandfather—and *Selti*—a common name for Tizraki cats—to run. Tears glistened on the child's pale, dirt-streaked face. His bright blue tunic had a rent down the centre, exposing a grazed belly.

Dhani unclipped her steel baton, testing its weight in her hand. Adrenaline flooded her mouth with a sharp, metal tang.

Behind the mask, the gunman's eyes bulged like fearful saucers. He gripped the gun with both hands, its muzzle cutting a shaky arc from the old man to the boy to the spitting ginger cat and back. Dhani took aim. *Maybe the Gods cared after all.* Either that or the gunman feared their judgement in the afterlife.

"Please, don't!" the old man begged, trying to rise on trembling arms. His great-grandson cowered, now wailing for his mother.

Shots popped off on the other side of the temple courtyard. Women, men, children screamed. A blaze of red Flame rent the air. *Another.* The wedding marquee fell, ballooning inwards like some great, dying sea beast.

Dhani drew back her arm, muscles tense, focus narrowed on the gunman and his shakier-than-a-twig-in-an-earthquake aim. The gunman twitched the weapon from the old man to the boy—then settled instead on the hissing, spitting cat.

Her entire being cinched. *Oh no, no, no, you don't.*

No one—*no one*—killed a cat in front of Dhani Karim.

She flung the baton with every fibre of strength she possessed. It spun through the air as the pistol cracked, the cat—

The cat!

Hindquarters bunched, the cat sprung *upwards*, a prodigious leap, claws extended, fangs bared, and attached itself to the gunman's thigh at the exact moment the spinning metal baton crunched into the side of his head.

The man dropped as if his bones had leapt clean out of his body leaving behind a fleshy sack. The pistol fell from his grasp, clanged on the paved walkway, and spun, coming to rest next to a potted miniature lemon.

The child's jaw swung, though whether it was at the sudden appearance of a wiry blonde-haired, copper-skinned Jhiriyan in a sea of raven Tizraki heads or the baton strike to the gunman's skull, Dhani couldn't say. She moved at once, ready to offer a hand up to the old man.

A *click-click* stopped her before she'd taken a second step. Another masked man emerged from behind a trellis on her left, pistol clutched in a white-knuckled grip. Its cold dead eye glared directly at her head.

"Time to die, Metalskin bitch."

A blinding flash of red Flame came out of nowhere, striking the gunman in the midsection. He screamed, dropping the gun and falling to the ground, clutching at his smouldering ribs, rolling about batting at his clothes.

Metres away, the old man leaned against a pot plant, shoulders heaving. His left hand glowed red with Deenjah. A gap-toothed smile split his grizzled beard.

Dhani scooped up the dying man's pistol and sheathed the unused blade. Heart still drumming, she closed the gap and offered the old man her hand.

"Thank you, " she said, pulling him to his feet. His great-grandson scooped up the ginger cat, eyes still boggling at her.

"Father Ulgan's blessing upon you," the old man said.

She thrust her chin at the nearest open gate, the same way she'd come in. "Go. Get to cover, outside if you can."

Then she sprang forward heading for the temple steps, pausing only to collect her baton and the first man's pistol.

Two bounding strides took her to the top of the steps and temple's broad balcony and its trio of ogee arches. Kyvil Yenidogat had disappeared. His attendant, unconscious or dead, lay in a rumpled black heap near a splintered wedding chair. Two masked attackers had fallen nearby, holes burned in their guts by shakandhli hurled at close and bitter range.

A wider scan of the courtyard and the wedding guests —and Dhani's heart seized in her chest.

The bride and groom lay dead amongst a dozen others, riddled with bullet wounds, blood staining the ground black beneath them. A gunman writhed nearby, shrieking in agony, clothes smoking, face charred black, his chest partly burned away. Many guests had gone, surging out through the northern gates. The remaining gunmen had a handful flanked, pinned in a covered stone walkway, cutting off their escape.

Fikret and Esmille were amongst them, cowering behind a pillar with several others, just as a masked man turned on them. Dhani raised the pistol, trying for a clean shot just as Fikret hurled a ball of red Flame at the man. At the very same moment, a second gunman rounded the pillar from behind and emptied a revolver into Fikret's back. Esmille's anguished scream was cut off in a spray of gore, shot in the head by the same man at point blank range.

No. No! Inside, Dhani tore. A rending, meat-cleaver to

the ribs and gut. The same searing pain as when Zandolan had given his life for hers, a hundred thousand red-hot knives to her soul's innermost eternal, tender core, over and over again.

No, not Esmille and Fikret. NO!

Her throat closed down, stifling a voiceless, silent scream. She staggered forward ready to unleash every kind of hell she could think of—and even those that didn't have names but stopped. There was not a *single* thing she could do. Not a damned thing save turn back time, run to the top of the steps quicker, shoot sooner. Be born Yargan and burn them all to flaming scraps of soot and ash.

Dhani hauled herself away from the sight, found a fallen shooter dead on the balcony and stopped to rifle through his clothes, searching for ammunition, fighting back a wave of anger.

Strips of cloth, buttons flew, a leather belt snapped through the air. A silk sash rent in two. Her fingers closed on a clip of ammunition and stilled. Her breathing calmed, the red mist of fury faded in her vision.

A sudden round of shouts and renewed gunfire pulled her attention to the temple's main gates. Cordite and dust-fouled air filled her nose. She blinked her shock away.

Handcuffs and Thin Man had rushed into the compound, guns blazing. They weren't bad shots. Not at all. The man who'd slain Esmille and Fikret fell immediately, spinning about in a gore-splattered arc. Several other gunmen turned, registered the pair of Jhiriyans and returned fire. Thin Man took down two more but was forced to dive for cover as the attackers began to rally. Handcuffs called his younger partner back. The dice were stacked against them, and he beat a hasty retreat back through the gate.

Dhani shook her head, clearing the fog of rage. *Find Yenidogat.* Save the barn-sized lump of meat if she could.

She rose to her feet, scrambled across the temple's outer promenade and into its cool, dark prayer hall.

Inside, it was strangely still.

The prayer hall, with its vaulted ceiling painted with calligraphy and frescos, its mosaic-tiled floor, stood empty. In the back of the building, voices stirred.

Pistol ready, Dhani took off at a run, crossing out of the main hall and through an archway into a smaller chamber. Offices lined the far corner. A pair of large rear doors had been flung open to the blistering afternoon sun. Outside, several horse drawn carts—covered tuchek wagons made for transporting people—stood empty.

She spied Yenidogat in the far corner and froze. Attended by three black-clad figures, unmasked, revolvers in hands, the priest was quick-footing it towards the offices, rattling off instructions. The trio of men nodded. One offered an opinion. Yenidogat grunted a *yes*.

Understanding dawned, a cold and resounding slap to the face.

Yenidogat, the cow-sized sack of wobbling chins, was part of Yevengik cu Bapa. She clenched a fist about the gun. Had to suck in a breath to keep from shooting the piece of overweight, scrotum-licking pond-scum square in the back.

Fury blackened vision, she clenched her jaw so hard, her molars ached. The mission might have changed, but the objective had not. *Get Yenidogat. Haul his arse to Regional Command.*

Dhani crept closer, darting behind a pillar, ears keening, pulse thudding in her neck.

"…*Them*…" The priest puffed as he spoke to the nearest gunman. His black cassock shivered as he moved. His fur-trimmed biretta was neatly tucked under one arm. "I don't care…get them all…" Yenidogat drew a huffing breath. "…to the tucheks…as fast as you can. Those Homelanders have Ha'filu written all over them. Place will be crawling with Secret Service before we can scratch our…"

The pair slipped into a room on the far side of the outer sanctum. The priest's voice was cut off as the door snicked shut. Dhani cocked the revolver's hammer and followed, padding softly across the prayer hall's tiles.

She placed her head against the door and listened. *Nothing.* Most likely, the priest had gone into his chambers to wait out the arrival of Ha'filu back up—or even the Territorial Militia given the amount of gunfire—and would feign innocence.

Her fingers whitened around the doorknob, a cold brass lever. She drew a long, calming breath and narrowed her mind to a single objective: *No emotion. No weakness. No retreat. Detain Yenidogat.*

Outside, the gunfire had ceased, replaced by the wails of the injured and dying. Time was running short. They'd send word to get the surviving gunmen out, probably through the temple and into the waiting tucheks.

She tensed her muscles and turned the lever.

The door swung inwards and she squared off, training

the revolver on each quarter before relaxing. The antechamber stood empty. Ahead lay several small rooms where the temple clerics would dress, store their clothing and personal effects. Voices carried from the room on her right, Yenidogat telling someone to "...*leave now and get word to Golan*."

Her lips flattened. *Well, if that wasn't an interesting connection.* Golan Fiyuret was the name of the man who'd threatened Temek Huyurgal when he'd refused to sell the land part of Koyulerin was built on. Kyvil Yenidogat had also tried to buy the same land. This was all starting to make sense.

Dhani took a step towards the room, revolver held level. A shadow from inside the room fell across the floor. She froze and waited. There was at least one person with the priest. She wouldn't hesitate to kill them or anyone else who didn't surrender immediately.

She took three steps. Two men burst from the room to her left, revolvers raised. They shouted a warning and cut off her escape. A second pair of men emerged from Yenidogat's room, pistols raised.

"Drop the gun, Metalskin," a gruff voice said to her left.

"Drop it," another shouted.

The man nearest to her slugged her in the gut with the force of a charging bull. Pain bloomed across her middle and she doubled over, clutching at her gut but not lowering the revolver. The man smashed his gun down so hard on the hand gripping her revolver, stars burst across her vision.

Dhani dropped the weapon, sucking sucking in air to regain control.

She was still clenching her gut as Kyvil Yenidogat appeared in the doorway, hands on his girth, remarkably unharmed. A smile oozed across his lips, like a slug sliding slowly across a wet and fleshy leaf.

"Ah, Izn Sarif, or should I say, Izn *Karim*." The creeping smile widened. Dhani's blood turned to ice. "Why I am not surprised to see you?" Yenidogat nodded to the men on her left. "Get her out of here. You know what to do, then. Just make sure you're not seen."

CHAPTER TWENTY-TWO

They took her knives, her baton, her hair skewers, cuffed her hands behind her back and pulled a greasy bag that stank of linseed oil over her head. The fools missed the bracelet that doubled as a garrote, along with the tiny lock pick and rake hidden in her brassiere—hardly surprising, though. With the exception of Touchy-Feely the guard on the Ha'filu compound's gate, Tizraki men weren't known for groping women's breasts.

Apparently satisfied, one of them wrapped a hand about her upper arm and shoved her forward. They marched her through two groaning doors, along a tiled corridor then pushed her down a set of five steps. Six steps later they manhandled her torso first into a cart.

"Shut up or I'll put a bullet in your head. Understood?" the gruff voiced man hissed in her ear. His breath stank of garlic and cinnamon-scented tabac. When she didn't respond immediately, a pistol's cold, hard muzzle was pressed to her temple. *"Do you understand?"*

"I'm Jhiriyan," she said. "You'll need to write it out in triplicate."

For her efforts, the man thumped her in the thigh with a fist, a blow hard enough to bring tears to her eyes. "Metalskin bitch."

The cart lurched as one man and then another jumped in alongside her. With a grunt, someone hauled a stifling tarpaulin over her. Dhani eased onto her side, drawing her knees up and inhaling a series of calming breaths. Her gut still ached from the initial blow near the Papat's rooms and her ankle complained, some childish grumble about not being fully healed. The linseed-flavoured sack itched her cheeks, the tarpaulin stank of horse shit, the cart's wooden boards dug into her ribs and left hip. A wry smile thinned her lips. *Life really couldn't get any better, could it?*

A man's voice hooshed the horses—or mules—and the cart lurched into motion, bumping over the uneven ground. Dhani bit down on her cheek, thinking quickly. *Yenidogat was involved in this right up to his fifth wobbling chin. He'd even known her real name!* The implications were damning, far worse than her current predicament.

Yet they made sense, too.

Everything from the turban-wearing tails who'd known exactly where to find her and Parvan Gorshayik to the ransacking of her room in Faissa to the murder of Temek Huyurgal—it all added up to an equation a mathematician might have penned. There was a mole within the Ha'filu's ranks. And not just any run-of-the-mill, sell-Imperial-secrets-to-the-Yargans-type mole, either. This particular mole had parked its furry, blood-specked behind firmly in Yevengik cu Bapa's burrow.

Somehow—*somehow*—she had to get a signal up to the General.

Of course, that was *after* she'd escaped, *after* she eluded the seething mob of Ha'filu operatives sent to bring her in, and *after* she'd bribed the government signal office to turn a blind eye to her name. She puffed out a breath. *So many afters.* She was exhausted already.

The cart bumped over something hard, jarring her back. Dhani gritted her teeth, counting the turns the cart took as the stiff suspension bounced along the ground. The journey was interrupted once as they stopped at the city gates, where a jangling exchange of coin took place. Then, the driver hooshed his animals and they trundled on again. *North and west.* As far as she could tell, they hadn't entered Izurum through the main Koyulerin gate. They'd travelled north, joined a main road, and followed it into the city though one of the north-western gates.

A few turns later, the cart bumped onto a paved street and the animals' hooves clopped loudly on the flagstones. Zidurat temple was her first guess as the destination, but the cart took a right turn, then a left, and pulled up after a further short, clattering journey along another paved street. She was hauled to her feet and marched into a cool, echoing stone building where the scents of dung and mouldering hay mingled with the musk of horses and cattle. A door opened and she was shoved down a set of ten stairs and into the chill of a cellar.

Her captor wheeled her through another door, then a hand pushed her roughly to the floor. Another hand grabbed her cuffs. Behind her, a chain clinked as it was threaded between the cuffs' own chain links. A padlock snicked into place. The bag was unceremoniously ripped from her head.

Dhani blinked grit out of her eyes and squinted into the gloom. It took a moment to register the shapes of two burly men standing over her in a small root cellar lit by a single oil lamp. One wall of the cellar was lined with shelves packed with sacks of potatoes and onions. The side she'd been chained against was made of flaking mudbricks and broken only by a pair of sturdy wooden uprights supporting the roof. A glance behind revealed she'd been chained to a metal ring bolted to one of the uprights. She tested the cuffs binding her wrists. *No give there,* and she eyed the bolt securing the chain. Not impossible to break out of, but it would be time consuming.

"Holler all you like," Gruff said. The man beside him tossed the hessian bag that had covered her head onto a shelf. "No one will hear you down here."

"So you won't mind if I sing?" Dhani raised her chin. Gruff ground his jaw but didn't reply. The other man remained mute and pale-faced, his gaze darting to the door and back several times. A thin sheen of perspiration lit his brow. *The man was nervous.* No doubt the guilt of killing innocent wedding guests and the Ambyturan's promise of an afterlife as an ever-burning corpse drowning in a vat of cow poop in the Ninth Hell was looping in his head. She filed the man's discomfort away for later use. A nervous man was a careless man—a man who might hesitate and, if pushed, listen to reason. Or he might simply up and run away at the first sign of trouble.

"Get her some water. She's going to be here a while," Gruff said to Nervy. Nervy nodded and disappeared. Once he was gone, Gruff tapped his holstered pistol. His mouth pulled a sneer so tight, it was a wonder he didn't sprain a muscle.

"I don't know what they plan to do with you, but let's get this straight. Make any trouble and you'll get a bullet in the brain." He scowled, hawked in his throat, and spat at her, the hot glob landing on her cheek. Dhani didn't give him the satisfaction of flinching. "*Jhiriyan filth.*"

As soon as he'd turned his back, she wiped her cheek on her shoulder. It didn't get rid of the stink of cinnamon tabac and garlic, just made it less intense. The nervous man returned with a metal bucket filled with water and set it down beside her. He licked his lips, swallowed, and hurried away. Both men seated then themselves just outside the door on crates they hauled from elsewhere. Nervy produced a pack of taroch cards and began to shuffle them. Gruff disappeared for several minutes, returning with a jug of wine and two glasses. He placed them down on a low table beneath the light of the flickering lamp and settled back against the wall. Every so often, his flat, baleful stare crawled her way. Dhani smiled politely in return.

Twenty minutes passed.

Then another ten.

The sounds of the card game were suddenly punctuated by a series of muffled thuds and a man's long, pain-filled groan. Gruff scowled over his shoulder, at some point elsewhere in the cellar. Nervy licked his lips. Dhani turned her head, trying to pinpoint the sounds. A muffled Tizraki voice swore and there was another series of thuds. Gruff sneered and made a comment. Nervy laughed, licked his lips again, and shuffled the cards. His tongue made another circuit of his lips.

Dhani waited until both men were engrossed in the game, then pulled at the cuffs, wrists flexing behind her back. The metal was snug and cool against her skin with little room for manoeuvering. She hauled at the chain links joining the left and right cuffs—the weakest part of the bindings—but they didn't budge. Next, she slumped forward using her bodyweight to drag on the metal ring anchoring the cuffs to the upright wooden beam. The bolt wriggled a little, enough that she'd be able to eventually work it free. It would take hours—but unless she could loosen it, there was no way she could bring her hands up far enough to reach her brassiere with its precious lock pick and rake.

"Ai, the Blasted Tower and Death," Gruff said suddenly. He slapped the cards down hard. "What kind of a hand do you call that?"

"Uh. A bad one." Nervy's cheeks paled even more beneath his beard. His eyes bugged at the cards. "Let's shuffle them again."

Gruff and Nervy played three rounds of taroch, emptied two glasses of wine, and complained about someone named Moltekiin taking far too long. The muffled thumps and groans from elsewhere in the cellar rose and fell sporadically and eventually ceased. Dhani counted the shelves and the bags of potatoes on the shelves, surreptitiously hauled down on the bolt anchoring the ring to the beam and then counted the bags again.

An hour had passed when the clomp of heavy boots and the sound of something large being dragged along the dirt floor stopped the game of cards. Gruff swore and stood up. Nervy's eyes goggled. He stood slowly and backed away from whatever was outside the door.

"Took long enough," Gruff said to someone Dhani couldn't see. "You get what you needed?"

"Eventually. Bastard had a hide like a bull camel," a new voice said. Another voice gave up a low, deep groan and murmured something unintelligible. "Couldn't beat the information out of him, though. Had to use Poppy instead." The speaker paused. "Put him in there with the Jhiriyan. You got another set of cuffs?"

Gruff grunted and disappeared. Two men Dhani hadn't seen before hauled the unconscious form of a large Tizraki into the cellar and dumped him on the floor.

After several moments staring at the man's battered face in the pasty light, recognition parted her lips. *Parvan Gorshayik.* One eye was swollen shut, his nose and mouth were caked with dried blood, his cheeks purpled with bruises. His naked torso glistened with blood from fresh cuts, more bruises and welts that looked suspiciously like chain. She sucked in a breath as Gruff returned with a pair of handcuffs and manhandled them into place around the Tizraki captain's wrists. Gorshayik also—unsurprisingly— had an atlevan band clamped about his left wrist, a metal cuff which cut off a Deenjin's ability to raise the Flames.

"The Papat wants us out of here as quickly as possible," the man giving the orders said. "The city gates have been closed and we're to disperse until the Majapayit is dealt with." He moved into view so that Dhani could see the speaker: a well-built man dressed in a stained black tunic. His knuckles where bound with bloodstained rags.

"What about them?" Nervy asked, eyes darting from Dhani to Gorshayik's inert form.

"I'll put a bullet in their heads, if you want." Gruff's fingers twitched for his pistol. "It's her fault all of this happened."

"Don't be a fool, Jartik." The man with the bound knuckles scowled. "They're Ha'filu. In the coming days, they'll be valuable hostages to Golan. Especially *her* if they need leverage over the Imperium." He moved out of view again. Gruff—*Jartik*—didn't shift. "Lock the door and leave them here. The Papat or Golan can decide what to do with them. In the meantime, we need to figure out a way to get the information to Golan whilst he's still at work…"

The man's voice faded as the door boomed shut. A padlock and slide bolt clanked. The cellar went dark, save for a few slivers of light leaking in through the cracks around the doorframe and the door's wooden planks. Then, the light vanished completely, plunging the cellar into inky black. Dhani sighed. Either they'd taken the lamp with them or they'd extinguished it. Her guess was the latter.

She waited until the soft thud of boots and muffled voices receded. When they'd stopped altogether, she listened to Parvan Gorshayik's breathing, slow and deep and even. The metallic stink of blood and stale sweat mingled with the earthy scent of potatoes and dirt. Faintly, a sweeter smell tickled her nose, the cloying scent of Poppy.

"Captain?" she said. *Nothing.* Then, hesitantly, *"Parvan?"*

Nothing again. Which wasn't surprising. If they'd given

him Poppy, he might well be lost in some bliss-filled dream world for hours. At least it saved her having to make conversation.

She gritted her teeth, blinked into the darkness, and began to haul at the bolt again. No use wasting time. The sooner she worked the bolt out of the wood, the sooner she'd be free.

"*Who…?*" Gorshayik groaned suddenly. He gagged and coughed up something that sounded like it had bones and a personality. "*Ai!* Karim, is that you?"

"Yes, it's me. Nice of you to drop by, Captain. Sorry I can't offer you wine, olives, or a feather bed."

He swore under his breath and coughed again. His cuffs clinked. A scrape of cloth and a further groan suggested he'd pushed himself into a sitting position. "Where are you? Are you chained up?"

"I'm about three metres away and, yes, my hands are cuffed behind my back. The cuffs are chained to a metal ring that's bolted to a wooden support beam. We're in a root cellar beneath a stable or a barn somewhere in Faissa, I think." She twisted the bolt to the right. "Are you badly hurt?"

"I'm not dead."

Dhani flattened her lips. The beating hadn't improved his manners or his mood. Most likely, nothing would. "Well then, I have good news and bad news, Captain. The good news is that I have a lock pick and rake."

There was a deliberate silence. He sighed and said, "And the bad news?"

"The lock pick and rake are in my brassiere. You're going to have to retrieve them."

"Holy Mother Yamir!" His cuffs clinked again. "I swear the Gods put you on this world to test me, Karim."

She grinned. Baiting him was oddly satisfying. "The Gods won't be too impressed by you groping my breasts, Captain. Though, if you attend prayer three times a day, offer up the blood of a bull yak, the liver of a Miresh sea snake and a thimble of canary gizzards, *and* beg their forgiveness…"

"Do you ever not…?" He swore again and changed the subject, voice tight with pain. "Karim, I'm not skilled at picking locks, especially in the dark."

"Aren't we lucky I happened to pass *Introduction to Blind Lock-picking in a Potato Cellar* with honours during basic Ta'Hafiq training?"

"Karim." He did not sound impressed. "*Can* you pick the lock?"

"What do you think?"

"*Ta'Hafiq*. Of course, you bloody can," he grated and began to move—crawling, judging by the long scrapes of cloth on dirt—across the cellar. His short, sharp breaths and occasional grunt marked his unsteady progress. After a few moments, he bumped into the wall. "Where are you?"

"Here." She rattled the chain anchoring the cuffs to the metal ring. "A little further to your left."

His hands scrabbled along the wall. He was near enough she could hear every slow, rattling breath. "We've got a problem," he said. "I'm going to need your help to solve it."

Dhani raised an eyebrow. *Her help?* Given how their

last conversation had ended, his asking for her assistance to solve his *problem* was a little presumptuous.

"A problem?"

"Yevengik cu Bapa are behind all of this. They staged a shooting in Geraktin Souk last night."

"I know," she said. "The whole city knows."

"There's more." His hand touched her shoulder as he reached her. He pulled away just as quick. "They were planning something else today. A shooting at a wedding, apparently. They're hoping the Majapayit will close the city's gates and make a public address." He stopped speaking and coughed, shifting to a seated position. Whether it was to add drama or to allow him to catch his breath, Dhani couldn't say.

"And?" she said, when pause became too long.

"When the Majapayit gives his public address," he said slowly, "they're planning to assassinate him and install Kyvil Yenidogat in his place."

CHAPTER TWENTY-THREE

The lock barrel gave a soft metallic click and the cuff securing Parvan Gorshayik's right hand sprang open. Dhani began prodding at his left cuff, taking care not to drop the lock pick and rake.

"I don't understand how Kyvil Yenidogat can end up ruling the city." She slipped the rake into the barrel and gently pushed. The cuffs were secured by a simple mechanism, a lock with a pair of teeth that inserted into slots inside a central barrel. Once she'd got hold of the lock pick and rake—after a considerable amount of apologetic fumbling on Captain Gorshayik's behalf—it hadn't taken long to free herself and then begin to work on him. "How can a priest take control without a coup and a show of arms?"

"Tizraki law," Gorshayik said. "If a ruler dies and there's no successor, one of the temples assumes control until a new leader is put in place."

"I've lived in Tizrak Yirda for five years. I've never heard of that law before."

"It doesn't happen often. It's a failsafe to stop the bloodshed you see in other places when a ruler dies without an heir, there's competing heirs or when succession isn't hereditary, as in Izurum's case."

"I don't see what difference it will make." She pushed the pick against the second tooth in the barrel. "Once the Imperium and Tizraki government get word that Yevengik cu Bapa is behind the assassination, they'll send troops down from Talmakhan and simply retake the city. They won't care how many people they kill. There'll be a bloodbath."

"That's exactly what Yevengik cu Bapa want." Gorshayik's voice was unusually curt, even for him. The left cuff clicked open and dropped into his lap. "If the Imperium attacks Tizraki people, it plays right into their hands."

"I see your point." For an instant, she stood back in Odesstra Souk the previous year, the harsh summer sun beating down on the bullet-ridden bodies of a hundred people, clouds of black flies buzzing in her ears. *Tizraki don't kill Tizraki*, she'd said to Zandolan, *I just don't understand. Fanatics kill anyone if it suits their narrative*, he'd replied, *even their own gods if it suits them.* Then, like a thief, the memories of Fikret chiding his son for being shy at the breakfast table and Esmille—very much alive—mending the rent in her wedding clothes, stole in. *Both innocent. Both dead.* Grief struck at her chest, a crippling, unexpected body-blow, and she slammed it away before the unwanted emotion became too strong to bear.

"I don't suppose the Ta'Hafiq trained you to unlock an atlevan?" Gorshayik said, thankfully distracting.

"No chance. You'll need a Deenjin for that."

He sighed and massaged his wrists. "We need to get to Shalamir and convince her to put Duyjarit Lurgak into protective custody. Then, we need to have her arrest Yenidogat as quickly and quietly as possible before he has a chance to disappear or cause some kind of public outcry that also plays into the hands of Yevengik cu Bapa—as the arrest of a well-loved priest most certainly will."

Dhani slipped the lock pick and rake back into the hidden pocket in her brassiere. *Should she tell him about breaking into Bethsehal Shalamir's office and the Ha'filu wanting to arrest her?* She decided to wait. The matter of their partnership still hadn't been resolved.

"*We?*" She raised an eyebrow. "As far as I remember, there is no *we*, Captain Gorshayik. I think your words were, *I never want to see you again.* And then there's the matter of your resignation from the Service."

"Circumstances have changed," came the gruff reply.

"That's not an apology."

He shifted, some part of him scraping against the adobe wall. "Circumstances have changed."

"You're on your own then." She pushed herself up from the dirt and brushed off her clothes. "You don't need me to convince Shalamir of anything—not that she'd listen to me anyway. However, I will advise you to be careful. I believe Yevengik cu Bapa have someone inside in the Ha'filu. I've been using an alias but Yenidogat knew my name."

Parvan Gorshayik was silent for a moment before rising to his feet.

"Karim," he paused. This time, it was most certainly

for effect. "I'm injured, I'm still light-headed from Poppy. I'm half-dressed and have numerous cuts and wounds which need attention. I require your assistance."

"And that's still not an apology, Captain."

There was a shuffling of boots as if he'd taken a step, started to take a second and decided against it. In her mind, she imagined him flexing his jaw and raking his fingers through his hair.

"Very well." He ground out every syllable as though each cost him a litre of blood. "I acted in haste. My words were uncalled for. I rescind them."

She sucked in her cheeks, trying not to laugh. It was the kind of stilted, non-apology she'd expect from some pompous Shaliaat barrister who'd lost an argument with a magistrate, but it was likely all she would get. That Parvan Gorshayik was incapable of saying *I'm sorry* was a conversation for another day.

"Very well, your *not-apology* is accepted. What's your plan, Captain?"

"Get out, clean my wounds, find something to wear and then go see Shalamir." He bumped his way along the wall, towards the door. "We may have another problem, too. I can't be sure."

Dhani placed a hand on the wall, making an effort to not roll her eyes. *Of course, there was another problem.* There was always *another* problem. "And what would the *other* problem be?"

Gorshayik inhaled before he spoke. This time, she was certain he raked his fingers through his hair. "Temek Huyurgal came to me with an interesting story. He told me he owned most of the land Koyulerin is built on and that a man named Golan Fiyuret tried to buy it from him. When he refused, Fiyuret had him beaten up and threatened. He went to the city constables who investigated, but they couldn't find any trace of a Golan Fiyuret. Huyurgal then told me a boy came to see him several days ago. The boy claimed a man named Scythe was plotting to assassinate the Majapayit and begged Huyurgal to do something about it. Huyurgal wasn't sure if the boy was connected to Fiyuret or trying to warn him, so he came to me because he didn't know who to trust."

"The men who were here before also mentioned the name Golan," she said. "I'll wager they're one and the same. And a boy, you say?"

"A boy about twelve, a student at the Bisantrik. If the boy's telling the truth, then I suspect he knows a lot more than he told Huyurgal. Possibly enough to expose Yenidogat and the ringleaders of the Yevengik cu Bapa group here in Izurum."

Dhani froze. Every hair on her body prickled. Abil Beriktiin's note flashed through her mind followed by the gaping horror of Fikret and Esmille being gunned down in an ocean of blood. She drew a sharp breath. She knew *exactly* who the boy was, and if that was so, Abil Beriktiin not only held the key to solving the mystery of Scythe and clearing her name, but he was also in mortal danger… along with every other person inside the city.

"The other problem you mentioned," she asked. "What's that?"

Gorshayik reached the door and shook it. The padlock on the other side of the door clanked. "The men from Yevengik cu Bapa spent most of today trying to find out what I know about Scythe and the boy who'd spoken to Huyurgal." He hesitated. Dhani's stomach churned one way and then the other. She knew exactly what he was going to say. "I may have told them everything under the influence of Poppy."

She stared at a point in the darkness, heart pounding as if she'd sprinted uphill. The parting words of the man with bandaged knuckles replayed in her mind. *I need to figure out a way to get the information to Golan whilst he's still at work...* She groped her way along the wall, thinking furiously.

Was it possible Golan Fiyuret, the man behind the conspiracy, was somewhere he couldn't be immediately reached? And, even more likely: was Golan Fiyuret the mole inside the Ha'filu? If that were true, and with the city in lock down, he'd be on double time, possibly pulling an all-night shift for Shalamir. There'd be a delay in him issuing commands—a delay they could exploit and turn to their advantage.

Perhaps she *could* find Abil—if he were still alive— before anyone else did.

"I think I know who the boy is," she said, blunt and dry, "and where to find to him."

—

A half hour later, they darted out a set of broad wooden doors and into the slanted golden shadows of late afternoon. Beyond the stable lay a flagstone-paved street flanked by a blacksmith's, two wainwrights and two leatherworkers' shops. Several other stables identical to the one they'd just emerged from stood further down the street, serving the city's many public cabs and carts, offering temporary lodging to animals whilst their carts, harnesses or hooves were being seen to.

"Where's the nearest gate?" Gorshayik asked as they passed the blacksmith's shop, where the smell of metal and charcoal and leather spilled out through the open doors into the open air.

"That way." Dhani pointed to the west. "The same way they brought me in."

He grunted, pulling at the dirt and grease-stained tunic stretched tight across his chest. After kicking the cellar door down, they'd lit the lamp and searched the stable's various storerooms. With the exception of a rumpled black tunic and a rat-eaten winter coat, hessian sacks had been the only fine couture on offer. After she'd torn trips of lining from the coat to bind his wounds, Gorshayik had—not surprisingly—chosen the tunic over the hessian sacks.

"About our plan," she said after they'd passed the blacksmith's shop. "Please explain to me just how you intend to walk straight into Bethsehal Shalamir's office and demand she take the Majapayit into protective custody?"

"I'll manage," came the terse reply.

"More likely you'll be *managed*...by a security detail and thrown into solitary confinement pending execution."

The scar on Gorshayik's cheek twitched. "You worry about finding the boy, Karim. *I'll* worry about Bethsehal Shalamir."

"That doesn't exactly fill me with confidence, Captain."

"*Find the boy*, Karim," he repeated like a door slamming shut.

Dhani scratched an itch on her thigh. The plan they'd come up with sounded good on paper—*if* you ignored annoying little facts like them *probably* being wanted for Temek Huyurgal's murder, Parvan Gorshayik's resignation from the Service and that she'd broken into Shalamir's office. Yet somehow Captain *I-have-a-condition* Gorshayik seemed convinced he could just walk into Bethsehal Shalamir's office and issue orders. Either she was missing something completely or Parvan Gorshayik's risk-meter was not only broken, it had been hacked at, stomped on, and ground to dust.

A few minutes—and a consultation of the linseed-scented mental map of her cart journey—was all it took to walk from the stable, cross one of the area's main streets and arrive near one of the city's nine major gates. The sun had dropped below the city wall by the time they arrived, the stinging heat beginning to vanish with it. The few people they passed along the way took one look at Parvan Gorshayik's battered face, bear-sized frame, and too-small, tattered clothing, and not surprisingly, kept their distance.

When they turned into the broad street flanking the wall and saw the gate, Dhani slowed to a stop.

Even at a distance of fifty metres, the sight of four men dressed in the camel brown of the Tizraki Territorial Militia standing guard at the gate was pause enough to reconsider the plan. She watched a woman approach one of the rifle-carrying guards, pleading to be let through because her children were outside. The guard captain shook his head, snapped that no one was to leave or enter the city, then sent the distraught woman away.

"Unfortunate," Gorshayik said as the woman trudged past, head down, wiping tears away with a dusty sleeve. He squinted with his one good eye at the gate and the broad wooden beam securing it, before looking up at the city's ten-metre-high wall. Another four guards sat on the parapets, lounging about in various states of *conscripted-to-be-here* boredom. "Can you climb the wall?"

"Well…" Dhani scanned the wall.

Above the gatehouse, the parapets stretched out for some way, a wooden promenade where marksmen could poke their rifles through gun slits in the wall, presumably to kill dark-skinned Loy hoards (*the Loy hadn't attacked Izurum for over a century*), invading Yargans (*who'd simply fend off the shots with Deenjah and blow their own holes in the wall*) or more likely, those poor, desperate souls whose only crime was their residence in Koyulerin. Beside the gatehouse were several stone fortifications strong enough to support small cannons. These stood empty save for a handful of amorous crested pigeons.

"Getting up from this side is easy," she said. "I just wait until it's dark and scale the fortifications near the gatehouse. Getting down the other side, however, won't be so easy. The walls are sheer and it's a long drop to the ground. I'll need to find a long rope and a secure point to hitch it to. That's going to take time." She glanced up at Parvan Gorshayik. For once, she didn't stare at the scar marring his cheek. "Time we don't really have."

"What about a drain or a sewer?"

"Not impossible." She scraped a fingernail

thoughtfully along her chin. "But I'll need to find the right drain. I didn't scope the sewers and drains when I worked here previously, so it could take some time."

Gorshayik ran a hand through his hair. His gaze strayed to a couple of children playing a game of knucklebones on the step of a nearby building. His brows knitted thoughtfully. "Do you have any money?"

Dhani tilted her chin. Every tunic she owned possessed a false hem where a small amount of emergency money could be stowed. It was standard practice for Ta'Hafiq. "A couple of five dironi notes in the hem of my tunic. Why?"

"Give them to me. I've got an idea."

She stared at his outstretched hand. "That would be, *give them to me, please.* Or even better, *Karim, would you please lend me ten dironi?*"

"Karim." His fingers twitched. "The money. I don't have time for your lip."

"You'll pay me back." She slipped the notes from her hem and handed them over. "*With* interest."

He murmured, "*Jhiriyan thieves,*" in Tizraki-accented Jhiriyan, then strode over to the children without looking back. The children froze and stared up at bruised, dirt and blood stained Gorshayik, gap-mouthed expressions hovering somewhere between *is this deranged man going to kill me?* and *run away!*

Gorshayik spoke to them for several minutes, singling out to the older of the pair, a boy, whose face zig-zagged from goggling terror to surprise at the sight of not one but *two* five dironi notes, then back to wide-eyed apprehension. The child's tongue made a circuit of his lips. After a pause, he nodded as earnestly as only a child could, frowning whilst he repeated something Parvan Gorshayik had said. Gorshayik made him repeat it twice more. The boy gave a final nod of his dark head before leaping off the step and running off down the street.

"Well?" Dhani said when he returned. "Are you going to tell me what that was about?"

"I've sent the boy to bring backup." Gorshayik turned his one good eye to the Militia guards. "The kind of backup *they* won't argue with."

The stone-wall tightening of his lips suggested he'd say no more on the matter. Dhani shrugged. He'd probably sent the boy to Regional Command, and if not there, then to call on other Ha'filu operatives he trusted, if indeed Parvan Gorshayik trusted anyone at all.

"You said you had an idea to get me through the gate quickly?" she said, changing the subject.

"I do." He crouched down, hissing in pain through his teeth as he fumbled at the heel of his left boot. When he straightened again, he held a folding blade small enough to fit into a carved-out niche in a boot heel—especially if you had feet the size of canoes. A click of a trigger and the blade sprung open, the metal carrying a soft red glow.

Dhani raised both eyebrows. "You had the blade charged by a Yargan?"

"The healer who treated my concussion."

She blew out a low whistle. "How much did *that* set you back? Ten dironi? Fifty?"

"Not your concern, Karim." His mouth thinned to a cold, hard *answer-sealed-behind-thirty-metres-of-rock* line. Clearly, she'd need to kill him—or worse—if she wanted an explanation. With time ticking and the fate of

244

thousands of lives at stake, the answer could stay entombed in Gorshayik's head for all eternity as far as she was concerned.

"So, your plan to get through the gate, Captain?" She wiped a smear of dirt from her cheek. "Tell me you have one and you're not just making this up as we go along."

His fingertips grazed the fleshy scar on his neck. His one good eye fixed on the gate and didn't shift.

"When the boy returns, I'm going to take you hostage and force them to open the gates."

CHAPTER TWENTY-FOUR

The boy came padding back about ten minutes later, made eye contact with Parvan Gorshayik, and nodded. With that, the big Tizraki pushed off the wall he'd been leaning against. Dhani followed, rising from the dusty, butt-numbing stoop she'd been sitting on.

"Before we start, Captain," she said, "two things."

Gorshayik turned about, nostrils flaring. Her own eyes —an irritating jewel green courtesy of her father—were reflected in his unnerving obsidian stare. "What?"

"I collected your pocket watch and your...ahh." She shifted under the soul-crushing scrutiny, studying the gritty flagstones under her boots, the cracks between them, a trail of single-minded, scurrying ants—anything that wasn't Parvan Gorshayik's irritated face. "And your wedding photograph from your room. They're safe with my things in the house I'm staying at in Koyulerin."

A long way away, a man coughed and a door slammed. A soft breeze stirred stray wisps of hair on her neck.

Gorshayik stood silent for several moments, swallowing twice before finally offering a hoarse and low, "*Thank you.*"

"And the other thing," she said. His gaze shifted and she eased out a breath she'd not been aware of holding. *Creator above! If Parvan Gorshayik had an entry in a dictionary, the definition would read, fifty kinds of lead-weighted, looming-shadow intense.* "What do we do if they won't open the gate? You do realise the guards will probably shoot you first chance they get?"

His expression closed, like a door slamming shut. "Are you religious?"

"Only when it comes to training and cats."

Without warning, Gorshayik wrapped one branch-sized arm about her neck and pressed the glowing blade to her throat. His other arm curled about her chest and cinched in against her still-tender ribs. Her spine popped, some piece of soft tissue sliding harmlessly over bone. She wrinkled her nose. Up close, his tunic smelled even worse than it looked—one part stale manure, two parts mouldy hay and three parts horse piss.

"Then start praying to the Gods that this works, Karim," he whispered, tightening his arm about her chest. "Otherwise, we're both dead."

"So there's no Plan 2 or Plan 3?"

"You're Ta'Hafiq." He grunted and began to shove her forward. "Think of something."

"And your backup?" she said, stalling. The street about them was empty save for the guards, the boy and his sister —and them.

"They'll be here."

She sniffed. "You'd better be right about that or I'll kill you myself."

"*Hush.*" He pushed her a little harder, steering her into the middle of the street. On cue, the guards' heads swivelled their way. One stood, a hand resting purposely on his rifle's stock. His face took on an *Oh-for-fuck's-sake, what now?* scowl.

"Look scared," Gorshayik hissed through gritted teeth. "Struggle."

Dhani complied, taking a deep breath, thrashing about under his arm and screaming, "*Let me go!*"

"Open the gate or I'll kill her," the big Tizraki shouted, loud and forceful enough it rattled her ribs. "You've got ten seconds."

"You can't pass," the guard captain shot back. The others jumped to attention, slinging their rifles from their shoulders and into their hands. The bored group of guards on the parapets turned about, suddenly interested.

"Majapayit's orders," the captain barked again. "No one is to enter or leave."

"I live in Koyulerin," Gorshayik shouted again. He used his chest to shunt her forward so hard she needed two scrambling steps just to stay afoot. "Let me pass through the gate and I'll release her unharmed." In her ear, he hissed, "*Struggle, Karim, or by the Gods I* will *cut you.*"

Dhani pushed back, launching herself into his chest, boot heels digging into a gap in the flagstones. She gave a guttural curse in Jhiriyan, then stomped a heel down his boot, making him swear. He rammed his hip into her back and marched her on again. Once more, she skated on gritty, manure-stained cobbles, found purchase, and strained her thigh muscles, forcing the big Tizraki to a stop. He immediately bumped her forward. The effect was a staggering, shuffling back-and-forth dance—albeit one drawing ever nearer to the rifle-clutching, nervy guards and the gate.

"He's crazy," she gasped after ramming a shoulder into Gorshayik's chest a fourth time. Her voice sounded ridiculous: high-pitched and breathy. "He's going to kill me!"

"Put the knife down and release her!" the guard captain ordered. He'd slung the rifle from his shoulder and now held it in both hands. His companions had done the same and stood to attention, four pairs of uniformly dark eyes affixed to Parvan Gorshayik. "Or I'll have to give the order to surround and shoot you."

"My wife and children are out there," he pleaded. Dhani had to admit she was impressed. Gorshayik sounded like he believed every word that left his mouth. "Let me through the gate and I'll release her."

The captain gave a signal and the guards raised their rifles. Dhani allowed herself to be shunted on again. By now, the guards could see Parvan Gorshayik's battered face and his dishevelled, ill-fitting clothes. Creator only knew what they'd make of his appearance. Tizraki tended to be a little superficial when it came to looks, though not as appearance-conscious as Jhiriyans. His present state of disarray, however, might serve only to earn him a bullet in the head—and one for her, as collateral damage.

"*Resist*," he said in her ear. His voice said he was enjoying this a little *too* much. She stomped down on his foot again. This time, he gave up an audible grunt.

"Keep still," he spat loud enough for the guards to hear, "or by the Gods, I'll cut you!"

"Let me go!" she shrilled. *"Please!"*

They were now close enough she could pick out the shimmer of perspiration on the guard captain's brow, the shifting of his fingers on the stock of his weapon, the way his tongue worried at a single point on his bearded top lip. That he was only a few years older than herself—thirty at the most—and his right eye had a nervous tick.

Gorshayik lurched to a decisive stop. Momentarily, his gaze flickered along the street, searching for the promised backup. Seconds ticked past. Dhani's heart thudded against her ribs. Her mouth tasted like blood and dust. The guards on the parapets raised their rifles and fidgeted, every moment as nervous as the young captain. *Tizraki don't like killing,* she reminded herself. *Ai, Creator above, hopefully the guards on the parapets also remembered that.*

"Open the gate," Gorshayik demanded. Dhani swallowed, shivering as the glowing blade dug harder into her flesh. "All I want to do is leave."

One of the guards leaned in and whispered to his commander. The captain listened for several seconds to whatever his subordinate was saying, stroked his beard, then nodded. He brushed at the perspiration on his brow. His eye continued to twitch. Whatever he was about to do, he was far from confident with the decision.

"Very well, we'll open the gate and let you through, but the woman must not be harmed." The young captain turned to those on the promenade and barked an order. "Watch above! Keep the gate clear on the Koyulerin side. We're letting this man through."

"They're going to shoot you in the back or the leg," Dhani hissed in Jhiriyan, not moving her lips.

"I know," Gorshayik replied. *"Play along. Backup is here."* He shoved her forward again so hard she tripped. The guards' fingers hovered over their rifles' triggers, ready to shoot.

"Open the gate," the guard captain barked. Two guards complied, setting their guns aside and hurrying to the sturdy wooden beam used to barricade to the metal gates. In seconds, they'd hauled the beam back and the gates began to swing outwards.

Dhani tilted her chin just enough to steal a glance up at the guards on the parapet. They'd all dropped to one knee, rifle butts cradled in their shoulders, barrels slid into the gun slits, ready to open fire on anyone on the Koyulerin side of the gates. *And Gorshayik's backup?* She kinked her neck, twisting about as far as she dared. Further down the street she saw them: five dark figures striding towards the gates.

Something in the way the quintet moved forced her to twist about again and do a hasty double-take.

You have to be kidding, she thought. *Creator's bright, shiny balls stacked on a silver plate, you* have *to be kidding me!*

She blinked twice just to be certain. A third time for no reason other than to satisfy her own complete and utter, jaw-smacking disbelief. The group were too tall and athletic to be Tizraki, too short and well built to be Jhiriyan. A fourth glance mapped their predatory gait and the sudden flare of the killing Flame about their left hands. *Yargans.* Curly-haired, boulder-shouldered, over-educated, Deenjah-sucking *Yargans.*

She blew out a breath. Creator only knew how, but Parvan Gorshayik had managed to summon the one kind of backup anyone with even a leaking half-thimble of commonsense would never challenge. It wouldn't matter even if the Camelskins *did* open fire, a Yargan could wield enough Flame to turn bullets to slag. Hell, a lone Yargan could hurl enough Deenjah to blow a hole in the city's wall the size of a warehouse. It was a brilliant distraction. One worthy of a Ta'Hafiq.

The gates groaned open, parting just enough for a man to pass through. The guard captain waved them on. He hadn't noticed the approaching Yargans yet. If he had, he'd have turned white or purple or maybe wet himself. Dhani's lips kinked upwards. *Perhaps all three.*

"Go!" the guard captain snapped at Gorshayik. "And you release her as soon as you're through the gate, understand?"

Parvan Gorshayik stood his ground, staring the young captain down. Dhani guessed he was stalling, giving his backup time to get close enough to be counted as a threat. "How do I know you're not going to shoot me in the back?"

"Don't argue, man! Get out or I'll shut the bloody gates." The captain flicked his hand. He shifted his weight between his boots. "Go!"

They approached the gates slowly. Gorshayik waited until they'd passed the captain, then whirled Dhani around, using her as a shield. This time, there was no need to feign surprise. She gasped as the gatehouse flew past in a blur, her boots skidding on the flagstones before she came to a complete about-face.

"*Be ready to take the knife,*" Gorshayik whispered. She waited for the world to stop spinning and gave a tiny nod.

He continued to edge back at crippled-tortoise pace. Five seconds passed. *Five more.* His breathing was tight; a series of quick, shallow puffs against her skin. They drew level with the gates. Dhani met the young captain's eyes, her own gaze wide, feigning terror. Dark stains ringed the captain's armpits, his larynx bobbed as he swallowed. He rubbed at his eye, annoyed by its twitch.

Right then, a woman's voice rang unexpectedly out, "*We will pass through the gate!*" A firm alto, she spoke with a confident *don't-fuck-with-me-I'm-Yargan* sing-song accent.

One of the guards whispered, *Yargans! Holy Mother's tits!* The captain's head snapped about, his skin blanching from warm light brown to cold ash grey. For the time being, he didn't wet himself.

"Gods above! Hold your fire!" he shrieked. "*Do not shoot! Do NOT shoot!*"

Dhani seized on the distraction and decided to take her chance. She elbowed Parvan Gorshayik in the ribs. "*Now. Whilst they're shitting their pants.*"

At once, the blade's pressure disappeared from her throat, the arm cinching her chest vanished. Gorshayik slipped the glowing blade into her right hand as he released her. Despite the charge of Deenjah, the knife was surprisingly cool against her skin.

"*Good luck,*" he whispered. Then, softly, "Take care, Karim."

She hesitated a fleeting moment, looking up into his deep, dark eyes—was that a flicker of *concern,* there and gone in an instant? She couldn't be sure. "See you soon, Captain."

With that, she turned and sprinted through the gates and into the gloom beyond the gate, praying to every god, demon, and spirit she could name that the guards on the parapets didn't shoot her in the back.

CHAPTER TWENTY-FIVE

A half hour later, Dhani slid into cover behind a rusting corrugated iron fence, throat dry and raw from inhaling a factory's worth of smoke, her back and underarms soaked with sweat. Ash and burning embers choked the air, some settling on the raffia shanties lining the narrow street and smouldering. Gunfire cracked close by, followed by a man's scream. She brushed a cinder from her cheek and stifled a curse.

It had taken exactly one fleeting, half-moment of dodging two uniformed groups of men and women charging *at* each other—rifles drawn—to realise the fool Majapayit had sent the Camelskins *and* the city constables out into the shantytown. Clearly, they'd been ordered to hunt down members of Yevengik cu Bapa. And clearly, the best way to do that—when they weren't attempting to kill each other—was to *burn Koyulerin! Burn it all to the ground!*

A glance up at a patch of dreary cobalt sky peeking through a blanket of billowing black smoke, and she hissed through her teeth. Her plan had been simple enough: go to Esmille and Fikret's shanty and see if Abil or even little Rivek had returned. Right now, however, with half of Koyulerin burning and the world's most shambolic gunfight clacking about like a broken wind-up toy, the shanty might as well have been on the far side of Soolaith. *Or the dark side of the moon.*

The *pop-pop-pops* of pistol fire resumed, the reports now loud enough they could only be one or two streets away. She flattened her back to the iron fence and considered a list of dwindling options: backtracking and blowing through time she didn't have, detours along shit-and-piss scented alleys, chugging down entire weather systems of dense, black smoke. *A holiday at Bayti, a Shaliaat resort town on the shiny white sands and azure waters of the Osmancik Sea.*

Backtracking it was. She huffed out a sigh. Both the holiday on the Osmancik and her plan to gatecrash somebody else's stuttering gunfight would have to wait.

She rose from her crouched position at exactly the same time several burly male figures clomped past on the other side of the street.

The trio couldn't have been more Tizraki if they'd tried: unimaginative dark blue, thigh-length tunics, thick raven hair, full beards and scuffed brown boots. Only the hunched set of their shoulders and the shiny new pistols clutched in their white-knuckled fists set them apart. Her eyes lingered on the weapons—and for an instant she was back in the temple, watching helplessly as Fikret and Esmille's lives were cut short.

The dull thump of grief knocked at her chest. Hate, an ice-cold chill, flooded every vein and then her capillaries. *These men were Yevengik cu Bapa.*

Her fingers twitched for blades that weren't there. She wrestled the urge to simply *kill* the trio, to cut their lives short by the most violent and ruthless means possible. *Slit them from cock to collarbone, cut out their livers and ram them down their throats.* Dhani closed her eyes and sucked in several calming breaths.

Find Abil. Save the lives of thousands of people. Nothing else that mattered—not even rejoining the Ta'Hafiq.

A series of popping gunshots rang out, near enough that the muzzle flashes made dull starbursts through her eyelids. Dhani opened her eyes and peered down the street.

The trio of predictably dressed, pistol-clutching men had slunk into cover, whispering and gesturing, unsure of how to proceed. Three more shots cracked in quick succession, their flare placing the shooters in a ditch near a row of iron shanties. An answering volley of five shots marked a second group of shooters in a lane directly south, laying fire on the group in the ditch. Smoke and fading light made it impossible to get a clear look at anyone save the trio who'd passed her by.

Another round of gunfire stung her ears. For a raw-nerved instant, a man's blond head poked up over the lip of the ditch, the revolver in his hand tapping out two more shots at the group in the lane. Dhani cursed and pulled back into cover, clenching a fist.

Ai Creator! Bloody Homelanders. Ha'filu no doubt. No one else would be carrying long-muzzled revolvers out here. No other Jhiriyan would be *stupid* enough to be out here, either.

Should she intervene?

She inhaled and immediately stifled a smoky, tickling dry cough. Life would be much simpler if she hadn't seen that flash of golden blond. Life would be much simpler if she simply turned and walked away. After all, she had only Parvan Gorshayik's Yargan-charged knife and her bracelet garrote as weapons and there were at least five armed assailants lurking in the street ahead. Besides, it wasn't as if saving a pair of Ha'filu operatives would do her any favours. Most likely, they'd cuff her and get her killed stumbling over their own bootlaces on their way back into the city.

The three Tizraki men she'd been watching retraced their steps, scrambling back along the street away from the gunfight. They took shelter in the doorway of a house just metres from where she crouched behind the fence. There, they began to whisper, loud enough she could hear every word.

"I'll cover you," one man said. He spoke quickly, panting hard. "You go in."

"How many rounds do you have left?" another man asked. The quaver in his voice said he'd rather be elsewhere. Dhani smiled to herself. A holiday in Bayti or simply getting the hell out of Koyulerin came to mind as options. "I've only got two."

"I've got three."

"Better finish this quickly before more Metalskins show up." A pause. "Cover us?"

"Aye," a third man said. He stuttered slightly, "B...be careful."

The trio separated, two men edging forward, the third remaining in the doorway, so close his revolver glinted in the failing light. He fidgeted, snuffling and scratching at his nose then switching his pistol from right hand to left.

Dhani considered the weapon thoughtfully. Right then, some bone-thin sliver of duty lurking in her mind's dustiest back corner chose that moment to jump up and shout *let's do this!* Her shoulders sagged. Call it dumb collegiality, the advantage offered by swiping a pistol or some gnat-sized chance of convincing the operatives in the ditch to help her search for Abil Berektiin, she needed to act.

She slipped the bracelet from her hand and unwound the wire garrote. The narrow steel thread blended into the gloom, dull grey, slender and strong. Eyes narrowed, she slid from her hiding place.

Three silent strides brought her to the man holding the gun. His compatriots were a dozen metres away, focussed on staying unseen. She tensed her core and tested the wire's tension. A knife would have been better—an unusually strong man might be able to fight his way free of the garrote until secured in place—but it did have the effect of incapacitating victims quickly: first through panic and then through loss of consciousness. The wire also had the advantage of being strong enough to slice flesh and sever blood vessels.

Ten seconds later she pounced. She looped the wire about the man's neck, hauling him out of the doorway and back into the front yard of the shanty. She wrenched hard on the bracelet's cool metal halves, pulling the wire until her arms ached. The man choked, dropping the gun and thrashing for thirty long seconds. The moment he lost consciousness, she eased him to the ground and snatched up his weapon. A search of his clothing turned up four more bullets but nothing else.

She hovered over him for another moment, watching. The wire had sliced through his trachea and bit into the carotid artery on the right side of his neck. A dark pool of blood spread beneath him. If he regained consciousness at all, it wouldn't be for long. A swift check of the pistol showed four rounds in the cylinders. She slipped a fifth in and cocked the hammer.

Without a backward glance, she slid into the street, pistol ready, intent on the fallen man's companions.

It didn't take long to reach them.

As she did, one turned about, a cursory check behind— or perhaps she'd been careless in her approach. *No matter.* She pulled the trigger, putting a bullet in the middle of his forehead at point-blank range. He went sprawling onto the dirt in a rain of red mist and pink gore. His companion swore and spun, already raising his pistol. For his efforts, she put a second round in the side of his head. The man wheeled away, thumping into a corrugated iron wall and smacking to the ground beside his friend.

Crack! Crack! Crack!

Several rounds of gun fire ensued, the people in the lane opening fire on the Homelanders in the ditch. The Jhiriyans returned fire, a flash of golden hair over the hollow's dirt lip, then retreated. Dhani made note of who'd fired. One assailant in the lane and the Homelander nearest her would be out of rounds. The other shooters would have no more than two rounds each without reloading.

She came to a stop and studied the lane where the

members—*Two? Three?*—of Yevengik cu Bapa were hiding. Her grip tightened on the pistol. She inhaled in a lungful of smoky air and blinked ash from her eyes. What she planned to do *might* get her shot, but her guess was a handful of Tizraki fanatics had likely spent more time chugging wine and telling tales in an inn than out on the shooting range. *Or so she hoped.*

Revolver ready, she broke from the lane at a dead sprint.

A cry went up and a bullet whizzed past, missing her by some distance. The telltale flash gave away the shooter's position. She returned fire as she ran, putting three quick rounds into the shadows where the man had been. A muffled scream said she'd hit someone, and the shooting immediately stopped. A man's cries and curses suggested that, for the moment, the surviving Tizraki were tending to their wounded compatriot. She leapt into the ditch and skidded to a stop.

When she realised just who was pinned down in the ditch, she nearly barked out a laugh. The Thin Man and Handcuffs blinked back at her, their not-so-immaculate long shirts and grey suit jackets now dirt smeared and soot-stained. The gap-jawed expressions on their faces said they were as surprised to see her as she was them.

"Karim!" The Thin Man brandished his revolver. Up close and in the eerie red, he looked only just old enough to have passed basic training. "I ought to cuff you and slug a fist to your gut for the trouble you—"

"Hanrif, shut it," Handcuffs, the older of the pair, said. A cut and a purple bruise marked the place she'd hit him in the chin. His accent said central Jhiriyan, most likely Da'id, the Empire's capital. "She just saved our lives."

Dhani opened the revolver's cylinder and fed her last three rounds into the receivers. She gave a shrug. "Sorry about this afternoon, gentlemen. I was running late for a wedding."

"You were at *that* wedding?" Handcuffs' expression sobered. "Terrible business."

"Unfortunately." She snapped the revolver's cylinder back into place.

"And you've been hiding out here ever since?"

"Working on my holiday plans like I expect you gentlemen were." Hanrif scowled at the comment whist Handcuffs' mouth thinned. Obviously, they weren't in the mood for humour. "What I can tell you is that Kyvil Yenidogat is up to his neck in this. I had the pleasure of discovering this when I went to see him at the wedding."

"The Papat?" Handcuffs' posture stiffened. He studied the pistol in Dhani's hand before doing the same to her face. "You're sure? We were told he'd been taken out a back door and rushed to safety."

"I'm not only sure of it, I've got witnesses to prove it."

"Bullshit." Hanrif—the Thin Man—curled his lip. "Why should we believe a word you say? We were told to arrest you and bring you in."

Dhani swung the revolver around. Hanrif raised his. Too bad he was out of rounds—and hadn't bothered to reload. "Ask yourself this, Hanrif: did I need to save your arse? You were outgunned and outnumbered two-to-one. It would have been easy for me to just walk away and let them kill you, but I didn't. Think about that." She glanced up at the fading streaks of orange in sky. Low on the horizon, the sun hung like an angry, bloodshot eye. Time was running short. She needed to find Abil Beriktiin—if he still lived—before anyone else did. Whether she did that alone or had help depended on what happened next.

She flashed a smile and began to rise. "Been nice chatting, gentlemen, but I've got to run. Someone far more important than either of you needs saving."

"Wait, Karim. One last question." Handcuffs held up a palm. He studied her face, cool blue eyes sharp as razors. "We were told you murdered your partner and the cordwain. I couldn't buy into it. What really happened?"

At least that *confirmed what she'd suspected.* Shalamir thought she'd killed Huyurgal and Parvan Gorshayik. Not that it was surprising. Presented with the same evidence, she would have concluded the same.

"Captain Gorshayik was very much alive when I left him at the southwest gate less than an hour ago. He'll corroborate my story about Kyvil Yenidogat's connection to the nationalists. As for Temek Huyurgal, all I know is that someone—most likely Yevengik cu Bapa—killed him for reasons I suspect have something to do with real estate. His death at the safe house was designed to make either Gorshayik or myself look guilty." She rose to a crouch. "Now, excuse me. I have to go."

Handcuffs continued to stare at her, brows furrowed. Dhani could almost hear the man's mind ticking over. Ten dironi down, he'd cut her a deal. And if he didn't, she'd be out of the ditch and on her way down the street.

"Does the name *Scythe* mean anything to you?" Handcuffs asked.

The question hung in the air between them. Handcuffs' gaze didn't waiver. Dhani returned the attention. *Was he the 'senior operative' Shalamir had running the case?* Even better, could he be Captain Khasain, the man she'd been ordered to report to in Parvan Gorshayik's place? Gut instinct said he was.

"Captain Gorshayik and I were supposed to find Scythe and bring him in for questioning, but I suspect you know that." A noise in the lane drew her attention momentarily, a scraping sound like an injured man being dragged out of harm's way. "I'm here looking for someone who can lead us to Scythe and verify everything I've just told you. Temek Huyurgal could have done the same but unfortunately he's rather dead."

"If we were to help you find this person, would you let us bring you in?" Handcuffs' brows notched even more. "If what you've told me is true, then you're innocent. You'll be tried and cleared."

"Khasain, are you mad?" Hanrif's eyes bulged. "She's wanted for murder and treason. We don't owe her a thing."

Handcuffs—*Captain Khasain,* and she could have punched the air—glared. "I've been in this game a lot longer than you, son. Long enough to know when someone's telling the truth and when they're not." He looked Dhani up and down. "Long enough to know when someone's pissed off the Regional Controller, too."

Dhani watched Khasain closely. Odds-on, if he'd worked under Shalamir for any length of time, he'd play by the book and be good for his word. And, when all was said and done, he'd done exactly what she'd hoped for and offered to help find Abil. Her attention shifted to rail-thin Hanrif and the white-knuckled death-grip he had on his pistol.

Whilst she needed the help, she didn't need Hanrif's trigger-happy finger putting a bullet in her back the moment her guard was down. The kid reminded her a little too much of herself a decade earlier, cocksure and always ready to overreact. The only difference was that Hanrif had much better clothing but considerably less street-smarts.

"I'll tell you what, Khasain," Dhani said. "You keep your guard dog Hanrif under control, help me to find the person I'm looking for, and when we're done you can march both of us straight to Bethsehal Shalamir, the Majapayit, heck even Safid Ereldemore himself, if you like." She held out a fist. "By the Four Winds?"

Khasain touched his knuckles to hers to seal the oath and nodded. "By the Four Winds, Karim."

Hanrif scowled so hard he probably twisted a cheek muscle. Dhani ignored him.

"Come on," she said. "Let's get out of here before backup arrives."

CHAPTER TWENTY-SIX

The smoke grew thicker and the light dimmer as they hurried towards the western section of Koyulerin, where Esmille and Fikret's shanty lay. After a few minutes, Dhani pulled a scarf from her pocket and tied it about her nose and mouth. It filtered the acrid air a little but did nothing to stop the tears streaming from her eyes. Khasain and Hanrif weren't so lucky, instead burying their faces behind their coat sleeves and smothering coughing fits.

They reached a left-hand corner where the lane they'd been following opened into a broader street obscured by even thicker smoke. A handful of smudgy shadows approached in the gloom, and Dhani took cover, pressing her back to a shack made of woven raffia mats and waited. Khasain and Hanrif snapped into the alcove alongside, following her lead. They were well trained, at least.

A minute or so later, a rag-tag group of soot and cinder-stained adults and children trudged past, bodies bent in the shoulder-slumped postures of the downtrodden who had nothing to begin with and now possessed even less.

Older children carried bundles of clothing, adults carried pots, pans, utensils. Dhani's jaw clenched. *Always the poor suffered.* After fleeing their homes, most of these people would head for the city gates, seeking safety, only to find themselves locked out and staring down the barrel of some uncaring Camelskin's rifle. And so the suffering continued.

"Can I ask you a question?" Khasain began, as the last small child had disappeared into the smoke haze, in a fit of coughing and stumbling.

Dhani shrugged. "Sure. I can't guarantee I'll be able to answer it."

"Were you a covert operative or a weapons specialist?"

"Next question."

"My guess is she's Ta'Hafiq." Hanrif's lip curled. The shack's door—a thin sheet of ratty, cracking plywood—creaked as he leaned on it. "Who else could pull a move like she did this afternoon?"

"Someone with a lot of hand-to-hand combat training. Like a specialist covert." Khasain's fingers brushed the bruise on his chin. He frowned. "Did you know you were supposed to report to me this morning, Karim?"

"I did." She ignored Hanrif's comment. The whip-thin kid and his suspicions could take a short hike off a steep cliff. "I was informed of the arrangement last evening."

"And Shalamir tasked you and Parvan Gorshayik with finding Scythe?"

Dhani nodded. "She gave us three days and four names to find him. Temek Huyurgal was one of the names on the list. Odd thing was, when we went to the archive to ask for files, we were told Huyurgal didn't have one."

Khasain's back stiffened. "That's nonsense. Two years ago, I read Huyurgal's file in relation to another case. Why would you be denied access?"

Further down the street, a series of cracks and a spray of burning sparks flew into the air as a shanty collapsed. Dhani waited until the whirl of glowing embers had faded before answering. "You tell me. But I did find the file eventually—in Shalamir's office."

"You broke in to get it, didn't you?" Khasain's mouth crimped back in a bemused smile. "That's why Shalamir ordered your arrest."

"I may or may not have broken into the Regional Controller's office. But then again, Bethsehal Shalamir may or may not hate me for simply having the temerity to exist." She brushed a smoking cinder from her sleeve. "I can tell you several interesting things, though. The file identified Huyurgal as the owner of most of the land here in Koyulerin. The file also stated that earlier this year, Kyvil Yenidogat attempted to purchase Huyurgal's land for the temple. Huyurgal refused. A few weeks later, a man named Golan Fiyuret tried to buy the land twice. Huyurgal refused both times, was beaten up and threatened with having his workshop burned down if he didn't sell to Fiyuret."

The smile faded from Khasain's face. His eyes traced the dusty, cinder-smeared ground as he no doubt connected *land in Koyulerin* with *Kyvil Yenidogat* and *Yevengik cu Bapa* and came up with the same conclusion she had. "So Yevengik cu Bapa are trying to get hold of the land here in Koyulerin?"

"My guess is they're running short on funds and want

to buy the land cheaply in order to collect the rent." She thought briefly about telling Khasain the rest of the story—about the group's plans to assassinate the Majapayit and install the priest in his place but decided against it. Parvan Gorshayik could collect the credit on that one.

"How can we believe anything she says, Khasain?" Hanrif said, leaning forward to aim his gun at Dhani's middle. "This all could be an outrageous lie and she's planning to lead us to some dark corner and kill us."

"Son," Khasain said calmly. "She could have shot us a dozen times already."

"I don't trust her."

"Get your head out of the Service Manual." Khasain waved Hanrif's pistol away. "We're working with her until I say otherwise. Understood?"

The kid's jaw muscles flexed. The weapon's cold, blank muzzle made a reluctant retreat to ground level.

"Who'd you piss off to get sent down here, Karim?" Hanrif snarled in retaliation. "General El'Meshid?"

Dhani peered around the corner and into a street which seemed deserted, but with the thick smoke and glowing flames it was hard to tell. Several homes were now ablaze and winter-weight curtains of black smoke obscured part of the street. She decided to ignore Hanrif's question. The answer was well above his pay grade.

"We should move on. The street's clear but there's a lot of smoke," she said. "Stay to the left. The place we're headed is two streets away to the west."

Khasain wrinkled his nose, staring at the black clouds billowing into the air. He brushed tears from his cheeks, smearing soot and ash in a dirty streak. Hanrif inhaled and buried his face in the crook of an elbow. Dhani broke cover, squinting to ward off the sting of smoke, swallowing to banish the raw, dry tickle in her throat. If it got much thicker, it would be hard to breathe and impossible to see. They'd probably be forced to turn back and waste more time finding another way to Esmille's.

They hurried along the street, darting from doorway to doorway, searching for a west-running lane. When Dhani glimpsed a half-dozen dark figures wrestling over something in the street just ahead, she waved them to a halt.

A woman's voice screamed, a heart-rending but unintelligible cry. A man begged the same words over and over again, *Don't take him, please, don't take him!*

"Cover," Dhani hissed. "Quick."

A shanty's recessed doorway presented itself, a space scarcely deep enough for one, let alone three. Not ideal, but it was better than the alternative—standing in the street, screaming *hello, I'm here!* They all shunted backwards, squeezing in against the building's pressed iron door.

The smoke cleared, offering a momentary view of four men shoving a group of Bisantrik-aged boys along the street. The boys had their hands on their heads, prisoner-style. A man and a woman stood wailing in the middle of the street, arms wrapped about each other, crying and pleading.

One of the men in the group drew her gaze, a younger man with a slight stature, deep-set eyes, and scrappy black goatee. She inhaled a sharp, jagged breath. Like a set of dovetail joints and slotted neatly into place, everything—*everything!*—made a sudden and undeniable sense.

Ziraat the tabac-chewing adjutant. Better known as Golan Fiyuret *and* the mole inside the Ha'filu.

She should have guessed.

In fact, had it been any more obvious, the clues would have walked up and smacked her in the head. A folk hero's name was an ideal pseudonym for a member of a nationalist cult—to say nothing of the snake-wrapped stallion hearth god on his desk. And, if she listened to the persistent niggle in her gut, he'd probably played a part in the oversight with Temek Huyurgal's file as well.

An instant later, she spotted Abil Beriktiin amongst the boys in the group and her heart jagged to a stop in her chest. *Oh, no. No. No. NO!*

"That's Ziraat Olucik, Shalamir's adjutant," Hanrif whispered, glaring at the short, well-groomed figure giving orders to the group. "What is *he* doing here?"

Dhani curled a fist. "I suspect that's Golan Fiyuret. He might also be *Scythe.* He's one of Yevengik cu Bapa's agents in Izurum."

"Then we need to take him alive," Khasain said, clearly unimpressed with the thought of the Regional Controller's adjutant being a nationalist mole. "Is the boy we're recovering in that group?"

Dhani nodded. "Second from the right. His name is Abil Beriktiin."

Khasain's lips thinned. He looked old enough to have children of an age with the boys being herded along the street. Most likely, he was imagining his own children as victims. "I don't understand any of this. I've seen Tizraki brawl when they're drunk and occasionally kill each other, but they're not premeditated killers. In fact, if I had to say anything about them, it's they're a nation of pacifists and cowards." His expression darkened. "Not the sort of people who massacre innocent people at weddings."

Fury burned in her veins. Whilst her life as an assassin was a mail-order catalogue of brutality and death, she'd never witnessed a massacre as cold and callous as that at the wedding that afternoon. She needed three long breaths before she could answer Khasain.

"Did you see the aftermath of the shootings in the Odesstra Souk?" she said.

The disgust on the man's lips worked its way upwards, wrinkling his nose and narrowing his eyes to slits. "Only in the newspapers and what came down through Service memoranda."

"When you're in HQ next time, ask them to pull file on the Odesstra massacre. Extremists don't do things by halves."

"Any chance we could circle about and ambush them before they get too far ahead?" Hanrif asked.

Khasain pointed with his chin. "Next left, then the first right. Should bring us out ahead of them if we hurry. We'll circle around if you bring up the rear, Karim?" He flashed a brief smile. "I've worked in this part of Koyulerin, too."

"We shouldn't split up," Dhani said.

"We don't have a choice." Khasain rubbed at his bruised cheek. "We don't have enough ammunition for a firefight and I don't want to put those boys' lives in any more danger than they already are. Surprise is our best weapon."

Whilst she agreed in theory, the possibility that more members of the sect roamed the streets nearby, probably rounding up boys who attended the Bisantrik, was a real one.

"Be careful, Khasain," she said. "Yevengik cu Bapa have more people on the ground here than I first suspected. Make sure you're not walking into a trap."

The older man nodded, the uptick of an eyebrow suggesting he'd noted the words and stored them away. "We'll circle around, take cover and move on your signal."

"I'll follow your lead, Khasain. For now." Dhani lowered her gaze. "Four Winds guide your path."

"And yours, Karim." Khasain gave a final nod before dashing around the corner with Hanrif shadowing him.

Dhani counted out a full minute before she moved, mapping a route along the street and when the smoke allowed it, watching the backs of the boys and their black-clothed captors recede. The man and woman retreated into their house, shoulders slumped in grief, clinging to each other. In the distance, a ruddy sun hung just above the horizon like an all-seeing, bloodshot eye.

Anger built in her gut, hot fury at the poor turning to fanaticism and religious extremes, at Temek Huyurgal for ignoring his tenant's pleas, a knuckle-shaking, sabre-rattling fury at those in power who turned a blind eye to the poor when they'd been sworn to protect the city's people. *But was it any different to Jhiriyah?* The girl she'd once been answered from an empty, long-forgotten grave. *No, you fool. From one continent to the next, this is ever the lot of the poor.*

She eased out from the doorway, darting across the

lane Khasain and Hanrif had turned down before slipping into the protection of a gap between two shanties. Her mouth tasted dry, of burning raffia, soot, and ash, whilst runnels of sweat streamed down her back, plastering her clothes to her skin. She made two more short sprints, using the thickening smoke to her advantage, gaining ground on the group of boys and men.

As she neared the cross street where Khasain planned his ambush, luck took a flying leap into a sewage-filled abyss and promptly burned itself in the fires of hell.

A gunshot rang out from the cross street and a man's body slammed into an iron fence with a resounding, final *thud!*

"No, wait. There's more of them!" Khasain's desperate shout echoed along the street in hard, hacking Jhiriyan. Gunfire erupted from the same direction, a *pop-pop-popping* sound. Another man screamed, his voice cut off mid-throat by a pistol's report.

Dhani ground her teeth and clenched a fist in frustration. Just as she'd suspected, Hanrif and Khasain had run into members of Yevengik cu Bapa, sweeping the side streets for children.

The group of men herding the boys began to run. Two rushed into the cross street, opening fire on Khasain and Hanrif. The others, including Ziraat the adjutant, took to their heels, shoving the shrieking boys before them, guns at their backs.

Dhani burst into a sprint, thighs straining, thumbing the revolver's hammer back. She focussed on the pair of men shooting into the cross street, desperate to end their assault on Khasain and Hanrif. Smoke poured from a row of shacks and blurring her eyes with hot grit and tears, she sucked down air and held her breath.

She reached the first man a few seconds later, a dark smudge in her smoke-stung vision, raised the pistol and shot him twice in the back. He fell, smacking an inglorious face-first into the dirt. A fleeting instant, and his bandaged knuckles and slab-like face brought a flicker of recognition. *The thug who'd beaten Parvan Gorshayik in the cellar beneath the stables. Moltekiin or something similar?* She aimed a boot at his ribs and kicked hard enough that several bones snapped. If the man hadn't been deader than a rock, he'd have screamed like a stuck pig.

Then, Dhani hurried on, searching the gloom for the man's accomplice. She found him crouched behind a fence just ahead, oblivious to his fallen comrade, focussed on the gunfight further up the street. Two strides brought her near enough, she couldn't miss. She pulled the trigger, putting a bullet in the back of his head. The man whirled in a spray of blood, bone, and brain, smashing a shanty's wooden door wide open and falling inside. For a moment, the satisfying scent of cordite filled her nose.

She took cover, pulse racing. *Three rounds left.*

A glance down the street revealed Hanrif writhing in the dust, clutching his gut as a pool of blood spread beneath him. A trio of bodies, all Tizraki men, were scattered about him. One of them twitched. Another groaned, holding a wound to his chest. Of Khasain, there was no sign. She cursed and wiped her streaming eyes. Hopefully, he'd had the sense to find cover and keep his head down for the time being. Her attention returned to

Hanrif. The kid groaned and tried to push himself up, calling for Khasain.

She sucked on a cheek but didn't linger. A wound to the gut could go either way. Hanrif needed a healer or a physician, not an assassin. Besides, saving Abil Beriktiin's life, along with capturing Ziraat Olucik was really all that mattered.

A swift check in the other direction and she swore. Golan—*Ziraat*—and the boys had vanished, most likely into a house or along a nearby lane. She dropped to a crouch, made a quick search of the nearest man's body, and came up with two more bullets. Both were the wrong calibre for her revolver, but she pocketed them anyway. A sweep of the ground nearby showed no sign of the dead man's gun. There was no time to search for it. Her heart thumped in her veins. Every second took Abil further away from her and closer to death. With a parting kick at Moltekiin's corpse, she began to run.

She'd covered just twenty metres when a gunshot sounded and a boy screamed.

CHAPTER TWENTY-SEVEN

D hani charged into the main street and pivoted mid-
stride, skidding on loose grit to follow the child's
scream. A second high pitched wail pierced the blood-red
gloom, coming from a litter-strewn lane that angled off the
street to the south.

She took off at a dead sprint into the lane, flying past
matching rows of patchwork raffia and plywood shanties.
One shack was already ablaze, its conflagration of flames
eating their way towards a second house. She flashed past
both, shielding her head with an arm and holding her
breath.

A third cry rang out, a child's piercing, pleading shriek,
followed by a single, resounding gunshot. Her chest
cinched, gripped by a breath-stifling horror she'd not felt
since the night Zandolan had been killed.

No. No. NO! Was Abil dead?

She pushed the thought away, praying it wasn't so. The
gunshot could have been a misfire, a shot at an enemy, a
shot at a mangy stub-tail rat—anything but a shot that

ended a child's life. That much she *had* to believe. She sprinted on, ploughing through a cloud of acrid smoke, gagging as she went.

This was supposed to be a nothing mission. A glorified pen-pusher's paper chase…

Her own words came to her as she ran, their irony not lost as she reached the source of the wailing, another raffia and wood-scrap house a mere three shacks down from the burning shanty. True, she'd been expecting life in Izurum to be slow and grinding ossification via paper cuts, boredom, or aching feet, not a fight to the death with a group of fucked-sideways-in-the-head cultists worthy of an organisation-wide Ta'Hafiq hit.

She slowed and used the smoke as cover, pressing herself against a shanty wall. A coughing spasm rose in her throat, but she swallowed hard and smothered it. Her eyes streamed with tears, her mouth tasted dry and rank. Another child's scream confirmed the next house was the place.

Dhani drew a slow breath, inhaling the scarf's sweaty cotton and blowing it out, taking her time to slip along the shanty's raffia and ply until she could make out the front wall of the adjacent house.

No emotion. No weakness. No retreat.

No matter what lay inside that house, she would deal with it.

The door was ajar, just enough to suggest someone leaving room to watch or poke a revolver's barrel through the gap. Her grip tightened on the pistol. She inhaled again, narrowing her focus to a pinprick. *If she were behind the door and ready to shoot, where would she stand?*

She picked her mark, took aim, and fired a single, chest-height shot into the door. A man screamed. Wood splintered inwards. A body thunked onto to carpet or a rug, a soft but definitive thud.

Dhani kicked the door's jagged remains open. She dived through and slid to the right, thumb on the revolver's hammer, ready to fire her second last bullet.

A large man with a thick salt and pepper beard lay sprawled on a threadbare rug, clutching his chest. A thin trail of blood leaked between his fingers and his gaze fixed on her, dark eyes wide and pleading. He gasped twice and stilled, blinking at her. Dhani lowered the pistol. There was no visible weapon in either of the fallen man's hands, and with a chest wound like that, he wouldn't be hurling Deenjah any time soon.

Shouts erupted from the building's rear. She jumped and spun, pistol ready, gripped in both hands. A man's voice sobbed, *"No, Golan, I can't…Please, don't make me shoot…Oh, Mother Yamir, Father Ulgan, I killed a child! Forgive me!"*

"Give me the gun, Jartik! We don't have time for this."

"No! I won't let you murder children."

There came a resounding *thunk!* from the rear of the building, the full thud of a body hitting a wall followed by the urgent scrape of boot leather on tile or hard-packed earth. Several grunts and a string of curses suggested Golan had decided to seize the gun for himself and was wrestling with Jartik.

She rubbed the back of her neck, torn between finishing off the man she'd shot in the chest and rushing along the dingy hall whilst the two men fought and she'd have the advantage. A decade of training warned against leaving an enemy—even one with a chest wound—at her back. Cold hard practicality argued she had two rounds left and two unwounded, dangerous targets ahead. Her only other weapons were the Deenjah-charged, spring-loaded blade Parvan Gorshayik had given her—and her bare hands.

Golan shrieked some unintelligible insult. Jartik growled, their footsteps thumping forwards and back. A chair or something like it crashed into a wall and splinted. A child cried out.

Wounded or not, she couldn't take the risk. She spun the revolver, crouched down, and smacked the weapon's butt into the injured man's temple. The blow stunned the man, his eyes rolling back in their sockets and his body slackening. Then, she was up and melting along the dark, narrow space that lead to the shanty's rear.

A single shot rang out and a child screamed. Fear spiked in her chest. She curled her fingers about a grimy curtain and reefed it aside.

Oblivious to her, Jartik and *Golan*—Ziraat the rat-faced adjutant—grappled in a small, windowless room which doubled as kitchen and dining space. Three terrified boys cowered in one corner behind a potbelly stove. When she registered one as Abil Beriktiin, relief flooded every wire-strung tendon and muscle in her body. Against the far wall, however, a fourth child lay dead, his head a bloody pulp from a gunshot. A table and chair lay splintered near a locked rear door, several pots and pans had been upended and scattered about.

She glanced back at the boy's corpse. Fury burned through her veins. *Kill Jartik, the child-murdering, gutter-*

licking coward. She raised her revolver, felt the trigger's metal stiffness bite into her skin and focussed the muzzle on Jartik's broad back. This close she wouldn't miss.

Right then, Jartik took a swinging right hook at Ziraat, smacked him in the jaw. The younger man went twisting backwards, slammed into the wall near the rear door, bounced once and collapsed in a blur of black clothing and blood spittle to the floor. Jartik, a much larger man than Ziraat, would have no trouble finishing him. Right now, however, he didn't seem keen to stick around. Instead, Jartik whirled about, ready to run.

Dhani recognised him instantly—the man who'd bound her and thrown her into the cellar. *The man who'd hacked a glob of spit on her face. A man who'd murdered a child in cold blood.* A bullet to the brain seemed too merciful, too quick, for such a man.

Jartik's eyes widened as he saw her, registering she not only had a gun, she now blocked his escape. His face screwed into a mask of hatred and he charged forward like some infuriated mountain of lard and gristle, pistol raised.

Crack!

Dhani squeezed the hard-sprung trigger before he'd taken his second step. The trio of boys screamed.

The shot hit Jartik dead-centre in the chest. He gasped and staggered, but his bulk kept him coming.

Crack!

She pulled the trigger again, putting her second and final bullet in his forehead.

The man's head blew apart, spraying the room in a shower of bone, brain, and gore. Jartik crumpled like a boneless meat sack, falling and losing grip of his gun. The piece clanged once and slid across the floor, coming to rest midway between Dhani and Ziraat.

There was scarcely a moment to draw breath. The gun clicked empty in Dhani's hand. She aimed its smoking muzzle at Ziraat, more for effect than anything else, as he pushed himself onto his elbows and shook his head. With her free hand, she tugged the scarf down, exposing her nose and mouth.

The adjutant blinked at her several times before his expression sobered, eyes goggling in disbelief. An instant later, his lip curled and be began to climb to his feet.

"Give up, Olucik," she said. "I'm arresting you for murder, treason against the Empire and conspiring to assassinate the Majapayit."

He didn't answer. Gave no sign he'd even heard her. He stood, wavering and grabbing at the wall, a fist-sized bruise blackening his cheek, his thick raven hair spiked like cock's combs in several places. Dhani eased back a little, turning side on. The adjutant's left hand twitched. His eyes flickered from her to the three terrified boys to Jartik's lifeless body. To the dead man's gun lying equidistant between them.

Would he dive for the gun or hurl the Flames?

Her guess was the second. Most Deenjin would choose Deenjah when faced with a Flame-mute Jhiriyan foe. Without lowering the gun, the fingers of her left hand closed about the blade tucked in her belt. Her heart pounded against her ribs. A tickle of sweat itched her nose. Steel charged by Yargans was rumoured to be able to cut through almost any kind of attack a lesser class of Deenjin could draw up. She *hoped* the rumours were true.

Otherwise, this might be the shortest of very short fights indeed.

Ziraat's fingers curled. His eyes took on a momentary glaze as he called up some combination of the Sha and Li to raise the Flames.

Deenjah it was. The blade sprang open beneath Dhani's thumb and she hurled it, aiming for Ziraat's belly just as he loosed off a blinding *blue* ball of energy.

There was enough time to register the adjutant's strange choice, that he'd hurled defensive *askandhli* rather than the killing Flame, shakandhli, before a force like a bull's kick struck her chest, slamming her into the wall.

The wind flew from her lungs. Her ribs crunched against the doorjamb, splintering the wood and sending pain spiralling through her torso.

In the same instant, Ziraat's screams filled the air, over and over like a toddler denied a sweet. *"Arrgh. No! No! Arrgh. No! Gods above! I'm burning. I'm burning!"*

Dhani straightened, cycling through a breathing exercise to unlock the winded spasm in her diaphragm. She moved, wincing at a spray of pain from her ribs and the stars popping across her vision.

When her head cleared, Ziraat the adjutant staggered about, staring at the Deenjah-charged blade protruding from his gut. His white-faced horror confirmed what she'd expected: the charged metal burned him *internally* as if he'd been hit by a blast of shakandhli. Sure, her aim had been a little off—she'd intended to hit his solar plexus—but there wasn't time to worry about that.

Ziraat's gaze flickered her way. With a snarl, he pulled the blade from his belly and flung it aside as if it were nothing more than a flea. He staggered forward, left hand flinching, expression glazing again as he tried to call up the Flames.

Please, no Deenjah. Dhani's pulse thumped in her ears, fear-flavoured adrenalin flooded her mouth. She sent the Creator a silent, final prayer, *Ai, Creator, I cower in wonder before your vast and all-powerful, sparkling self! Favour me here, and I give you my word: I'll sleep with a Yargan if this works.*

The adjutant's face crumpled. His confused frown and deathly-white cheeks told her everything she needed to know. He couldn't draw Deenjah and couldn't figure out why. She almost punched the air. She would, of course, have to sleep with a sack-of-bulging-muscle, *We-Are-The-Superior-Race* Yargan, but it didn't matter. *It worked. The Yargan-charged blade actually worked!*

The adjutant wheeled about a second later, attention falling on Jartik's gun.

They both moved in the same instant.

Ziraat pulled a blade from a pocket, no larger than a paring knife but one whose gleam left no doubt about its sharpness. He slashed at her wildly as they converged on the gun. Dhani pivoted in the last instant, Ziraat's wild thrusts meeting with empty space.

Still in motion she kicked low, smashing a boot into his shin. From the corner of her eye, she caught the gap-mouthed, astounded faces of Abil and his two companions, still backed into a corner with nowhere to go.

The adjutant howled in pain. Dhani snapped around, wrenching Ziraat's wrist up and twisting it hard enough that his bones cracked. He shrieked like a stuck weasel, loud enough that her ears rang, but didn't release the knife. Abil and the other boys took their chance, darting out from behind the stove and heading for the rear door.

"*Bitch!*" Ziraat hissed through bared teeth. Then he lunged, throwing all his bodyweight at her.

It was an unexpected, desperate move. She dodged the adjutant's onslaught but tripped on one of Jartik's legs and fell backwards, slamming to the floor in the narrow gap between the potbelly stove and a set of wooden shelves. A cascade of white-hot pain bloomed in her chest, a city of lights popped in her eyes and faded. Ziraat pounced, his body crashing down and pinning her in place. He didn't hesitate, gripping the knife with both hands, tendons and muscles straining as he drove it towards her exposed neck.

Dhani wrenched a forearm up to block the onslaught, halting the blade just millimetres from her flesh. She winced, pushing with every fibre of strength against Ziraat's double-handed assault. A vein pulsed in the younger man's temple as his dark eyes locked on hers, wide and wild. Up close, the scrubby goatee still didn't suit him.

"*Die, Metalskin bitch,*" he grated, bunching his wiry muscles and thrusting down with his entire body weight.

Her arm began to tremble, quivering with effort. She searched about for something—anything—to use as a distraction or a weapon. Hemmed in as they were, her options were few. She couldn't head butt him without impaling herself on the knife, and there was no room to swing and smack her fist into the straggle-bearded weed's temple. Worse, whilst Ziraat might not have been built like a bear, he had the advantage of weight and position.

Which meant she needed to figure something out—and figure it out fast.

Ziraat grunted and squeezed down, hands shaking with the effort. The knife's tip grazed the layers of scarf, pressing down against her skin. She made a last-ditch effort with her forearm, heaving upwards and forcing the blade back. The adjutant's lips twisted into a vicious smile, knowing well that in a war of attrition, victory would be his. Somewhere, a long way away, a door latch clicked open and a hinge creaked. *The children were out, at least.*

As her arm began to fail, she made a frantic search for something to use as a weapon. Her eyes found nothing save a knife sharpener hanging on the wall, well out of reach and small pot of ashes next to the stove.

A pot of ashes…

With her free hand, she stretched, found the pot, and palmed a fistful of ash and grit. The powdery mix ran fine and cool through her fingers. *Hopefully, it would do the job.* Then, she closed her eyes, held her breath and hurled the ash into Ziraat's face.

The man's reaction was instant. He flinched and cried out, the downward pressure of his bodyweight momentarily easing. With the hand that had thrown the ash, she reached up and jammed her thumbnail into the adjutant's left eye socket as hard as she could.

Ziraat screamed. The knife fell from his grasp, clunked on the floor, and slid out of reach. He howled in agony, shifting his weight and fumbling desperately for the dropped blade. A soft pop and a flush of warm liquid on Dhani's cheek said she'd caused an eye injury the man wouldn't recover from. She smacked a fist into his temple.

Once. Twice.

The third blow was enough to dislodge him. Dhani rolled, bringing a knee up and flipping him off her body.

She swiped the knife from the floor and sprung to her feet, grabbing a fistful of the man's hair. With an almighty reef, she pulled Ziraat's head back as he clawed at his ruined eye, pressing the blade to his exposed throat.

"Enough," she panted. "Yield or die. I don't need you alive, Golan."

The sudden click of a gun's hammer sent a chill through her core.

She froze. Ziraat swallowed, trachea bobbing against the blade.

Without easing the pressure of the knife on the adjutant's flesh, she looked up to see Abil Beriktiin holding Jartik's revolver in a pair of wavering hands. The boy's eyes were red and puffy, his cheeks smeared with tears, dried blood, and gore. His expression was cold and blank. *Shocked* most likely, which was easy to understand. The child had endured more pain in a day than most Jhiriyans experienced in a lifetime.

"Step aside, Yelanda. I want to kill him," Abil said, voice hard and flat. The gun's muzzle shook, but the set of the boy's shoulders, the clench and flex of his jaw said he'd come to the implacable decision that Ziraat the rat-faced adjutant needed to die and die *now*. Dhani chewed on a cheek. *Creator above,* she hated negotiating. Especially with kids.

"I know you're angry, Abil," she said as softly as she could manage, "but I suspect the Ha'filu would like to interrogate him and sentence him to death."

287

"He made the other man kill Marel." Abil's eyes flashed to the other boy's corpse, sprawled against the wall. "He deserves to die." The boy's words faltered. "They...murdered my parents and the guests at the wedding."

"I know," she said meeting his gaze. "I was there, and—"

Footsteps pounded at the front of the shanty, a hurried, urgent cadence. Her shoulders sank. If this was another of Ziraat's thugs, she'd need more than a prayer to the Creator and handful of ash to get out of the predicament.

"*Karim?*" a man called in Jhiriyan. Dhani blew out a breath. The voice was Khasain's. "Are you here?"

Without warning, Ziraat took advantage of the distraction, ramming himself into her gut and grabbing at her hand. *Oh no, you don't.* She struggled, feeling the blade bite into his skin as he writhed and she twisted her fingers into deeper his hair.

Crack!

A shot rang out. The bullet whizzed by so close its stung Dhani's cheek. She flinched. Ziraat stopped struggling, becoming suddenly, irrevocably bone-statue still.

Abil's face lost all trace of colour. The revolver's muzzle omitted a thin, smokey smear. The boy stared past her, eyes probably fixed on a bullet hole in the wall just to the left of her head. His arm fell to his side but he didn't drop the gun.

"Sorry." His lip quivered. "I've never fired a gun before."

"*Creator's bright shiny...*" Khasain pushed through the

flimsy curtain, on point, gun leading. He took one look at the room, at the smoking weapon in the boy's hand and lowered his weapon. His gaze made an arc from Abil to Jartik's body to Marel's corpse before coming to rest on Dhani and Ziraat. One side of his mouth kinked back a crooked smile.

"I see you've got everything under control, Karim?"

"It is now." Dhani exhaled and, for a moment, closed her eyes. "I think it finally is."

CHAPTER TWENTY-EIGHT

Dhani heaved out ten pushups, counted ten seconds and four splattered drops of sweat on the floorboards beneath her, then squeezed out ten more. The last ten hadn't been on the agenda, but then, she had nothing better to do. Midday had come and gone for the ninth day in a row. House arrest, no matter how comfortable, nagged like an itching scab.

Partway through her fourth circuit—she'd just started tricep dips on a chair—the lock rattled and the door swung open. Aydan Khasain stood framed in the brilliant light, a shaft of afternoon sun gilding his already golden hair. His neat, white longshirt and royal blue coat suggested formality, which could only mean one thing. The great, clunking iron cogs of the Imperium had turned, and after days of silence, finally metered out her judgement, no doubt wrapped in a regulation brown, wax-sealed envelope. Her gut flipped one way then the other.

"Your presence is required." Khasain wrinkled his nose. "Though, I'd wash and change first."

Ten minutes later, smelling of lemon soap and dressed in a light blue longshirt with an itching Mandarin collar, Dhani stepped into the blazing sun. A deep breath brought with it the scent of dust, the faint perfume of orange blossom, the nostril-searing heat. About her, Regional Command's compound with its orderly grid of one and two story blockhouses, pistol ranges and predictable bougainvillea-covered walkways looked no different than it had over a week ago, when Khasain had walked her in.

A pair of uniformed guards fell in behind them. Khasain waved her along a walkway to the left, towards the central bungalow where Bethsehal Shalamir's office lay.

"Abil and Rivek?" Dhani began.

"Doing as well as can be expected," he said. "We were able to locate an aunt, a younger sister of their father. She's taken them in." He slowed, fiddling with the gold marriage bracelet on his right wrist. "The family has been relocated to Geratkin. Abil will attend school in Mursik, and when the time comes, if he wishes, will attend university in Istanakhand. Rivek will be offered the same."

Dhani pulled at her collar, trying to ease the itch. *Good news,* though the raw sting of Fikret and Esmille's deaths would take far longer to heal. In the aftermath of the fight, they'd bound Ziraat Olucik and accompanied Abil home. There, they'd found Rivek unharmed, attended by the same ancient woman she'd been with at the wedding. The old woman turned out to be a neighbour and, though happy to care for Rivek for a short time, had no room in her already overcrowded shanty for two more bodies. Khasain had taken the children instead, bringing them home to his wife and two children in Geraktin. Finally, it seemed, other arrangements had been made.

"I appreciate everything you've done for them, Captain," she said. "I counted his parents as friends."

"Abil asked to see you every day." Khasain's hands fell to his sides. His brows notched. "I wish I'd been able to do more for them. The massacre at the wedding…"

"How is Hanrif?" In truth, she didn't care how Hanrif was. Sure, he'd taken a bullet wound to the abdomen but his suspicious, by-the-rulebook attitude had been fun for all of three seconds. She'd asked the question to distract Khasain from reliving the slaughter at the Koyulerin temple. No doubt he was there, every night and half his waking day.

"He's sore but recovering." His mouth kinked into a half-smile. "Not so eager to charge in, guns blazing from now on. He's fortunate Captain Gorshayik knew a Yargan physician with experience treating bullet wounds."

Yes, how very convenient. Dhani narrowed her eyes. Best to keep her suspicions about Parvan Gorshayik's Yargan healer to herself. Khasain didn't seem the type to care about somebody else's bedroom partners, anyway.

They turned a corner and the Regional Controller's office came into view. Her stomach flip-flopped. Whether a noose, a firing squad or a *see-you-later* letter awaited, she couldn't say. Knowing her luck, it would be the latter. Which was, as far as she could discern, just marginally better than being dead.

"So who's passing judgement?" she whispered as they reached the blockhouse's wide, tiled verandah and creaking screen door. "How far up the Service's ranks did this go?"

"I've been ordered not to say."

"Tell me it's not Sharafaa Ereldemore." Dhani's gut dropped like a sack of rocks down a well. The thought of facing the Empire's heir—technically the head of the Ha'filu—filled even her with ice-cold dread.

"It's not Sharafaa Ereldemore. The compound would be crawling with Service brass, Imperial guards and Ta'Hafiq. And besides, it's a full two-week journey from the Homeland."

"She visits Istanakhand and Erissat regularly."

"She's not here." He opened the door for her. The pair of guards stopped as well. "Inside."

In place of Ziraat Olucik, a young Tizraki woman sat behind the foyer desk. Though her gaze lingered on Dhani a little longer than necessary, she directed them towards Bethsehal Shalamir's closed door with a pleasant smile. "Go ahead, Captain Khasain, Operative Karim. You're expected."

When they reached the office door, Khasain came to an abrupt halt. "This is where I leave you. Knock once and go in." He frowned. "By the way, Imril Huyurgal was asking after you as well. Something about a meal?"

Her lips parted. With everything that had happened she'd completely forgotten about Imril-nephew-of-Temek and his offer of wine and a meal.

"Ahh. Well." A flush of warmth rushed to her cheeks. "If I survive this, and you see him again, let him know I'll be happy to take him up on his offer."

"I'll do that." Khasain touched his fingertips to his heart and saluted. "Good luck, Karim."

Dhani's chest tightened. She returned the salute and murmured a word of thanks. Without looking back, Khasain turned and left.

A knock on the door and she gripped the handle.

No emotion. No weakness. No retreat. She repeated it three times and still didn't believe it. Of course, this could all be for nothing and she'd simply be facing Bethsehal Shalamir, her two gold nibs and too-clean desk. Shalamir would be furious she'd had to cancel her journey home to Jhiriyah for her brother's wedding. After which the day—and anything left of her career—would take a swift and bloody dive into the gaping jaws of death.

Bethsehal Shalamir wasn't waiting inside, however.

It was General Behzad El'Meshid.

He'd been perched on the front of the desk, arms folded, and rose to greet her. His blue longshirt matched her own, falling to mid-thigh as he stood, fastened by a single row of ebony buttons and a hem embroidered with understated gold fancywork. His pants were charcoal grey, his boots gleamed like glass. As tradition demanded of Shaliaat, he wore his dark blond hair unbound, just below shoulder-length.

Dhani began to salute, but he cut it off, holding both hands out to greet her. Cool relief faded to warm embarrassment as she took in Parvan Gorshayik standing off to the right, attention welded to his boots. Despite the company, she had no choice but to take the General's hands.

"Dhani," the General said, his steady grasp closing

about hers. For a fleeting instant, she was eighteen years old again, meeting him for the first time from the drug-numbed confusion of a sanatorium bed. Her legs, ribs, collarbones, and right arm were broken, her body a mass of cuts, bruises, and abrasions. She'd abused him for saving her life, screeching she'd have rather died with her brother. Thankfully, he hadn't listened. He'd politely blamed her pain medication.

"They've treated you well?" His voice enfolded her like a father's embrace, soothing, calm and warm. She'd never heard him raise it, but when your family sat so far up the Imperial Cedar you could probably gaze into the Emperor's nostrils, you didn't need to shout. People simply sat up and listened.

"A bungalow reserved for visiting dignitaries. Room to train. Ceiling fans, slatted glass windows. Insect screens." She smiled. "Can't complain."

"I'm sorry this has taken rather longer than I would have liked. Messy business." He released her hands and gestured at a pair of utility brown leather chairs set before the desk. "Please sit." He angled his chin at Parvan Gorshayik. "You, too, Captain. Please sit and that *is* an order."

Gorshayik came forward and folded himself into the chair. He inclined his head to Dhani then returned to studying the floor. Odds-on the General had given him some kind of silk-touched dressing down—for what, however, she could only guess.

Behzad El'Meshid returned to his perch on the edge of the table. He straightened a sleeve cuff, considering it for several seconds. The fan ticked overhead. Behind him,

Shalamir's once spotless desk was stacked with files, scattered papers, bottles of ink and the General's battered but familiar, brown-zippered folio. His House shorfa—his noble's silk scarf—bearing the El'Meshid lion, lay draped over the back of his chair. On the wall behind the desk, the Emperor's sepia portrait considered them with a tired, perfunctory stare.

"As you've both been somewhat indisposed, I'll fill you in on what has happened." The General fiddled with his cuff again, a habit he privately despised. "I'm sure you're both aware that Ziraat Olucik has been warming the bench in solitary confinement for the past week. What you may not know is that Kyvil Yenidogat was arrested attempting to flee the city after the Majapayit cancelled his scheduled public appearance, thanks to the warning Captain Gorshayik delivered. Yesterday, both Yenidogat and Olucik confessed under the compulsion of Deenjah to conspiring to commit treason and attempting to overthrow the government of Izurum. There were also charged with murder. This morning, the Majapayit ruled they both be put to death by public execution. Twenty-four other men and women, all from Koyulerin, were also arrested. Most will likely be sentenced to death."

How predictable. Dhani ground her jaw. The Majapayit could mete out death when his own position was threatened but happily turned a blind eye to the underlying problem even when it bit his pony-sized arse. "If the Majapayit and his ilk actually *did* something for the people of Koyulerin instead of sitting on their perfumed behinds, groups like Yevengik cu Bapa wouldn't exist." She crossed her arms. "The Colonial Government needs to lean on him *and* people like Temek Huyurgal. In Erissat, House Rumahlah directly intervenes to assist—"

"Erissat is not Tizrak Yirda, and you know as well as I do that the Colonial Government's policy is to not intervene unless it has no other choice, but I will pass on your concerns." The slight rise of the General's chin said the subject was closed. Dhani curled a fist then released it. They'd had the conversation a hundred times. A hundred times, the answer had always been the same. "In time, I hope the situation will improve."

The General swept on, changing the subject. "Nonetheless, the Majapayit wishes to personally commend both of you for your efforts in circumventing a coup that would have most certainly resulted in the deaths of hundreds, if not thousands of innocent people. He has requested you attend him in a private audience this evening." He paused, fingers brushing his shirt buttons. Dhani could hear a continent sized *BUT* coming, as sure as the sun set in the west. "However, there are a number of internal, disciplinary matters to which I must first attend."

She stiffened her spine. Parvan Gorshayik's chair creaked as the General's attention swung his way.

"Captain Gorshayik, you will not abandon a mission to pursue your own agenda without first consulting a superior. This is the first and the last time I shall reprimand you for this. Secondly, unless your orders state otherwise, you *will* communicate to both your partner and immediate superior *any* intelligence you acquire about any mission assigned to you. Is that understood?"

Dhani stole a glance at the big Tizraki. That he'd withheld information about their mission was hardly surprising, but his *abandoning* the mission to pursue his own agenda? She raised an eyebrow. That *was* interesting news. If nothing else, it made some—slight—sense of the note she'd lifted from his pocket.

"Yes, Shulim General," Gorshayik said with a slow dip of his head. "I understand."

"Furthermore when you are wrong, you will admit as such." Behzad El'Meshid folded his arms and canted forward. "None of us are perfect and it is not a crime to be incorrect. You will make mistakes in the future, Captain. I will make mistakes in the future as well. It's called being human. Admit your mistakes, own them, learn from them and move on." Gorshayik flexed his jaw, the scar on his cheek twitching the twitch of a man unlikely to ever accept his own infallibility, much less his mistakes. The General ignored it and continued, "Finally, you will talk to someone about your condition. Preferably a doctor with some experience treating these kinds of illnesses."

"General, I cannot—"

Behzad El'Meshid raised a hand. "Parvan, we have just arrived at an agreement. If you wish me to honour it, then you're going to talk to a physician about your condition. Otherwise, there is no agreement."

Dhani had to hold herself back from turning to stare at Parvan Gorshayik. No doubt there'd been some discussion between the pair prior to her arrival; her guess was the *agreement* involved Parvan Gorshayik's attempted resignation and whatever it was he'd been planning on doing. Clearly, whatever it was, the General had some interest in it.

Gorshayik clasped his hands. "Of course, if there were

such a physician—"

"You know very well such physicians exist." The General's clipped Shaliaat accent rose in pitch. "No excuses. You need treatment. This is my last word on this matter."

The discussion with Parvan Gorshayik now ended, Behzad El'Meshid's attention turned to Dhani.

"Operative Karim." She sat to attention, fixing her gaze just to the right of the Emperor's portrait. "Breaking into a superior's office is a crime worthy of court-martial and dishonourable discharge. As is breaking into the home of a citizen and holding a child hostage to elicit information. And yes, we did receive a complaint."

She clamped her jaw shut lest it slap the floor in disbelief. Her only other option was to throw her head back and snort in outrageous laughter. *Jursek Cerevin, gods bless his whiny-voiced, bucket-hurling soul, had made a complaint.* Perhaps she'd pay him a second midnight visit and hold a cold spoon to his throat, out of sheer spite.

"In the first instance, Shulim Bethsehal noticed an irregularity in the files in her possession—files she never requested from the Archive and files critical to your mission." The General paused. "Once Captain Gorshayik informed her of the events following the Koyulerin wedding, she agreed your burglary, whilst irregular and unlawful, was justified."

Dhani leaned forward. "And did Shulim Bethsehal also tell you she didn't want myself or Captain—"

"*However,*" Behzad El'Meshid cut her off with a penetrating sky-blue stare. "I will remind you, Operative Karim, that Internal Affairs is not the Ta'Hafiq. You've been accustomed to taking whatever actions were necessary to complete a mission with the full protection of Imperial law. In this branch of the Ha'filu you do not have that luxury. You *will* familiarise yourself with the Service Manual, you will follow regulations *and* you will follow the instructions of your superiors. You will not break into the homes of citizens and hold children or anyone else at knifepoint. Is this understood?"

"Yes, Shulim General." She breathed out a tiny sigh of relief. Sure, she'd pissed off Bethsehal Shalamir, but she'd dodged both suspension and dismissal. What it meant in terms of the rest of her career remained to be seen. "But I'd still like to state that the Regional Controller said—"

"I assure you Shulim Bethsehal made it clear to me she did not want either yourself or Captain Gorshayik transferred to her command. Several times. You may find her opinion less dismissive when she returns from the Homeland, though you're both going to have to work hard to earn her trust." He considered his nails. "I posted her here to clean up Izurum Regional Command. It's an unenviable task and she's doing well. I realise she has some affection for regulation—"

"*Affection?*" Dhani choked. "Look up *love* in the dictionary and you'll find a daguerreotype of Bethsehal Shalamir's marriage to the Service Manual. And whatever you do, do not look up *lust.*"

The General refolded his arms. His lips thinned. "Izurum Regional Command requires someone both incorruptible *and* able to lead with a firm hand. That person is Bethsehal Shalamir, no matter what your opinion, Dhani."

She ground her teeth. For now, the discussion had ended. In private, there'd be much more to say about hot-for-a-deposed-emperor, married-to-the-regulations Bethsehal Shalamir. "Yes, Shulim General."

The fan's click grew momentarily loud. Behzad El'Meshid cleared his throat and began anew. "Lastly, Operative Karim, I'm aware that you consider your role in Internal Affairs to be little more than the shuffling of papers about a desk. I've also been apprised of your opinion that the role offers neither challenge nor advancement to your existing skills."

"I may have revised my opinion a little. The role entails *some* paper shuffling combined with other...activities." Dhani studied the rug, shifting her boots. "My existing skills weren't particularly challenged, though."

"Then perhaps you'll find your next mission somewhat more..." The General raised an eyebrow. "Challenging."

He reached around and pulled several files from the top of a stack. Gorshayik leaned forward, the most animated he'd been since she'd entered the room. Perhaps the bag of hornets in his rear end had finally shifted.

"We have received intelligence about antiquities being trafficked in Tizrak Yirda's far south."

This piqued Parvan Gorshayik's attention even more. He leaned forward a little further and asked, "What kind of antiquities?"

"Aretellian artefacts."

Dhani sat back, the sudden blood rush in her ears filling the room's silence. The Aretellian were the long-vanished, god-like race who'd once ruled the world, changed the bodies—and blood—of its peoples and harnessed Deenjah. A civilisation far advanced beyond any that now existed, the Aretellian had turned on each other in a devastating civil war, wiping themselves out save for a single survivor and a swathe of humanity with them.

The General wrapped a knuckle on the top-most file. "A number of Aretellian artefacts and a few well-made fakes have appeared in several marketplaces in Tizrak Yirda's south. As you might understand, the Imperium cannot take the risk that some of these artefacts may be dangerous—especially if they fall into the wrong hands."

Wrong hands and *dangerous* could only mean one thing. *Yargans.* Dhani sucked on a cheek. The Imperium and the Yarga had been engaged in a centuries-old race to recover as many Aretellian relics as they could. Whilst the Imperium currently had the upper hand in terms of military and political might, the Yarga was the nation most likely to figure out how to use Deenjah-based Aretellian technology *should* any of it actually work after two thousand years.

"You said the south, Shulim General?" Gorshayik asked. "Whereabouts?"

"The artefacts appear to be coming out of Agara."

Dhani's shoulders drooped. Agara, a mountainous nation the size of a rumpled handkerchief, not only abutted Tizrak Yirda, but it also shared a border with the Yarga. Which meant high-altitude cold. Nipple freezing, blizzards-in-winter, oxygen-starved cold. She hated the cold. *Hated it.*

"I'm proposing a covert mission run out of Burukalin, located near the Tizraki-Agara border," the General continued "A man named Guillermo Mancidi, an Irduni national living in Agara, is the likely origin of at least some of the artefacts. He's our best chance to learn where these artefacts are coming from and seize the source *without* raising the suspicions of the Yargan government." He paused, gaze shifting between Dhani and Parvan Gorshayik. "If you agree to undertake this mission, you'll be authorised to act independently, with only a weekly report to Regional Controller Shalamir."

"Independent?" she asked. "How independent is *independent*?"

"There will be certain guidelines." Behzad El'Meshid raised an eyebrow. "But you will largely be free to pursue the mission's objectives at your own discretion. Captain Gorshayik, I already know your answer will be yes, but I need your *partner's* agreement as well."

The General's emphasis on the word *partner* sent a buzz down Dhani's spine. *A warning to Captain Gorshayik?* Perhaps the big Tizraki still had a hornet jammed firmly up his rear end about working with her? Whatever it was, she'd ignore it for the time being. She'd take Gorshayik's moods *and* Agara's nose-bleeding cold over Bethsehal Shalamir's regulation fetish any day.

She exchanged a glance with Gorshayik. His mouth *almost* tweaked upwards in a smile—but not quite. A twitch of the corners was close enough. Dhani turned back to the General.

"Aretellian artefacts, dying of cold or altitude sickness. *Yargans.* Sign me up." She held out a hand for a file. "When do we leave?"

EPILOGUE

Five months later…

Guillermo Mancidi raised a shaking hand and stroked the fur about his doublet's collar. The gesture loaned him an even more furtive, foxlike air. Any moment now, he'd start digging a burrow. Or stealing chickens.

"He's here tonight," Mancidi whispered, conspiratorially.

"Who?" Dhani asked.

"*Troccatti.*"

Her mouth went dry, a sudden chill iced her limbs. *Was Mancidi bluffing or telling the truth?* She scanned the smokey cantina, studying faces and clothing, searching for an Irduni, a Chandroli or someone similar to the girl who'd tried to kill her in the lane the previous night.

Locals filed in and out of the room. The group of acrobats wiped their mouths on napkins and laughed amongst themselves. Moushaan Farrokhshal and the members of his geological expedition were still pouring over maps under the light of their *screw-you-I'm-a-rich-Jhiriyan* brass deenjili lamps. The pair of shadows in the corner hadn't moved. Save for the same pair of loved-up female Irduni caravan merchants who'd been in the cantina last night, mouths welded to each other's faces, there were no other russet-haired, freckle-dusted Irduni or Chandroli in the room.

She glanced up at the stained map of Soolaith on the wall, considering her next words carefully. Where the continent-crossing span of the Yargan mountains loomed directly south of Agara, someone—probably Yargan—had written, '*We will rise*' in defiant Massayalam. Next to it another hand had printed, '*Fuck the Imperium*'. Somehow, both seemed fitting.

"Tell Troccatti I recommend the goat dhal. The yak is far too chewy." Dhani set the goblet aside. She had what she needed and the conversation was going places she didn't particularly like. "Thank you for your company. I'll see you tomorrow night."

Mancidi lifted his chin. His voice was cold. "My people consider it very rude to leave a glass of wine unfinished."

"I don't drink when I do business."

"I'd prefer you made an exception. For my patron's sake."

The warning in his words didn't go unnoticed. His stare didn't waiver. Dhani glanced across the room. The cantina's main door opened. Six people filed in with a blast of cold, snowy air, weaving their way towards the bar. The shadows in the corner of the room had somehow up and vanished. The skin on her neck shivered.

She eased back onto the butt-killing crate, fixing her gaze on Guillermo Mancidi's fox-like face. *What was this about? Allowing Troccatti to size her up? To give him time to kill her?* Or did Mancidi have some other agenda, something she could only guess at?

The scent of Mancidi's perfume invaded her nostrils along with a sudden waft of tabac leaf. She checked the back corner again. The booth where the shadows had parked their gloomy, black-as-a-mineshaft arses still stood empty. Her pulse fluttered in her neck. *Where had the pair gone—and so quickly?* A knot of local women obscured her view of Parvan Gorshayik and his game of taroch, just inside the cantina's front door. She slipped a hand about the dead hillman's pistol tucked in against her waist. Her other hand formed a fist about the goblet. None of this felt right.

"Don't expect me to drink it all," she said, finally.

With his chin, Mancidi pointed at the table where the members of the geographical expedition were seated. He gave an oily smile. "Perhaps you'd prefer the Tizraki wine that your Homelander compatriots are drinking?"

"Tizraki make the best wine in all Soolaith. Perhaps all of Caledon."

The Irduni laughed again, a genuine, bubbling sound. "You haven't tasted Irduni wine, then?"

"Can't say that I have."

"Come to dinner at my home tomorrow night and I'll treat you to some. You may change your opinion about who makes the best wine in the world." He paused and glanced at Salish. The girl was chewing on her lip, looking anxious or even slightly ashamed. *Or perhaps she needed to pee.* When your face was a locked in permanent shade of sour lemon, who could tell?

"I have something I'd like to ask you. A favour," Mancidi said, abruptly.

"Oh?" Dhani glanced at the vacant spot in the far corner. Her pulse began to pound in her throat. She slipped the pistol from its holster, her movements hidden beneath the coat in her lap. Whether Mancidi thought it was impolite or not, she *had* to leave.

"This is quite forward, and I apologise for my rudeness," Mancidi continued with a smile, fingering the gold embroidery on his cuffs. "Salish admires your skills. She talks about you endlessly when we're alone. Has done from the moment she met you, although I think some of it is because she's fascinated by all things Jhiriyan." The fox-man paused again, now stroking his narrow chin. Salish's cheeks flushed bright pink. "I was wondering if you'd teach Salish to pick locks? Perhaps take her on as an apprentice?"

The request took Dhani completely by surprise. "An apprentice? I don't—"

She was momentarily distracted as the group of acrobats stood up to leave. One threw a coin on the table with an exaggerated flourish before hurrying after his companions. As he turned, he bumped into one of the new arrivals headed for an empty table, spilling the woman's ale. The newcomer swore a loud, fluent string of profanities. The acrobat apologised, bowing low and tipping her another coin.

Dhani would have dismissed the foul-mouthed woman immediately, but in a sliver of lamplight the woman's footwear gleamed like a beacon. *Shining black leather.* Those who'd entered the cantina alongside her all wore the same well-made boots and dispassionate, slab-faced stares. One by one, they noted her, Guillermo Mancidi, and the members of the Jhiriyan geographical expedition. One by one, their postures stiffened to attention.

Her hand tightened on the pistol, Mancidi's question and Salish's pleading expression forgotten. The Thulkar's thugs had arrived, and she didn't need a second glance to know that beneath their sheepskin coats, every one of them carried a shiny, six-shot pistol just like the one in her hand.

The door thudded shut as the last of the acrobats filed out. Mancidi was watching her, still waiting for a reply. Salish was biting her lip, dark eyes imploring. Dhani stared into the wine. Made a quick decision. *The Thulkar's thugs had turned up to spoil Troccatti's party right when the mysterious Troccatti was in the room.* This could be interesting.

"Don't look behind you, but we've got company," she said, offhand. "Six of the Thulkar's thugs just walked in. All armed. Middle of the room. I suggest we cut behind the bar and leave via the kitchen."

Salish's shoulders sagged. Mancidi opened his mouth to say something—

The inside of the cantina exploded in a ball of flame.

WHAT HAPPENS NEXT?

Find out in
VALLEY OF LIES - Book 2 in the Imperial Assassin Series.
Sign up here and be first to read *Valley of Lies*:
http://bit.ly/Assassins-team

GLOSSARY

Nations/Continents

Erissat - (eh-riss-AT), the name of a Jhiriyan colony bordering Tizrak Yirda to the east.

Jhiriyah - (jih-REE-yah), the name of a continent (east of Soolaith), the single nation which populates that continent and the empire. Jhiriyah has twelve colonies, all of which are located in Soolaith.

Loyodz - (LOY-odds), a desert area, largely unmapped, located to the south of Tizrak Yirda.

Soolaith - (soo-LAYTH), the name of the continent on which *City of Whispers* takes place. Also called '*the Continent*'.

Tizrak Yirda - (tizz-RACK YAIR-da), the name of the Jhiriyan colony in which *City of Whispers* takes place.

The Yarga - (YAR-ga), the name of the largest nation on Soolaith, spanning all 14,000 keloms of the mountain range of the same name. Home to the most feared people on the Continent, *Yargans*, who previously dominated most of Soolaith.

Places

Atoulibba - (at-TOO-lib-a), the industrial portion of Izurum, located in the city's south.

Ciyurit - (chee-OO-rit), the section of Izurum where the Jhiriyan colonial administration and Ha'filu Region Command are located.

Faissa - (FYE-suh), an area in the eastern part of Izurum.

Geraktin - (geh-RACK-tin), a large area in the north-central part of Izurum; home to the city's largest souk.

Istanakhand - (is-tana-KARND), the Tizraki capital, located on the western end of the Osmancik Sea.

Izurum - (iz-OO-rum) - a small city of approximately 40,000 people located in the southern-central part of Tizrak Yirda.

Koyulerin - (koy-OO-ler-rin), the shanty town located on the south side of Izurum, outside of its walls.

Odesstra - (oh-DESS-tra), Tizrak Yirda's second largest city, located on the north-western side of the Osmancik Sea.

Mursik - (mer-SICK), the sector of Izurum where the wealthy live and often work.

Osmancik Sea - (oz-MAN-chick), a large, land-bordered sea in eastern Soolaith, like the Mediterranean in Europe.

Talmakhan - (tal-MACK-arn), the capital of the region in which Izurum is located.

Tergayit - (ter-GAY-it), a poorer area of Izurum, located in the city's south.

Zidan - (Zi-dan), the name of the river directly to the north-west of Izurum as well as a working class area in the city's west.

Zidurat - (zid-OO-raht), the name of the central section of Izurum.

Titles

Jhaliaad - (ja-lee-ARD), the Jhiriyan word for *emperor*, used for both male and female occupants of the position.

Jhalifarriset - (ja-lee-FAR-iss-et), the Jhiriyan word for the heir to the empire (usually the Jhaliaad's eldest child), used for both male and female occupants of the position.

Majapayit - (mar-jah-PYE-eet), the Tizraki word for the ruler of a city.

Papat - (puh-PAHT), the Tizraki word for priest.

Recip - (reh-CHIP), the Tizraki word for a junior priest.

Shalisar - (shall-ee-SAR), the Jhiriyan word for *lord*, used for both the female and male heads of noble houses and their firstborn heirs.

Shulim - (shoo-LEEM), the Jhiriyan word for *earl*, used for both the female and male younger children of a Shalisar. Unlike a Shalisar, a Shulim does not pass their title on to their children.

The Jhiriyan Castes

Jhiriyan society is divided in to five hierarchical sections, largely based on occupation. The system is called *the Mawat* (MAA-waht). The Shaliaat and Kishaat castes have strict written rules governing behaviour, dress, hair, marriage and duties.

Shaliaat - (shall-ee-ART), Jhiriyah's noble caste, made up of seventy-eight families who rule the seventy-eight provinces of the Jhiriyan continent.

Kishaat - (kish-ART), the financial, wealthy mercantile/industrial and upper bureaucratic caste.

Vashatriya - (vash-at-TREE-uh), the bureaucratic (white collar), small business, skilled trade caste. Dhani is now considered a member of this caste.

Sastriya - (sas-TREE-uh), the working/farming caste.

Gishatriya - (gish-at-TREE-uh), the caste of unskilled labourers and petty criminals. Dhani was born into this caste.

General Terms

Ambituryan - (am-bee-TOUR-ran), a Tizraki religious text.

Aretellian - (a-ret-TELL-ee-UN), the name of the long extinct, godlike people who created Deenjah.

Askandhli - (as-KARN-dlee), the blue-coloured protecting Flame / the Flame of maintaining.

Ashishqa - (ash-EESH-kuh), opium smoked in a hookah or similar.

Besantrik - (bess-AN-trick), the name of the religious schools often found within Tizraki temples.

Bopa - (BOE-puh), the Tizraki word for great-grandfather.

Caravanserai - (car-uh-VAN-seh-RYE), a place where caravans made up of strings of camels, ponies, yak or other animals used to transport goods can gather and stay within a city or town.

Chhadi - (ch-haa-DEE), a kind of incense used by Yargan people.

Deenjah - (DEEN-jah), the name of the power / magic in the *Imperial Assassin* world.

Deenjahi - (deen-JAH-hee), the very rare individuals who are connected permanently to the Flames of Deenjah.

Deenjili - (deen-JEE-lee), anything powered by Deenjah, like the lamps in Mursik.

Deenjin - (DEEN-jin), any person of <u>any</u> race who can raise Deenjah.

Dewari - (de-WAH-ree), the name of the lettering used to write Massayalam, adapted from Yargan.

Dironi - (dih-RONE-ee), Jhiriyan currency, a gold coin.

Drukilyi - (druk-EEL-yee), the Tizraki word for a Deenjin healer.

Drukpa - (DROOK-pa), the Yargan word for a Deenjin healer.

Ha'filu - (ha*FILL-oo), the name of the Jhiriyan secret service. The apostrophe indicate a glottal stop. You cut off the sound with the back part of the tongue on the roof of the mouth.

Kaffai - (KAFF-aye), the universal word for coffee.

Kofte - (KOFF-teh), spiced lamb meatballs.

Kelom - (KEE-lom), the universal work for kilometre.

Massayalam - (mass-SAY-a-lam), a creole / common tongue first used by traders but now spoken widely across Soolaith (the Continent) between people of different races / languages.

Naan - (NAHN), the universal word for flatbread eaten in both Soolaith and Jhiriyah.

Peshak - (PESH-ack), a unit of Tizraki currency, usually a copper coin.

Shakandhli - (sha-KARN-dlee), the red-coloured killing Flame / the Flame of destruction.

Souk - (SOUWK, like 'south'), a large marketplace.

Tabac - (ta-BACK), the universal word for tobacco.

Ta'Hafiq - (ta*HA-feek), the Imperial Assassins, a branch of the Ha'filu.

Taroch - (ta-ROCK), a game with 78 illustrated cards developed from ancient tarot cards.

Tarandhli - (tuh-RARN-dlee), the green-coloured healing Flame / the Flame of creation.

Ulaya - (you-LAY-uh) an oil Yargan people use in the ends of their hair.

Yevengik cu Bapa - (yev-eng-ICK CHU bah-PUH), a Tizraki term meaning *people and fatherland*. The name of the nationalist cult in *City of Whispers*.

THANK YOU SO MUCH FOR READING
CITY OF WHISPERS.

Before you go, would you do me a favour? If you enjoyed the book, please leave a review on your favourite book review site or book retailer?

A review as simple as: *This book was action-packed and fun. I recommend it for people who like assassins, fantasy and action novels* is all it takes to help authors like me spread the word about our books.

Thank you once again for reading, and a special THANK YOU from Dhani, Parvan and all the other invisible people in my head for leaving us a review.

―――――

VALLEY OF LIES - Imperial Assassin Book 2

A fast-paced, adventure fantasy for those who like snarky, kick-ass heroines and hurt-me-bad action with a touch of gunpowder and magic…

Expelled from the Imperial Assassins for a murder she didn't commit, Dhani Karim is granted one chance at redemption: spend two years as a lowly covert operative in the Empire's Secret Service whilst she tries to clear her name.

Partnered with Parvan Gorshayik, a man with a

mysterious and brutal past, Dhani is sent to a far-flung mountain town on a routine intelligence-gathering mission.

But when Parvan's unauthorised quest for vengeance leads to an ancient artefact with the power to destroy nations, Dhani is forced to make a choice.

Should she walk away from the rogue mission—and sacrifice her one chance to rejoin the Imperial Assassins— or help Parvan recover the artefact from the hands of a group planning to bring down the Empire itself?

Before she can decide, she's thrown into a deadly race against time.

Agents from the Yarga—a powerful military nation— are also seeking the artefact and will stop at nothing to secure it for themselves.

And, unlike the Continent's other peoples, the Yargans possess both the magical strength and knowledge to use the weapon. Yet, without the Yargans' help neither Dhani nor Parvan will be able to defeat the group who's stolen the artefact…or the powerful form of magic the group possesses – a magic that shouldn't exist.

Valley of Lies by Katt Powers coming April 2021.

Sign up to the Assassin's Team and be first to read the book:
http://bit.ly/Assassins-team

ABOUT THE AUTHOR

Katt Powers was born in Sydney, Australia.

After a time living in the Southern Highlands of New South Wales, she worked as an anthropologist in the Northern Territory for many years.

A decade ago, she retrained as an archaeologist specialising in human remains and Aboriginal archaeology. She now works as a senior archaeologist for a large ecology and heritage consultancy. She is of Aboriginal descent and is deeply grateful to have spent over 20 years protecting Aboriginal heritage.

Katt currently lives on 24 acres in the Murray-Mallee region of South Australia with her husband, two very naughty dogs and lots of prickles.

She does not like Vegemite and has never seen the movie Titanic.

More from Katt:

IMPERIAL ASSASSIN SERIES:

City of Whispers

Valley of Lies

The Night Lily (Coming mid-2021)

The Diamond King (Coming late-2021)

CONNECT WITH KATT

Sign up for the Assassin's Team newsletter and get a bonus novella, short stories, maps, special offers, and the odd, random picture of my dogs here: **http://bit.ly/Assassins-team**.

I'm very active on Instagram, where I'm a keen Bookstagrammer and love talking about books. Come and say hi at **@kattwritesworlds**.

If you'd like to email me (especially if you find a typo) and chat about the books, you can get in touch at katt@kattpowers.com.

Ingram Content Group UK Ltd.
Milton Keynes UK
UKHW040958100523
421436UK00029B/391/J